~A NOVEL~

MAUREEN FRANCIS DOYLE

outskirtspress
DENVER, COLORADO

A Journey in Time
A Novel

v2.0 r1.0

Outskirts Press, Inc.
http://www.outskirtspress.com

ISBN: 978-1-4787-5870-9

PRINTED IN THE UNITED STATES OF AMERICA

To my husband, Ron, for his love, constant support, patience and painstaking honesty

A Note Before You Begin the Journey

Have you ever wondered how writers of historical fiction choose their subjects or why they were inspired by a particular project? My father died in 1998 and on his deathbed, he asked me to find his long-lost brother. I found him, but unfortunately, he had died one year prior. My father and his brother grew up in an orphanage in Detroit, Michigan in the early 1900's. We grew up knowing virtually nothing about his side of the family and he rarely shared his memories. His past was one vast expanse of nothingness.

Once I found his brother, I became compelled to find the others. It took fifteen years of searching, making calls, writing letters and doing continual research, but one by one they seemed to come forward just as if they wanted their memories preserved and their voices heard.

In 2012, just before a research trip to Kingston, Ontario, Canada, I received an email from Kevin Hoeg through Ancestry.com sharing that he believed we were cousins. Since I had plans to visit Canada, he graciously volunteered to meet me in Kingston from his hometown of Toronto. As it turned out, Kevin's grandmother, Mary Ellen Garrett Cavanaugh was the niece of my great grandmother, Catherine Garrett Doyle. Kevin had known my great aunt, Annie Doyle, prior to her death in 1975. He gave to me photos, family stories, the family bible, and other mementos from the Garrett and Doyle families. He also introduced me to another cousin, Margaret Thompson who was a distant relative to the Doyle side and who shared with me many valuable documents including the land lease and baptismal certificates of the Doyle family in Ireland. I am deeply indebted to both for their thoughtfulness and willingness to share what they knew. I would also like to thank Colum O'Rourke of County Wicklow, Ireland for his time and interest in reviewing the accuracy of my Irish history and Bernie Schein, my writing coach and author in his own right for his encouragement, patience and grand sense of humor.

I continued to travel back in time through research and found that my great great grandfather, Thomas Doyle had leased land from Samuel Astleford in 1829. After Thomas' death, the potato famine ensued. Thanks to Jim Rees for his book *Surplus People*, I researched the Fitzwilliam Clearances and found out that millions of Irish had fled Ireland from 1847 through 1856. As Jim writes, "The Irish potato famine of the second half of the 1840s was a catastrophe of immense proportions. It has been described as the worst social disaster of nineteenth-century Europe." There is a saying that describes the horrific time period: "One million dead, two million fled." I discovered that John Doyle, my great grandfather did in fact leave Ireland during this period at the age of twenty-six. I found his courage and determination to be extraordinary. Inspired by my newly discovered ancestors, I believe I have given a voice to their indwelling spirits to tell their story since my father never could.

With a few exceptions, most of the characters in this novel are fictional and their actions are based on events that may or may not have happened. However, the major narrative arc is based in fact and historical truth. My hope as the novelist is to be your guide through the time period, the challenges and the joys and extreme heartache that was common to people of that time. I can take you safely through the death and destruction during the potato famine, the danger and extreme risk of traveling in steerage to an unknown destination, past the early death of so many from lack of medicine, basic knowledge or epidemics. We can tiptoe together into the bedchambers to experience the warmth and safety between two lovers – opening and illuminating a vanished world so that for a few hours at least, you can experience the successes and failures of a great man. I hope this story of John Doyle will inspire and delight you.

May 1848

Dear Mamai,

Charlotte has agreed to write this letter for me. I hope it goes without saying that the hardest thing I have ever had to do was leave my family at the Shillelagh Workhouse.

I pray everyday that you all are doing well. Please be reassured that I'm going to do everything in my power to get to America and will send back for you as quickly as possible. I must admit I was heartsick to leave our home even though I know we had no other choice except to stay and perish. Samuel and Charlotte offered to give me a ride to New Ross to catch the ship instead of me doing the journey on foot. Mamai, you would not have believed all of the people that we passed. I only recognized a small handful from Coolkenno and Shillelagh. I felt so grateful that I had a ride. It will take them many days to travel on foot to New Ross. I saw so many old people and children trying to keep up carrying everything that they owned. There were even a few that had died on this journey from starvation or sickness and their bodies were left on the side of the road. People stopped to cover up the dead but had no choice but to leave them. Samuel and Charlotte have been able to tell me stories along the way of buildings that they recognized or shops where they have bought things. We stopped in Fern and I thought of you and Dadai. We passed the cathedral that I believe you were married in. How I wish you were traveling with me. I know it's been many years since you were in County Wexford. I must go for now. I will write to you when I reach the ship before my voyage. Love to you and the rest of my family.

John

Part I

Chapter One

Wicklow, Ireland

1835

Courage does not always roar.
Sometimes, it is the quiet voice
At the end of the day saying,
I will try again tomorrow.
Author Unknown

There is nothing colder than an Irish winter. John stood in the frigid air pulling his thin coat around him feeling the cold seep through the cloth. He choked back the tears that were determined to spill onto his red cheeks. The smell of burning turf from his neighbor's roof circled around him making it difficult to breathe. The whinny of a horse and a lonely sheep bleating in the distance could be heard as if in a desperate plea for help. He ran around the burning embers searching for life inside what was left of his neighbor's home. Besides the distant sounds of barn animals, he heard nothing but the crackle of burning turf and fire.

John ran back to his home in search of his father.

Dusk was settling in making it difficult to see but he had traveled this road so many times, the light of day did not hinder his efforts. He saw no one on the short journey but a few lonely farm animals that hadn't made their way back to their barn.

"John, what is it? Why are you so out of breath? Asked his mother, Winfred wiping her hands on her apron.

"I need Dadai, Mamai! The MacGrath's house has been burned down."

"He knows, John. There's nothing we can do. No one died in the fire. Just leave it alone."

"But Mamai!!"

"Don't 'but me,' John…enough!"

He couldn't leave it alone and couldn't understand the injustice. He stood there and looked at his mother incredulously. *How could you just leave something like that alone?* Kicking the chair in the kitchen, he stormed out of the room. He climbed the ladder up to the loft and lay there thinking most of the night.

"John, come down for supper," his mother yelled from the bottom of the ladder.

"I'm not hungry," he mumbled to himself, barely audible from below.

Winfred looked at her husband, Thomas and her children at the table and said shaking her head, "That boy's temper will get the best of him."

The tears stung his eyes as he wept into his blanket.

He knew that someday he would live as a free man and that his family would not fear the Loyalists or anyone else. Over and over in his mind he envisioned the remains of the house smoldering angrily in the dirt and when sleep finally set in, he dreamt he heard the cries of his friend, Willie MacGrath, coming from the house.

Before the first light of the day, John could hear his parents stirring below the loft. "John," Winfred yelled up to the loft. "Its Good Friday and Mass starts in an hour. Wake your sisters and Thomas Jr. and get ready for church."

St. Mary's Catholic Church was only two miles from their home, not a bad distance to walk when the air was warmer. Even though it was March, the wind howled, blowing gusts of ice and snow. John was the last one outside. The air was glacier perfection to someone that was dressed warmly, but with each step John's legs became block-like and he could no longer feel his feet. He worried that if he took off his thin-soled leather boots, his toes might remain in the boot. Way ahead of the rest of the family, his three sisters had already turned the corner and could no longer be seen. John's mother, Winfred, carried baby Joseph in her arms, his weight slowing her walk. His younger brother, Thomas walked a few steps behind him. Unlike John, he had a head of dark wavy hair that accentuated his deep-set eyes. He was an inquisitive little boy and completely idolized his older brother. John glanced back to Thomas Jr. and smiled. If he squinted his eyes from the blinding reflection of the sun on the snow, he could see the distant ruins of St. Finian's Monastery. The tall steeples, though crumbled with age, rose above the hills harboring the secrets of history. Since medieval times, the majestic monastery had fallen into ruin abandon. John liked to stand on the summit of Aghowle Hill and catch a glimpse of the Irish Sea and the looming Wicklow mountains.

Thomas Sr., John's father said, "Boys, I hear the church bells and we can't be late, so pick up your pace."

John tried imagining that it was spring to get his mind off of the pain in his legs and the visions that he carried from the day before. He loved the springtime in Ireland, the land that boasts forty shades of green. Under a blanket of dew, those shades of green would shimmer like emeralds.

The family entered the church and made their way into the family pew going around the cluster of people also running late for Mass. John sat down on the hard bench and a patch of sun filtered through the stained glass window warming his face, but his frostbitten feet still ached. He started to itch from his wool clothing and now thawing body when his mother poked him and gave an expression of disapproval. Father Byrne, meanwhile, walked up the isle led by servers in starched white soutanes carrying two large white candles that flickered when they walked throwing shadows on the ceiling. Lightly showering the congregation with holy water, the priest waved the thurible of holy incense giving off thin, gray wisps of fragrant smoke. John sat quietly on the pew and watched as the priest announced the Stations of the Cross though he was more interested in watching the shadows that appeared on the stonewalls than he was in hearing Father Byrne read from scripture. His stomach began to grumble, his body itched and his feet still felt numb. The incense filled his nose and he started to sneeze. He was physically uncomfortable and mentally preoccupied. When John thought he could no longer sit still, the small church opened it's doors marking the end of the Mass and the congregation slowly began to file out.

"Good morning, John." Walking a few paces behind him wrapped in a thin black cloak was Aideen Murphy. Her once soft features and youthful look now looked drawn and pinched.

"Good morning, Mrs. Murphy."' John didn't know what to say to her. She was another victim of a house burning a few months back and the depth of her anguish clung to her. Aideen's husband, James and young son, Quinn had been trapped in the house, burning them alive. James had been accused of assisting the Irish rebels. Now homeless and alone, she was forced to move in with her in-laws and her future looked dim. John missed

Quinn. He was a regular when they played cricket at The Hurling Bank.

John smiled hiding his pain, not knowing what else to do and ran to catch up with the rest of his family.

"John," his father called out. "I want you a part of this." Thomas, John's father stood with a small group of men huddled together talking softly. Since many locals were loyal to the British crown, the Catholic villagers were forced to hold meetings under a veil of secrecy. John stood close to his father listening to the whispers of the men from his village planning a meeting at the Donegal farm to discuss the recent political riots and pillaging affecting everyone in the village.

Thomas Sr. was a respected and trusted member of the community. Even though small in stature, he carried an air of confidence. His hair was as black as the vestment worn by the priest giving Mass and he displayed a large, strong chin, deep set dark eyes and a nose of topographical complexity.

John, the eldest of his six children, seemed much older than his fourteen years. He had a fierce determination and independence that became more evident as he aged. He was the strong quiet type but was quick to temper. He was a complex series of contradictions - strong and insecure at the same time. Broad shoulders, weathered skin from working long hours in the sun and a firm square jaw like his father. His brown wavy hair only accentuated his serious eyes and a warm smile that would make any woman's heart melt.

As the family walked home together, Thomas cautioned, "This gathering must be kept secret. We will be discussing local Loyalists and potential uprisings. These issues must not be shared with anyone. You never know whom you can trust anymore." He was honored that his father would want him there.

That night, John slept lightly fearful of falling into a deep sleep and not hearing his name called.

Hours before dawn, Thomas whispered, "Son, it's time to get up." Quickly and dressing quietly, John made his way down the ladder. He followed his father outside into the cold, windy morning air hours before the sun would gently lift itself over the mountains. They ran through the snow-covered ground taking cover behind the trunks of large trees as they made their way to Patrick Donegal's barn. The meeting was already in session when they entered the small outbuilding.

"As long as the British are in power, we'll remain impotent servants to them!" Patrick said passionately. All eyes went to Thomas and John as they entered the cold barn. The only light that glowed in the dark came from one small candle that everyone crouched around. As John took a seat on one of the bales of hay, he looked around and recognized all twenty-five or so men from church to include his friend Bryan, Patrick's son. The hay felt slightly damp underneath him, increasing his chill and sending a cold shiver through his body. The barn air was thick with the musty smell of animal dung and mold. Shadows flickered on the men's faces from the wick on the candle. A small field mouse scampered across the barn floor in search of a hiding place and warmth from the cold outside. John's wandering attention was interrupted as he heard his father's voice.

"I know I am not the only one to say that I feel they want us to choose between our religion and our freedom and I will not do that!" Thomas said with intensity. "We have every right to our Catholic religion and should be permitted all of the other freedoms that the Protestant and British people have! The British politician's, specifically Robert Challoner, say that our rights our protected from the 1829 Emancipation Act, but we know we still aren't really free. We can own land now but no one can afford to purchase it our wages are so low.

Everyone nodded in agreement and Thomas continued, "As you all know, only a week ago, near our farm, the MacGrath home was burned to the ground. The Loyalists believed that Liam MacGrath was involved with a group of Irish rebels from Dublin! The family barely escaped with their lives. When will this stop? It wasn't but days ago, another suspected Irish rebel's son was found swinging from a tree with a leather strap around his neck. These Loyalists are lynching and burning anything in their path. Will we be the next victims of this violence?"

Patrick spoke up, "I think we are all in agreement that we cannot afford another revolution. We lost 30,000 people during that one summer of 1798. I heard in the village that a Catholic Association is being formed in support of Catholic Emancipation. There will be a fee of one pence a month per family for all of us to participate. Surely, we can afford that small sum for the support that we need. But we must get more people involved and spread the word to do this peacefully! It will take all of us fighting for change to make this happen."

The meeting continued with a heated discussion about the new groups being formed all over Ireland to throw out British rule and the rebel riots conducted by some of the Irish.

John didn't say anything during the meeting but on the way back he asked, "Dadai, we aren't headed for another uprising are we?"

"I don't know. I certainly hope not but we don't really have any of the rights that the British and Protestants have and that needs to change. I do not want to see the death and destruction that we saw during the rebellion though. Too many lost their lives. John, I'm only telling you this because I think you're old enough to hear it but the Loyalists have started something again called pitch capping. It's been outlawed but it's occurring again. Do you know the farmer, O'Reilly from Aghowle?"

"Yes, Dadai, I know of him?"

"His son was captured a few days ago and they shaved his head, put a cone-shaped cap on him and poured tar into the cap. Ripping the cap off, they intentionally removed part of his scalp. He died a tortuous death. It is so horrendous; no one is talking about it. That is how bad the Loyalists are becoming against the Irish, John. Even though we are not rebels, we could be next."

John couldn't believe what his father was telling him. He felt a fear he had never felt before but at the same time, he felt anger and wanted to retaliate. They walked quietly back to the farm each in their own thoughts, just as the sun began to glow orange and red upon the earth.

Chapter Two

Thomas and Winfred

1807

You will never do anything in this world
without courage. It is the greatest
quality of the mind next to honor.
Aristotle

It was the spring of 1807, when Thomas and Winfred Doyle moved to the crossroads of the Crablane, County Wicklow. They packed everything that they owned into a small horse-drawn wagon and traveled north from County Wexford.

"Thomas, I've never seen so many beautiful pink blossoms on the crabapple trees," Winfred said with enthusiasm. Just adding to the beauty was the deep green of the meadows and the purple of the distant mountains. The countryside was picturesque and breathtaking.

Thomas and Winfred passed St. Michael's church and noticed a farmer tilling a small plot of land. He pulled the horse off to the side of the dirt road and told Winfred to stay put. Walking up to the wooden fence he yelled,

"Sorry to interrupt. Could I have a minute of your time?"

The farmer put down his plow and walked over to Thomas.

"Good day. My name is Thomas Doyle and I'm just arriving from County Wexford and would like to lease a few acres to farm. Do you know who I could talk to?"

"You are on Fitzpatrick land," the farmer replied. "They might have acres for you to lease. It's the large farm at the end of this road before you turn to the left. Can't miss it. My name is Flinn, Joseph Flinn. Welcome to the Crablane."

Thomas tipped his hat and hopped back into the wagon. He continued down the dirt road to a large farm that had a rock wall running down along the road. The two homes on the property were quite large and made out of stone. The windows were open and lace curtains blew gracefully in the gentle breeze. Thomas and Winfred could hear a dog barking in one of the many barns warning of their arrival. A very large man with thinning hair and a very long mustache walked out of the stone house. He walked with a slight limp and had an unusual gait swinging his shillelagh fighting stick as he walked. He was dressed rather nicely, not like the typical Irish farmer.

"Good day," Thomas smiled pleasantly.

"What do you need?" the man replied with a heavy British accent and pursed lips.

"My name is Thomas Doyle and this is my wife Winfred and we're arriving from County Wexford. I'm interested in leasing some land to farm and was told you might be able to help me."

Winfred thought to herself looking at this austere man, *I'm not sure I like the looks of him.*

"My name is Henri, Henri Dowling and I'm a land tenant appointed by Lord Fitzpatrick of England himself. Do you have any experience farming because I have no time to train an Irishman," and with that, he threw back his head exposing a mouth full of decayed teeth and guffawed loudly. He then belched, swung his shillelagh and said, "Lord Fitzpatrick lives the majority of the time in England even though he is responsible for some land in Ireland and thanks to the King of England and in his Lord's absence, has entrusted me with managing his land."

"I do have experience. I've been a farmer all my life. You won't have to train me, I promise you that,"Thomas responded ignoring the insult.

Henri gave him a dubious look and started walking towards a small outbuilding. Thomas glanced at Winfred and followed Henri to wherever he was taking them.

"I have seven acres you can rent, but just a few rules first." Henri walked ahead as if deep in thought and then stopped, turned and looked Thomas in the eye. He stood way too close for Thomas' comfort and as he stood staring at Thomas his breath made him wince. It smelled strongly of tooth decay and Irish spirits.

"I will keep a watchful eye on all transactions since I report directly to Lord Fitzpatrick. If you choose to sell your leased land to another Irish farmer, I must approve it because ultimately Lord Fitzpatrick will approve it himself...but he trusts me explicitly. If your widow decides to remarry," Henri stated looking under hooded brow to Winfred, "we must approve of her new husband."

"I'm hopeful that won't be an issue for sometime," Thomas replied with a hint of annoyance.

"Well, you don't know that now, do you?" Henri asked swinging his stick and throwing his head back for another loud and boisterous guffaw.

As much as Thomas and Winfred had ill feelings already about their new landlord, Thomas needed land and a home for his family. They reluctantly signed the agreement with Henri Dowling.

Luckily for Thomas and Winfred, Lord Fitzpatrick was in Ireland at his nearby estate and was able to approve the lease agreement within a couple of day's time.

The crossroads of the Crablane only contained a handful of houses and two churches. Coolkenno was the closest village and Shillelagh, the closest large town, had a population of only 186 and only twenty-two houses, most of the residents Catholic farmers. Even thought quite small, the Doyle's had one of the nicer homes in the area. The little wooden farmhouse had a thatched roof which Thomas constantly repaired to keep out the rain and winds from the north. Cold and slippery under their feet was the hob stone floor and though their small home was quite comfortable the thin walls were drafty and porous to the elements; hot in the summer and cold in the winter.

It wasn't long before the family grew and John was born. Winfred gave birth with the help of a neighbor that had bore fourteen children of her own. John was a healthy baby who arrived ready to take on the world. Thomas and Winfred agreed that there wasn't a better or finer looking boy in all of Ireland.

One year later, Winfred gave birth to Bridget followed by Rose, Catherine, Thomas Jr., and Joseph, one right after the other.

As the family expanded, so did the small farmhouse. They occupied three rooms. The kitchen was the central unit but behind the fireplace a large room opened up with a small window where all of the children took their first breath at birth and now where Winfred, Thomas Sr. and Joseph slept. One small room stood at the other end with a loft above it reachable only by a moveable ladder. It became a rite of passage to be old enough to climb the ladder, which meant you could now sleep with your siblings in the loft. Like the vines of a tree, all five children curled together protected from the winds that howled around them. Above the loft there was no ceiling, only the roof and trees supporting the thatch, which had become black with age and turf smoke.

As the days became longer and the air warmer, the Doyle family sat outside on an early summer evening, watching the sunset and enjoying the symphony of crickets and an evening owl in the distance. Sitting around a small fire, Thomas played the fiddle and Winfred brought out her box accordion and sang, her voice was considered the best in Ireland. She was the personification of strength and that strength affected all those around her. Thomas handed John his fiddle reflecting on how he handled the instrument as confidently as a seasoned musician. Winfred watched tenderly as John caressed the strings welling with pride. She realized that if John had the opportunities like the wealthy landlord's children, he could go very far in life.

Winfred glanced at Rose; she was the shyest in the family and a fragile young girl. The coloring of her skin and hair blended together as if a passing cloud had fallen over her, throwing her under a shadow. Her large brown eyes had a trace of sadness in them. She had a depth that most didn't understand - what some would call an old soul. More interested in being near Winfred than socializing with her sisters, she was quiet and soft spoken, born like a seashell with everything resonating inside her. She had the kindest spirit of any of them but was also the most fragile having been sickly on and off since birth. Winfred had gone into labor one month early and delivered a tiny infant that Winfred thought resembled a rosebud, which is how she arrived at the name Roseanna. Rose came into this life not screaming like most infants but whimpering almost apologetically. Despite Winfred's fears that they would lose her shortly after her birth, the little girl persevered. Thereafter, with each cold winter though she would become ill from one thing or another but she never complained, not wanting to worry anyone or cause any problems.

Together as a family, sharing beautiful music together against the backdrop of the deep green mountains was how they spent their evenings under the stars. But, they could all feel the north wind starting to blow. The life that they cherished swirled with change; like watching summer gracefully turn to autumn knowing the cold winter lay just beyond. They watched as one by one, the leaves of the mighty oak gracefully fell and slowly swirled to the ground only to lose their color and decay.

On one crisp early October evening, Rose came in from taking the dirty dishwater outside leaving the door open behind her. A frigid gust of wind blew into the family home, snuffing out the candle and leaving them all to an early winter chill that smelled of nothing but cold, illness and change.

June 1848

Dear Mamai,

We arrived at the ship without incident. It was an exhausting journey but I know that once I am aboard this vessel, it ultimately brings us closer to being together. There are hundreds of people trying to board these ships to America. Mamai, I must warn you that people that arrive ill or even looking ill are denied boarding even if they have purchased a ticket. It was heartbreaking to see families that were denied boarding because of an elderly parent or young child that looked ill. I'm sure they had spent their last little bit of money for a ticket and would now be worse off than before if that's even possible. Luckily, Charlotte and Samuel once again, were able to secure passage for all of us since they are traveling first class. I have not been aboard yet, but I am confident that the accommodations in steerage will be adequate. I want this letter to post before I board since I don't know how long it will take us to sail to America. Charlotte will not be available to write more letters for me since she will be in a first class cabin but I'm hopeful that I will find another willing person to assist me so that I can continue to write to you. My love to you and my family.

John

Chapter Three

Samuel and Charlotte Castleford & The Lord Fitzpatrick Estate

1840

Life shrinks or expands
in proportion to one's courage.
Anais Nin

Much to Thomas and Winfred's delight, they received news that Lord Fitzpatrick had dismissed Henri Dowling from his position as Landlord. Henri and his wife Rebecca, an unapproachable woman who looked down her nose at anyone who was not British or loyal to the crown were returning to England and Samuel and Charlotte Castleford would be taking their place. Thomas prayed that his new landlord would be easier to get along with. So, it was like a breath of fresh air when Samuel and Charlotte Castleford arrived. Samuel and Charlotte lived in Yorkshire, England when Samuel was asked to replace Henri Dowling. In hopes of gaining favor with the British Crown, he agreed to move Charlotte to a small estate near the crossroads of the Crablane.

Thirsk, the little town in Yorkshire, England where Samuel and Charlotte had lived was a place full of character, whose pretty little red roof houses clung to the rocks, right down to the shoreline. Fishermen went out in their boats early in the morning until they pulled in their catch coming in from a long day of fishing just before the sun went down. A bustling political town, if a bit small, the town elders held Charlotte and Samuel in humble esteem due to Samuel's political connections to royalty. Thirsk was a busy town whose large cobbled square was crowded each Monday with a farmer's market. This village had developed into an important coaching stop at the center of a crossroads and was noted for its many coaching inns. Charlotte loved the Dower House and the Golden Fleece Hotels of all the inns in town, and delighted in narrating legends of ghosts and spirits who haunted their well-worn rooms. When the Golden Fleece was first built, a chambermaid had been murdered mysteriously as she cleaned one of the rooms. The manager of the inn found her young body face down in the soaking tub, her throat slit from side to side. No one ever found her murderer, though a traveler passing through from London to the coast became the suspect. Many visitors claimed to have witnessed the maid walking the halls carrying a candle, and those that had seen her said that she was crying and acting as if she was searching for something or someone.

Charlotte and Samuel attended St. Mary's, an Anglican Church every Sunday morning, a towering medieval building whose perpendicular gothic architecture and eight-foot tower stood erect with dramatic height over the village. Typical of gothic style, there was a large pointed arch in front with a ribbed vault, and a flying buttress that protected its height. The tower housed the ringing chamber containing eight bells. Charlotte loved to hear the ringing of the bells fondly known as "The Bells of St. Mary's."

One of their favorite pastimes was watching cricket, which was already a thriving sport in London and now a growing rural pastime. Samuel had a reputation of gambling large sums of money much to Charlotte's irritation and disappointment. "Samuel, if you won more often, I probably wouldn't care that you lose more money than you win."

He would always reply, "Charlotte, when you're making the money in the family, you can spend it the way you wish."

Charlotte also thoroughly enjoyed riding horses and hoped to someday be an accomplished equestrian rider.

She found the excitement of a racetrack irresistible and would even bet her own money from time to time even though what she wagered seemed quite small compared to her husband. The Thirsk Racetrack was Yorkshire's most beautiful track, sitting between the NorthYorkshire Moors and the Dales.

Before leaving Thirsk for Ireland, Charlotte paid one last visit to the track to say farewell to her trainer. Standing outside brushing a beautiful dark brown Hackney was its owner and rider, Phillip Ramsdale.

"What a lovely animal you have there. Tell me about him?" asked Charlotte.

"Mrs. Castleford, what a nice surprise. Yes, this is Messenger. He's a Hackney horse, elegant high stepping breed that possesses good stamina and can trot at high speeds for extended periods of time. Beautiful isn't he?" replied Phillip obviously proudof his new purchase. Messenger had a dark brown coat like that of a mink with a black mane and white around its ankles. Directly between his big brown eyes was a black star. Charlotte gazed at the horse wondering if Phillip would let her ride Messenger. She wore her hair back in a tight knot with a very high black riding hat, a tailored black bodice, masculine neckwear and flowing black skirts and was the essence of style and beauty. On her delicate hands, she graced black calfskin riding gloves and carried a riding crop in her left hand.

"Phillip, what if I took him for a little jog around the track?" asked Charlotte. Phillip looked at her questioningly but based on the lessons she had had, surely she could handle this horse.

"Please be my guest," replied Phillip. He helped her up on the horse bareback and handed her the reins. Charlotte looked so smart sitting on top of that beautiful horse. She leisurely trotted him around the track and brought him back to his owner. Phillip helped her off the horse.

"Thank you Phillip. That was just delightful!" exclaimed Charlotte. "I also came to say goodbye. Samuel and I are leaving tomorrow for Ireland. He has been selected by Lord Fitzpatrick to be a land manager for a time.

"I'm sorry to hear you'll be leaving Charlotte. You'll be missed I can promise you," he said with a smile. "Please visit when you return."

Reluctantly, she left to go back to her home to get ready for her upcoming move.

Samuel and Charlotte prepared for their travel by carriage to Liverpool, a journey that would take ten hours to cover the 115 miles with stops in a few of the small towns that they passed through. She had servants packing all of their clothes and mementoes that would be coming within the week of their arrival, but they had decided to leave the furniture behind.

"Charlotte I can assure you that your new home will be furnished to your liking and if it is not, we will buy new. I promise, Darling. Besides, don't you think that sixteen trucks of clothes is a bit excessive?" asked Samuel.

"I'm only taking two trunks with us on the ship to Ireland. Are you sure that the other trunks will follow quickly? What if something comes up before they arrive? What if I need a gown that I don't have with me or matching shoes?"

"You're worrying over nothing. I've been assured that the same people that take care of Lord Fitzpatrick and Lady Wentworth's belongings will take care of ours. We have nothing to be concerned with. Tonight we will spend the night in Liverpool at the Throstles Nest Hotel and bright and early in the morning, we'll catch the sailing ship across the Irish Sea to Dublin."

"How long will the sailing be?"

"About ten hours."

"I've never been to Liverpool, Samuel, and I'm not sure I care to see it now. The hotel will be lovely, I'm sure. I know we have a long trip from Dublin to Coolkenno so I hope the ship is comfortable and restful."

After a wonderful night at the Throstles Nest Hotel complete with a gourmet supper in one of the finest restaurants in town, Charlotte felt refreshed and ready for the next leg of their journey. Once on board, she stood by the railing waving to the people on the dock. This was a small sail ship and could only accommodate one hundred people. The Norbank moved out on schedule and slowly Liverpool and the bustle of the city and dock glided out of sight, giving way to the rolling blue waves of the Irish Sea.

Almost immediately, Charlotte was overcome by nausea from the rocking and rolling of the ship, and chose to stay in her room. Samuel, on the other hand, enjoyed the fresh air of the sea and eagerly struck up conversations to anyone within earshot. By afternoon, tea and crumpets were served to the guests and luckily Charlotte felt well enough to come down and enjoy them. Nevertheless, she felt anxious to get to Dublin and then Shillelagh and to her new home near Coolkenno. After an exhausting sail and another long carriage ride, they arrived after dark to a small but quaint two-story stone house with flowers lining the walkway.

Samuel said cheerfully, “This is lovely don't you think?”

“I'm too tired to care and it's too dark to see anything. I'll make judgment in the morning.”

Much to their relief, someone had already spent hours preparing the house for their arrival, cleaning and dusting and preparing the bed with fresh, crisp linens. Samuel blew out the wick in the candle casting a soft light by the door, and the two fell fast asleep.

Early the next morning, they woke to a rooster's crow, birds chirping and the little Irish curtains billowing from the breeze coming through the window. The tranquil beauty of the morning convinced them that this would be a cozy home for the two of them until it was time to go back to England.

Charlotte was a charming and demure woman at the age of twenty when they moved to Ireland. Even thought she loved Thirsk, she was happy to get away from England and the politics and thought the Ireland countryside exquisite.

Samuel was a slight man, only about 5'7", but his personality outsized his short stature. He had gentle hands and graying hair but kind eyes. He was quite a bit older than Charlotte and had a lifetime of experience over her. When he first laid eyes on his delicate creature, her smile warmed him like a hot toddy on a cold evening. He longed for many children with her to fill their large homes, but unfortunately, discovered that she was unable to have children of their own.

Despite the absence of heirs, Samuel kept busy and believed he would enjoy working for Lord William Fitzpatrick, knowing that his new boss was a well respected royal Lord that had agreed to pay Samuel handsomely for moving and managing his land.

There was a knock at the door soon after they arrived. Charlotte's maid answered the door to a liveried attendant of Lord Fitzpatrick who bowed and said, "An invitation for Samuel and Charlotte Castleford."

Passing the invitation to Samuel, he excitedly shouted to Charlotte saying, "We've received an invitation to a weekend at the Wentworth Estates. It appears that Lady Ann Wentworth loves to ride and has invited us to enjoy a morning out exploring the Irish landscape."

"Oh! How lovely," cried Charlotte.

"And, I've been invited to a fox hunt with Lord Fitzpatrick!" Fox hunting, a new sport to Ireland brought over from England was Samuel and the Lord's favorite pastime. Samuel relished each chance to dress in his finest Melton wool hunt coat and breeches on a crisp morning, climb onto his Field Hunter, and chase a fox with his dedicated hounds leading the way.

When the Lord and his lovely wife Lady Ann Wentworth traveled to Ireland, Charlotte and Samuel frequently received invitations to lavish parties at the Wentworth Estate.

Coming home after their first elaborate weekend with Lady Ann Wentworth, Charlotte decided it was time to visit her new tenants. She walked over to Winfred's with some hot cross buns and fresh grape preserves.

Knocking on Winfred's door, Charlotte has a big smile on her face when Winfred answered.

"Well hello. I'm Charlotte Castleford the wife of your new landlord, Samuel. I baked a little something for you."

Winfred was thrilled to meet such a friendly woman after her long experience with Henri and Rebecca.

"On my, come in, come in, Mrs. Castleford. God bless ya. How nice. Please have a seat." Winfred welcomed her by pulling out the chair. Charlotte sat at the kitchen table and Bridget, Rose and Catherine walked in. Winfred introduced the girls to Charlotte. "Look what Mrs. Castleford has brought over for us."

"Please, call me Charlotte."

The girls eyed the buns hungrily but had the manners to refrain.

Charlotte loved to talk and Winfred appeared to be willing to listen.

"I went to the Wentworth Estate this weekend. My, what nice hosts the Fitzpatrick's are. Lady Ann invited Samuel and me for a hunt. She works tirelessly when she has guests. It must be exhausting," Charlotte shared without taking a breath between sentences.

"Doesn't she have help?" asked Winfred.

"Of course, but she attends to every detail. They invited thirty people to their estate, probably one hundred people total including the servants. She had a large breakfast for everyone before the men left for the hunt. I actually wanted to go on the hunt but the women stayed behind and read by the fire and gossiped. It was quite lovely. She had a luncheon in the High Lodge where the men joined us, an elaborate tea during which we were regaled by a Viennese trio and then a fabulous dinner that night. I had to take sixteen dresses for the four days, which was a change of clothes for every event. It was so tiring!"

Bridget and Catherine both thought how delightful a weekend like that would be. How they would love to get dressed up and have tea.

Winfred smiled and said, "Charlotte, not enough time in the day to take care of sixteen dresses. I'm sure your maids got a real workout."

Charlotte just laughed. "Well, I'm on my way, Winfred, girls. Have a lovely evening."

She left and John walked in about that time. "I see you met Mrs. Castleford. What did she want, Mamai?"

"To introduce herself and to talk and rub it in about her parties at the estate. I can't imagine, John, can't imagine," replied Winfred with a sigh. "But, she seems nice enough and brought us something she called hot cross buns."

John slathered a bun with graph preserves and took a bite, saying despite a full mouth, "I'm sure she means no harm. She's probably lonely over there with no one to talk to but her maids."

"She's a kind woman but frivolous. I don't understand that kind of thinking."

"Neither do I, Mamai. But anything is better than Henri the terrible and Rebecca."

"Where have you been by the way? You've got dirt all over you."

"I was playing cricket; Thomas, Willie Fenlon, Daniel Doyle, Bryan Donegal, Willie MacGrath and the rest of my friends. We played against a group of boys from Coolkenno. We slaughtered them," John said smiling.

"Stay away from the Donegal boy. Between his mouth and your temper, you're lookin for trouble."

Chapter Four
Typhoid Fever

1845

Keep your fears to yourself,
but share your courage with others.
Robert Louis Stevenson

In the year of 1845, Shillelagh experienced an unusually cool summer. The rain came down in buckets and seemed to go on for days. When it finally stopped for a short time, the sun didn't come out long enough to dry the soil. Thomas Sr. and John left the house early and walked the short distance to the land they farmed. A layer of dew blanketed the grass and a light fog covered the green hills.

Thomas stopped suddenly and breathed deeply. *What is that smell,* he thought to himself? He glanced down at the crop of potatoes that were laying in the brown soil. "John, come take a look at this," he said with a furrowed brow. Both men got down on their knees and Thomas lifted the brown leaves gently in his hands.

"What is it, Dadai?"

Without looking up, Thomas replied, "John, this is not good. This is blight. It could take out the whole crop." The leaves were as black as the bottom of a well and they hung loosely on their stems. Thomas and John walked the seven acres and even though the disease had not spread throughout, Thomas would lose everything if he didn't stop it quickly.

Within as little time as a month, the disease spread throughout the whole county. The wet climate gave rise to ubiquitous mold and a strange-looking fungus that appeared on new potato sprouts, if the new buds came up at all. Thomas farmed more than potatoes which enabled him to continue to put food on the table but many of the farmers in his area found it more and more difficult to provide for their families and as the situation grew more dire, some began to even fear starvation.

Families were known to scrounge through garbage searching for a morsel or two. Some resorted to catching rodents like small field mice just to feed their hungry bellies. Winter was coming and the situation would only get worse.

One morning, Winfred heard an unexpected knock at the door. It was Margaret O'Brien from church.

"Margaret, what brings you here this mornin?"

"I'm sorry to bother you Winfred. I was wonderin if you'd like to join me. I'm going to check in on the Douglas family. They weren't at church as you know and

I'm afraid something is going on with them!"

"Let me fetch my shawl." Winfred and Margaret walked down the dirt road. There was a chill in the air even though it was June and an eerie silence. "Margaret, you don't think it's the fever do you?"

"No, I don't. I don't believe anyone in the family has had a fever. That's why I want to check in on them. If I thought it was the fever, Winfred, I wouldn't take the chance nor would I let you risk it." Margaret was something of a local medical expert in the area. Her grandmother and mother had taught her about healing herbs and she had remedies for everything from bee stings to morning sickness.

They walked the quarter mile to the Douglas home, a small wooden structure with less land than Winfred or Margaret had. There was a well out front and a worn out Frances was at the well filling a bucket. She had an apron on and looked exhausted.

"Frances, we've been worried about you and the family," Margaret said with concern.

Frances looked up from the bucket, "I'm okay. I'm worried about the rest though. They've all come down with bad stomach pains and diarrhea. I've been cleaning all morning. No sooner do I get one cleaned up another one starts."

"Any fevers, Frances?" Margaret asked.

"The children only have slight fevers. I've sent

Patrick for the doctor but haven't seen him yet. He's not feeling all that great either but he's still working and I'm worn out."

Frances had sent her husband to fetch Doc Clanny and while the three stood in the yard, they rode up on their horses. "Good morning, ladies. Patrick has been telling me you have a house full of ill children."

"Oh, I'm so glad you're here. Every one of them has stomach pains and diarrhea," Frances explained.

"Let me have a look at them." Doc Clanny climbed off of his horse and tied the reins around a tree limb grabbing the medical bag dangling off the saddle.

Doc Clanny was an older man in his 60's with winter-white hair that he covered with a dark blue Irish flat cap. His gentle eyes looked fatigued but he wore a kind smile. He genuinely cared for people especially children. Most of the doctors in Ireland would not treat patients if they couldn't pay first with money, but he would accept a few vegetables from their garden instead or anything they were willing to part with.

"Frances, do you want us to wait?" Winfred asked.

"Yes, please." Doc Clanny, Patrick and Frances walked towards the house and Frances quietly told the doctor what had been going on with the children. It occurred to Doc Clanny as he entered her home that one of his patients, George Baley of Quarry Street of Shillelagh, had been suffering from cholera. Diagnosis was difficult because there was confusion over the symptoms of the disease. Various typhus-like illnesses had long been described in Ireland as typhoid and Doc Clanny did not realize that cholera, which was making its insidious first appearance in Ireland, was a completely different disease nor did he understand how the contagion spread. A group of doctors from Britain had recently speculated that the malady might be caused by contaminated water. These children and their symptoms looked very similar to the Baley family symptoms.

Doc Clanny examined the first small child that lay on a tattered makeshift bed on the floor. The child was wet from fever. He gently pinched the skin on his arm and noticed the loss of elasticity. He put his fingers on the child's neck to check the pulse and knew the heart rate was much too fast to be normal.

He examined the rest of the children and asked Frances and Patrick to step outside with him. "I believe your children have a disease called cholera. We don't know much about it but there is a thought that it could come from contaminated water."

Frances gasped and put her hand to her mouth. She glanced over to the water well and pump and asked, "Oh dear God, it could be from the well?"

"That's a possibility. We don't know how to treat it at this point. I would suggest not using this water source for a few days." The doctor gave them orders to lime-wash their house in an attempt to clean it up. Frances was crying as the doctor rode away.

When she broke the morbid news to Winfred and Margaret, Winfred compassionately replied, "We'll get people from church over here to help you. We'll bring you water, Frances. Don't worry."

By the time people arrived the next morning to help, all of the children had died, taken by death's cold hand during the night. Frances grew ill that day, too ill to bury her children and she died two days later. Her husband was dead within the week.

Later that summer, Rose, didn't come down from the loft. Winfred was starting breakfast, the fire was going, a pot hung on the hearth and no one had seen Rose. "Girls, did Rose come down with you?" Winfred asked.

"No, Mamai, come to think of it, she didn't," Catherine replied.

Rose was always the first one up so Winfred worriedly said to John, "Go up and see if Rose is still in the loft."

John climbed the ladder and saw Rose curled up under the blankets but noticed immediately that her coloring didn't look right.

"Mamai, come up, Rose doesn't look well," John shouted from the loft.

Winfred climbed the ladder quickly and took one look at Rose. "Get some water quickly!"

John got a cold cloth and water and took them up to Winfred, whose worry was palpable. "Go outside and find your dadai and tell him to find Doc Clanny."

John came back in after frantically finding Thomas and giving him the message. Winfred had John and the girls bring Rose down the stairs which was difficult carrying her down from the loft and lay her on Winfred's bed. She kept a cold cloth on her face but throughout the day, the fever only got worse. They waited for Doc Clanny but by the middle of the night, her fever was inducing seizures, and by morning she was dead. The sudden loss stunned the whole family, who was plunged into grief beyond words. By the time Doc Clanny finally arrived, he took one look at Rose, was told her symptoms and thought it might be cholera again but he was discovering people in the area coming down with typhoid fever. They buried Rose in the Kilquiggan Cemetery and it was the saddest day of their life.

John overheard Thomas and Winfred talking quietly through sobs after the burial, "Thomas, I'm afraid Rose had the fever. What if it takes more of our children?" Thomas tried to comfort Winfred but he had the same fear. Typhoid Fever was spreading through the villages and they didn't know what was causing it or how to stop it. Little did they know, it was caused by bacteria that had contaminated their water that in turn was tainting their potato crop. John, like his father did not show emotion but deep inside, he hurt terribly and also was afraid.

Two weeks to the day of Rose's death, Winfred cradled Joseph in her arms grieving in disbelief that she was gone. She hummed an Irish ballad as tears ran down her cheeks. She thought back to Rose and her sweet demeanor. Always willing to help, always cheerful. Winfred smile at the memories and felt heartsick at the same time. Her awareness was suddenly back to Joseph as he began to cry. *My God he feels hot*, she thought as the anxiety began to wheal up in her. She picked him up and held him to her breast. Laying him down on the bed, she pulled up his shirt her hands shaking. Rose-colored spots appeared all over Joseph's chest. The spots that she feared the most. "No, my God, No!" Winfred cried out loud. "Not another one of my children. " Within just a few days, Joseph was buried next to his sister on a dreary summer morning. The Doyle family was dwindling and it became more difficult to carry on as they always had. They continued to work their land and dying potato crops. They would wake early in the morning and work late until the evening. The long hours kept them busy and their minds occupied. Two of their dairy cows had died, straining their milk supply. In the late fall of 1846, John noticed that his father was working slower than he usually did. He didn't seem to have the stamina that he was used to seeing.

"I'm worried about him, Thomas," John shared with his brother. "He's not eating and seems very tired. Maybe he's just worn out from worry and grief."

The north wind began to howl and it quickly became very cold. A falling snow began to blow in and around the front door. John and Thomas had been put in charge of keeping turf on the fire. Winfred didn't like the fact that they had to build fires so early in the season. She feared that they would run out of turf before the end of this cold winter. John and Thomas decided not to mention any of their concerns to Winfred, but Winfred knew her husband well enough to know he wasn't his usual self.

The next morning, the boys worked in the barn when John heard Winfred call for them. They could hear the urgency in her voice. The snow crunched under their shoes and the holes in the soles exposed their bare feet. John pulled his coat tightly around him.

Winfred was standing near the door as the two boys walked in. The air outside was so cold that they quickly closed the door to keep the wind out. The house, drafty and dark, made it easy for the wind to whistle below the door like hungry wolves trying to enter in pursuit of its prey. The air inside suddenly reeked of illness and defeat.

"Boys, it's your dadai!" Winfred cried softly to herself, holding her rosary to her lips and silently pleading for Thomas' recovery. They followed Winfred into the bedroom and she wept openly. Thomas had worked hard all of his life and was much too young of a man to be dying. John could hear his labored breathing and with each cough, he feared it would be his last. He kneeled by his father's bedside and held his hand. As Thomas struggled to open his eyes, John knew he had something to share with him while he still could. John leaned toward him and gently held the cloth to his forehead. Thomas burned with fever.

"John, Thomas whispered. You must promise me something?" He struggled with each word and John could hear the rattle of each breath.

"Anything Dadai," John whispered with tears in his eyes.

"You are my oldest son. Promise me that you will go to America and take our family. Protect them, John, and provide for them. Will you promise me that, Son?"

John was moved but knew that his father relied on him. He wasn't sure how he would accomplish this but he replied, "I promise you, Dadai."

With that promise made, Thomas closed his eyes and took his last breath.

In the early months of 1847, John and Thomas Jr. desperately tried to keep the farm going. They continued to attend church each Sunday but the congregation was dwindling. Some died of Cholera and Typhoid Fever and many more from starvation. It seemed like the Doyle family was attending a funeral a couple times a week. It became common to see the black wagon going down the dirt road past the Doyle farmland and on to St. Mary's Church.

Bridget felt a keen responsibility being the oldest child to try and keep the families spirits up. She was also the redhead of the family that only made her more beautiful. Her hair fell in waves around her shoulders and framed her dark green eyes. Attending the funeral of Joseph Flinn's son, Edward, she patiently waited for Willie Fenlon to arrive. They had been best friends for as long as she could remember and had been courting for over a year. His sense of humor and inner strength always left her feeling like anything was possible. Bridget stood in the back of the church. She was dressed in an ankle-length cotton dress and high-topped laced shoes whose holes had been patched with deer hide.

"Bridget, I'm glad you waited for me. I have news."

Bridget looked at him apprehensively. What is it, Willie."

"My family is thinking about moving to the Shillelagh Workhouse."

"Willie, that's so far away?" Her eyes welled with tears.

"It's not that far. We can't go on much longer like this.

We have little to put on the table and we hear that the workhouse is filling up. Don't worry, Bridget. Nothing is carved in stone yet.

Willie wiped her eyes tenderly and they walked into church.

Sitting down next to John, Bridget noticed the far away look in his eyes. The last words from his father kept haunting him. John knew he had to get out of Ireland and take his family with him or they would all surely perish.

Chapter Five
Time to Leave Ireland

January 1848

Most of us have far more courage
than we ever dreamed we possessed.
Dale Carnegie

John contemplated with grave seriousness the enormous responsibility for his family now that he was the man of the house. Standing 5'11" tall with broad shoulders, he had beautiful, serious eyes. Even though he could be pleasant and had a pretty good sense of humor, he tended to be conservative and reticent. He said little unless he had something to say. During the difficult and challenging times of his life, he relied heavily on his faith.

As Winfred and John left St. Mary's one Sunday morning, Winfred walking slowly next to her son said, "Don't you think it's time you took a wife?"

John stopped in the road and with a serious expression on his face said, "Mamai, I'm surprised at you."

"Why? You're not getting younger and Keline O'Connor is a nice woman."Winfred was not one to talk so openly about romance or relationships so this discussion surprised John.

"I agree Keline would make any man a lucky man but it won't be me. I would not consider marriage unless I had a future that was secure and could provide for my family. I want to own a piece of land someday and build my log cabin and fill it with children. That's what I want for my future and when I know I can provide that, I'll take a wife."

Winfred could tell by John's demeanor that the discussion was closed. John did think about Keline. He loved her beautiful hair and she was kind and thoughtful and had a cute sense of humor. He took every opportunity to talk with her the few chances that he had but knew in his heart that he couldn't encourage a woman he couldn't take care of. The day would come when he would have a wife and he hoped many children but it wasn't now. He believed in hard work and when he did relax it was with his family and the music that they shared.

"John, would you play the fiddle for us?" asked Catherine after the evening meal. "It reminds me of Dadai." Catherine, John's older sister sat big-boned and brawny with soulful brown eyes and long lashes that hid her deepest secrets. Her beautiful lips told it all. She mindlessly tugged on her long dark hair that was braided down her back and thought about Daniel. Daniel was the love of her life. He carried the same last name and everyone had teased that they were related but they weren't. Daniel had just shared with her that leaving Ireland had been a discussion in his family.

"Catherine," Daniel whispered to her only days before. "If I leave Ireland, you will leave Ireland with me as my wife." Catherine smiled to herself as she thought of this wondering if she should share it with her family and how they would respond. She decided for the time being to keep that secret to herself.

In January of 1848, they endured a particularly bad winter. Snow fell heavily throughout the area making travel impossible. Carts and horses couldn't make it through the heavy snow and deep rutted roads. Father Byrne started a relief committee of the healthy congregation to assist in getting a supply of food and turf to those that couldn't get out. He asked John to go with him on one of the visits. They had collected a meager amount of oatmeal and potatoes and an even smaller amount of turf and made their way through the snow to a farm up the hill near Aghowle. Father Byrne knocked on the door of the small farmhouse with no response. They pushed open the door peering into the cold dark room. Lying on a bed in the corner of the room was a family of six frozen to death. John couldn't believe what he was seeing. Some of the children lay with their eyes and mouth open as if they died hoping for one bite of something to sustain them. Both men looked at each other in helpless desperation.

In response to the starving and destitute Irish, the British Government created relief committees in and around Coolkenno. Soup kitchens were constructed but the lines became so long that they would eventually run out of food and have to turn starving people away. They only had enough food to last maybe another month.

A few months later, during Sunday Mass, John sat next to a neighbor, Ryan Donaghue from Coolkenno. "I'm taking the family and we're going to the Shillelagh Workhouse if we can still get in."

"I've heard stories about that place," John replied.

"Well, it's not the best answer, but it's better than starving," Ryan said with worry.

"I've passed it a few times but never been in it. It looks foreboding. I wish you the best though. Anything to take care of our families."

After mass, Winfred, John and his sisters were eating breakfast when there was a knock at the door. It was Sam Castleford. He had passed Thomas Jr. out at the barn milking the last cow they had left.

"Good morning, John, Winfred, girls. John, we need to talk about a business matter. Could we talk privately?"

"Of course." John had taken over all of the duties of taking care of the garden and barn and paid Sam rent for the land they lived on.

They walked outside and Samuel said, "I have some

bad news. Charlotte and I have decided to leave Ireland. We've already informed Lord Fitzpatrick of our decision. As a matter of fact, they're looking for volunteers to leave and passage will be paid. Not only that, Lord Fitzpatrick has promised parcels of land for the Irish to farm in America. I believe we're ready for a new start. If you go too John, you'd be able to own land instead of rent. We're on a sinking ship and I don't see it improving. We've lost so many acres to this damn fungus and it's spreading. No one knows what it is or how to stop it. We'll starve to death if we stay another year. Charlotte and I could go back to England anytime we want but I think it would be political suicide."

John was stunned. He listened intently but all the while he could hear his father's voice and pleading request to take the family to America.

"There's a town meeting tonight. Many farmers are going to learn how to get to America. I would be honored and relieved if you would join me."

"Of course. I'll go and see what's it's all about. I don't know what to tell my mother. We've discussed America but she only knows Ireland. I'll take Thomas with me tonight and we'll hear what they have to say and make a decision. How much time do we have?"

"Probably not more than a month."

"Thanks, Sam, and please give my best to Charlotte." John walked to the barn to talk to Thomas. He had his head down, deep in thought. There had been talk amongst the farmers in town about how difficult the voyage to America was and how some never made it to the other shore, or at least the family never heard back from them.

"Brother, why so serious?" Thomas asked.

"Samuel and Charlotte are leaving for America. We'll have to move."

"What?" replied Thomas in shock. "America, when?"

"Less than a month! There's a meeting tonight at the town hall to tell us how to sail to America. We're going. We have nothing left here and everything to lose if we stay. I can't handle one more death in the family. Don't mention anything to Mamai, Catherine or Bridget just yet. Let's hear what they have to say tonight and then we'll make a plan.

John finished his chores for the day and was tired and hungry. He filled the wash- bowl with clean water and cleaned himself up as well as he could. Putting on a clean shirt, he stood in front of the looking glass as he buttoned the buttons.

"Where are you headed, John?" Winfred asked.

"Thomas and I are going into town tonight. We have a few matters to clear up. We're meeting Sam there. You have nothing to worry about," John assured her.

The air was cool as they stepped out to walk the distance to the town center.

"John, Thomas," Winfred called after him. "Would

you boys like something to eat before you go?"

"No thanks, Mamai; I don't want to be late. Keep a plate for us, will you?"

"Sure I will," she replied concerned about what they might be up to.

John held his head down as he walked the dirt road next to Thomas. Both men trudged in silence, lost in their own thoughts. In the background, the crickets sang a melodic tune and the spring evening held the fragrance of apple blossoms as the sun lowered itself below the horizon. When they arrived at the town hall, there was already a line forming to get in.

"Standing room only, John!" It was Ryan Donaghue. John was surprised to see him at this meeting.

"Must be a popular topic!" John replied back. The two brothers inched their way into the back of the small room, which was buzzing with the chorus of men talking to each other and greeting old friends. John and Thomas stood quietly in the back, nodding hello to a few that they knew. They were two of the youngest in the room but had as much responsibility as anyone there. "Gentleman, ladies," the fellow in the front yelled out. "My name is Skipper." Skipper was a very tall thin man who looked like he could use about fifty pounds to balance his lanky structure. Pushing back the long gray hair from his face revealed the weathered look of a man who had spent many years at sea. His loud, deep voice carried even to the back of the crowd. The clothing he wore was as worn as the expression he carried.

As he stood in front of this large, inquisitive crowd, he pulled his cap down over his ears as if protecting himself from a possible assault.

"May I have your attention, please? Thank you for coming here tonight. I know you all are most anxious to hear about voyages to America. The ships are filling fast. Each ship will hold approximately 200 people in the belly of the ship. If you have the money to reserve passage above the belly, you're one lucky gentleman or lady. The passage takes approximately three months and leaves out of New Ross Landing. There will be two ships leaving each month; one on the first of the month and one on the fifteenth. You can sign up tonight but you must have a down payment, which would be half of the passage, and it is first come, first serve to get on the ship. If you make a down payment and get to the ship and your name is not called at roll call, you have to wait for the next ship. If you appear ill, you will be turned away until you are well."

A loud buzz of excited speech filled the room. John just listened. He didn't have the down payment, didn't know he needed it. Finding out that it would be sixty shillings and he only had twenty meant that he would have to find a way to earn the money needed. Samuel had also mentioned that Lord Fitzpatrick was paying passage for some to leave Ireland. John looked around the room for Samuel. He put his hands in his pocket and listened for the curator to quiet the crowd.

"Keep it down, keep it down. While on the ship, you'll be given food and milk once a day but you may bring your own. Keep in mind, you will only be permitted one trunk per family to bring on board. This can be food or your family keepsakes; it's up to you. Once you arrive in New York City, you will be given an examination and only the healthy will be allowed to enter New York. You must, and I repeat *must*, have an address or plan when you arrive. You will be asked what your destination is and you must have an answer or you will be turned away."

An uproar came from the crowd. John stood wondering how this was going to be accomplished since he knew no one in the America. He shoved his hands deeper into his pockets and the lines in his forehead grew more furrowed as he tried to come up with a plan. He glanced over to the crowd by the door and there was Sam Castleford. He gave a small wave and John and Thomas inched their way over.

"Sam, what do you think about all of this?"

"John, your passage will be paid for by Lord Fitzpatrick. Charlotte and I are booking passage. We're leaving on the next ship. It's 47 miles to New Ross Harbor where the ship will be embarking. My brother,

George is taking us in the carriage if you want to join us. It would save you the tiresome task of walking," shared Samuel.

Thomas stood listening with anxious expression. "John, are you thinking of leaving us soon? What will we do – where will we live?"

"Don't worry, I won't leave unless I know you all are taken care of. We'll figure something out. Sam, plan on me joining you. I have much to do in the meantime. I have twenty shillings which would be enough to get me to the ship," John shared.

"John, your father and I were good friends and you've been a loyal tenant. I'll do anything I can to help you." Samuel replied.

"Thank you. Thomas and I have much to plan," John said looking like he had a lot on his mind. John and Samuel signed their name on the roster of people who planned to board the next America-bound ship while Thomas anxiously watched. When Skipper questioned John about his deposit, Samuel vouched for John that Lord Fitzpatrick would pay for his passage and he purchased two first class tickets for Charlotte and himself.

"Well Samuel, it looks like this is really going to happen. I'm glad we're in this together," John smiled as they walked away.

"Good evening, gentleman," Samuel replied.

John and Thomas got back late that evening. The full

moon cast a silvery glow on the path, guiding their way. They didn't say much to each other on the walk back. Both were deeply troubled and anxious over what all of this meant.

"Thomas, if we can get Mamai and the girls and you in one of the workhouses until I can send for you that might work. At least you'd have a roof over your head and food to eat?"

"Mamai would never agree to that, nor Catherine or Bridget," answered Thomas.

"Everyone is leaving. I think the quicker we go, the better off we'll be. I'm going tomorrow to the Shillelagh Workhouse. I hear there's a line to get in so possibly Sam can help. The hard part will be telling Mamai and the girls. Thomas, I need you to stay here with them until I can send for all of you."

"I don't like this, John!"

"I don't either but this is what we have to do. I don't see any other options." The next morning, John walked the distance to the workhouse, only to get turned away.

Chapter Six

The Shillelagh Workhouse

April 1848

God grant me the serenity to
accept the things that I
cannot change, the courage to change
the things that I can, and the
wisdom to know the difference.
Reinhold Niebuhr

The Shillelagh Workhouse, one of the largest in Ireland, had been built to accommodate 400 inmates but soon became full to overflowing. They had been designed not to encourage admission but to discourage it. By the beginning of April 1848, the workhouse in Shillelagh was declared full.

John had not even ventured beyond the exterior, but merely stared at the line to get in. He was sure most would be turned away including himself.

Feeling discouraged, he left the line and walked back to Sam's house.

"Good morning, Charlotte. Is Sam home?

"He's traveling to the Fitzpatrick Estate, John. How can we help?"

"I need his assistance in getting my mother, Thomas and my sisters into the Shillelagh Workhouse. They're full and the list to get in could take months to work through. If I'm to leave in less than a month, I need to make sure my family is taken care of," John shared anxiously.

"I'll talk to Sam when he returns," Charlotte replied with a smile.

"Thank you. Please no mention of this to Winfred or my sisters until I know that it's settled. There's no sense worrying them if this isn't going to happen." He knew Charlotte liked to talk and her ability to keep it quiet would be difficult. John could only hope.

By the end of the week, Sam had drawn on his connections to secure John an interview at the workhouse. John showed up on a cool April day filled with hope and trepidation. Standing outside breathing the fresh air, he was impressed with the enormity of the place. It consisted of three horizontal blocks, a large brown stone structure with a big wooden door and windows in the front. There was a large wall surrounding the main building but he could see smaller buildings out back. The line of people outside to apply to get into the workhouse was fifty deep. He heard someone yell that the priority to get in was old age, sickly people or physically disabled, or children and next came the unemployed. John shoved his way to the front of the line.

"Hey you bloke, get to the back!" someone yelled. A guard with his hand on his stick approached John.

"I have an appointment!" John yelled.

"Who do ya have this appointment with?" questioned the guard.

"It's with Mr. Jonathan Murphy"

"Come this way."

John heard the yells and insults as the large wooden door closed behind him. Once inside, he glanced around. The guard told him to have a seat on the wooden bench. John sat directly outside of the admissions office. The guard took it upon himself to point out where the porter's office was located, along the probationary wards and the guardians' boardroom. Within a few short minutes, a man walked out of the admissions office and called John in.

"Mr. Doyle, welcome. My name is Jonathan Murphy. I understand that you have been recommended by Samuel Castleford, is that correct?"

"Yes sir, I'm planning passage to America with Mr. Castleford and his wife Charlotte and I need beds for my mother, Winfred, brother Thomas and my two sisters," John replied.

"How old is Thomas and your sisters?"

"Sir, Thomas is thirteen and a hard worker, Catherine is nineteen and Bridget is twenty-five."

"Is your mother lame or insane?"

"No sir, she's able-bodied."

"How long do you intend for their stay?"

"I'm praying not more than one year. I'll then arrange passage for them to join me in America."

"You realize there are many people ahead of you in line but if your family is willing and able to work, I'm sure we can find something for them and of course, you came highly recommended," Mr. Murphy stated.

"Yes sir, that would be most gracious of you," John said breathing a sigh of relief.

"Let me show you around." John followed Mr. Murphy out into the main hall. "The main building holds the dormitories, the school and the dayrooms and master and matron's accommodations. Thomas will be in one building and the women in another. The third building through that courtyard is the infirmary and the lunatic wards. We have a dining hall which doubles as a chapel. The small buildings outback are the kitchen and the washrooms."

John noticed that the building he was standing in was relatively quiet and the wood floors and everything else he saw seemed very clean. It was certainly better than nothing. God willing, it would only be for a year. This could work.

"Mr. Doyle, when will your family be arriving?"

"Within a two week period," John replied.

"Very well, we look forward to their arrival."

The large crowd outside started yelling at John as soon as he opened the door. He feared they would get violent. Ignoring their insults, he pushed his way to the dirt road. Once outside of the throng of people, he felt a sense of relief that he was able to find his family accommodations while he would be away. He had Sam to thank for that. Now would come the difficult part, telling his mother and sisters.

Thomas was working in the yard when John returned to the house.

Eagerly, he looked at John and asked, "Well, how did it go?"

"You're in," replied John.

"It's hard for me to be excited about this. Mamai is going to be very upset."

"Thomas, it's not permanent. There are more opportunities in America than here. As soon as I get there, I'll start working on getting you all out. This will work. Help me tell Mamai."

John and Thomas walked into the house apprehensively. Winfred and Bridget were talking casually as they prepared supper. A boiling kettle gave off a low rumble and exuded the aroma of cooked onions and cabbage. Thomas and John sat down at the table.

"Mamai, we have something to tell you," said John sheepishly.

Winfred turned around, wiped her hands on her apron and said anxiously, "What is it, boys?"

"Sam and Charlotte are leaving for America and closing the farm," John replied.

"Oh my dear God!" Winfred cried pulling out a chair to sit before she collapsed. Bridget started to cry.

"Where will we go?" asked Winfred. "We have so little as it is."

"Mamai, I'm going to America with them. My passage has been paid for by Lord Fitzpatrick and I have made arrangements for you, Thomas, Bridget and Catherine to live in the workhouse for hopefully no longer than a year."

"A year John, that's so long," Winfred said with defeat.

"I know, but that will give me time to get to America, find land and send for you all. We're leaving Ireland, Mamai. There's nothing left for us here. Do you remember Dadai's final words to me? Take care of the family and leave Ireland! I know this is our country but we've already lost so much. In America, we'll have a new opportunity," John said, trying to convince her.

Thomas just sat quietly, afraid to say anything.

"John, you don't know that for sure. I've heard stories about the ships. They call them coffin ships for a reason. What happens if something happens to you and then what?" Winfred cried.

"Mamai, if I don't take this chance, something will happen to me here. If illness doesn't get one of us like the rest, we'll starve if we have another bad winter. We have no potato crop to speak of. We have to trust in God to help us through this," John pleaded.

"When are you leaving?" Winfred asked.

"Two weeks from tomorrow."

Trying to remain positive, Thomas added, "Mamai, it's going to be okay. We'll be together. Bridget, I hear Willie Quinn and his family are trying to get into the workhouse as well."

"I know Thomas," he shared it with me months ago

"It's our best option," John said stoically.

Winfred sat down with an enormous heaviness in her heart. She didn't know what was worse, leaving Ireland and her deceased husband and her children's graves or taking the chance of losing John on the voyage. What if they got to America and didn't like it or John couldn't find work or illness was worse there? Sadness and anxiety overcame her.

The news was told to Catherine when she returned home from visiting the Widow Murphy. She was relieved to know they would all stay together but she was worried about John. Catherine did not react like everyone had expected.

"I'm not surprised," Catherine replied. "Everyone is thinking of leaving. Daniel is talking about leaving and taking me to America as his wife!"

Everyone looked up at Catherine.

"What?" asked Winfred. "Catherine, has Daniel asked you to marry him?"

"Not exactly. But if he leaves, I'm leaving with him."

Bridget chimed in, "Willie's family was told that they would have a room in the Workhouse within the month and as upset as they are, they know that it 's better than starving."

No one felt like eating that evening and everyone retired early with much on their minds.

Preparations for the next two weeks were quickly underway. In the urgency of the moment, John was forced to sell their last cow for a pittance. The leased land paperwork was taken care of with Sam Castleford and they packed the little they had. Winfred had her mother's rosary and a few things from the kitchen. John had his father's fiddle but asked Winfred to keep it until he sent for them, protective of the few objects of sentiment he had inherited.

On a chilly, foggy April 15th, the family climbed aboard the loaded wagon and huddled together as John drove them to the Shillelagh Workhouse. The air was heavy with sadness in leaving the little house that they had always known. They left their furniture – the beds they had lain in, the chairs in which they had sat on so many idle evenings, so many jovial suppers - and couldn't look back. As they neared their destination, the church bells of St. Mary's tolled with a brassy timbre and the familiar sound registered as a sign that someone from above was guiding and protecting them or perhaps there was just another death in the village of Coolkenno.

John pulled the wagon around back to avoid the crush of onlookers - the poor souls that still waited for a vacancy. The new inmates, as they would be called upon arrival were instructed to use the back entrance only. He prayed he was doing the right thing. He felt horrible for dropping them off and heading out.

Thomas saw the look on John's face and spoke up, "Don't worry about us. We'll be fine until you send for us."

John appreciated the encouragement and said, "Thank you, this is really difficult for me. I will miss you all terribly."

John helped his sisters out of the wagon and gave them each a hug. He hugged Winfred and promised, "Mamai, if it's the last thing I do in my life, I'll send for you."

"I trust that, John. God be with you in your travels. Know we will pray for you daily," Winfred replied, choking back tears.

With that, he had to leave so that no one saw the tears in his own eyes. Though overcome with fear and sadness, he knew he had to push through it. Nothing would be gained by breaking down now. Gathering his resolve, he turned the wagon around and headed back to the farm.

Life in the Workhouse

Thomas, Winfred and the girls walked through the large wooden door to be greeted by a rather large man in a dark brown suit and clean linen shirt. "May I help you?" he asked directly to Winfred.

"We're the Doyle's from the crossroads of the Crablane. Mr. Murphy is expecting us," Winfred spoke up confidently.

"Ah, yes, please come right this way," the man directed. He led Winfred and her children down a long hallway.

They had never been inside this building as long as they had known it was here. It seemed more like a prison to her than it did a dormitory.

"We'll get you checked in and you'll meet with a relief officer. You'll fill out the records for admission and then you'll receive a physical by one of our medical officers." Winfred was appalled "medical officer"? She had never taken off her clothes in front of anyone, including her husband. The look on the girls' faces showed the same terror.

Thomas said, "Mamai, it will be okay. Just remind yourself that this is temporary."

Winfred's eyes got dark and her lips became pursed. She didn't want to get thrown out before they had even been admitted. She decided it best to keep her feelings to herself.

The four of them were led into a room and were instructed to have a seat on one of the many benches in the room. A large cluster of people waited in line before them.

The gentleman launched into his instructions, "Inmates will be separated into groups according to age and sex. No contact will be permitted between married couples. Parents will have reasonable access to their children and if in their presence, will control their children without inconveniencing the workhouse administration."

The administrator, who had a large beefy mustache, held a clipboard in his hand and looked over his glasses as he spoke in a no-nonsense tone. After about one hour, the Doyle name was called and Thomas went forward. Sitting at a small table with a stack of papers in front of him was Shamish McCormick. Small, wire-framed glasses sat perched on a round little face with a pointy nose. Thomas had never seen glasses like that.

"Mr. Doyle," the young clerk spoke, "is your entire family present?"

"Yes, sir we are."

"Their names please?" asked Shamish.

"My mother, Winfred, is over there along with my

sisters Bridget and Catherine and me, Thomas."

The clerk checked their names off of the list. "Do you or your family have any known illnesses?" asked Shamish without looking up from his clipboard.

"No, sir."

"Anyone insane?"

"No, sir."

"Have you broken any laws or wanted by the authorities?"

"No, sir."

"What goods have you brought with you?"

"We have our clothes and my dadai's fiddle. That's all," Thomas replied.

"You'll not have any need for your clothes since we will provide those for you and you are welcome to keep the fiddle but I doubt you will be leaving with it. There is no place to keep something like that and we can't control the thieves."

Thomas immediately felt sick and a churning anger began to rise up inside him the longer he stood there answering incessant questions. John had given them that fiddle for safekeeping. He couldn't bear to think someone might steal it.

"Please sign here or put an X that you understand everything that has been told to you today. Then, please bring your family up and I'll go over the rules."

Thomas called for Winfred and his sisters. Hesitantly,

they walked to the desk looking at Thomas anxiously.

Shamish had them take a seat and he proceeded to tell them the rules.

"Welcome to the Shillelagh Workhouse. I'll go over a few things with you and then you're welcome to ask questions when I'm finished. Agreed?"

Everyone nodded yes. Winfred showed no expression.

"You will leave this office and be taken to an area to bathe. Thomas, you'll be on the west wing with the men and, ladies, you three will be on the east wing with the women. At no time, will the men come to the east wing or the women to the west wing under any circumstances. Breaking this rule will get you bounced out immediately. Is that understood?"

They nodded in solemn agreement.

"Once you have bathed and have put on your new clothes, you'll be inspected by the medical officer. Until it can be confirmed by a medical attendant that you are free of disease, you'll be staying in our probationary ward. That is also where you will receive your meals. After approximately two weeks, if you are released, you'll be assigned to the regular ward and given a bed. Your meals will then be in the dining hall. At that time, after it has been determined that you are capable of working, you'll be assigned a job for the duration of your time here at Shillelagh Workhouse. What questions do you have for me?"

The girls wanted to sob but were determined not to cry in public or in front of Winfred or Thomas. With cold, bureaucratic haste, Shamish escorted them out of the admissions office. He led Thomas to the left and Winfred and the girls to the right. A large woman dressed in a dark cotton gray dress with a white apron and a gray cap on her head greeted them.

"My name is Hilda and I will be in charge of you until you leave the probationary area." Once in a small private room, she told them to take off all of their clothes behind a small screen in the room. Winfred at first refused.

"Ma'am, you must do this and bathe, put on clean clothes, or you'll be sent out," explained Hilda quite impatiently.

Winfred had nowhere to go if they sent her out, so she begrudgingly complied. Bridget became very angry as she listened to the dialogue between Hilda and her mother. "Mamai, I will help you," Bridget said as she threw a look of repulsion towards Hilda.

Winfred sheepishly turned so that Bridget could unbutton her dress. She wanted to weep as Bridget placed the garment and discarded underclothes on a pile to be burned. Winfred turned again and tried to cover herself with the small towel that was given to them. Never in her life had she felt so helpless and shameful to be so exposed in front of her daughters and a perfect stranger. Equally, Catherine and Bridget had a difficult time with the whole procedure but decided to ignore the leering eyes of Hilda. It was only a matter of time when they would be leaving the Shillelagh Workhouse behind them and into the arms of the men that loved them.

After they bathed, Hilda gave them their new clothing, an outfit very similar to Hilda's that included a gray cotton dress, a shift, petticoat and other undergarments and a formless cap designed to fit everyone. Hilda began checking them for fleas, working her grimy fingers through their hair. Then the clothes that they wore to the workhouse were taken away and burned, another trace of their past life disappeared, turned now to ash. Hilda led them down the hall to the medical examiners. As Winfred sat outside the door and waited for her name to be called and for her two daughters to finish with their physical, she could hear the doctor talking with patients through the thin walls. She thanked God that she didn't have any ailments. Four people were sent down to the infirmary; one was lame, another had episodes of convulsions, another suffered from sore eyes that were bright red and oozing pus, and one poor unmarried woman discovered she was pregnant during her examination.

The doctor brought them in one by one, asked them a serious of questions and then gave them each a thorough medical exam.

Since they all appeared relatively healthy, he was about to check them off the list and send them to the probationary ward when the medical doctor asked, "In the past year, has anyone in your family been ill or died from typhoid or the fever?"

Winfred froze, not wanting to lie, but terrified of being sent away. Her mind raced.

"Speak up, woman," the doctor said with irritation. "In the past year, has anyone in your family been ill or died from typhoid or the fever?"

Catherine looked at Winfred and said, "Mamai, it's been more than a year since Dadai died."

The doctor continued to stare at Winfred. It became so quiet in the room, Winfred could hear a clock ticking on the doctor's desk.

Finally, after an excruciating silence, Winfred replied, "No sir, not within a year."

The doctor signed his name and said flatly, "That will be all."

The three women walked back out in the hallway and waited for Hilda to take them to their next stop.

Chapter Seven

Probationary Ward and Employment

April 1848

We gain strength, and courage,
and confidence by each experience
in which we really stop to look
fear in the face...we must do
that which we think we cannot.
Eleanor Roosevelt

Winfred and her daughters entered the probationary ward and found twenty other women dressed just like them, all wearing a look on their face of dismay over their current conditions. Winfred didn't recognize any of them, despite having convinced herself that surely she would know someone.

Late in the day when they arrived in this ward, they felt tired and hungry from the emotional morning. They stood in line to receive a cot with a sheet and blanket and instructed to make their bed. Once they achieved that, supper would be served within the hour. As Winfred made her bed, she struck up a quiet conversation with the woman who would be sleeping next to her, named Sally O'Shea. Sally was from Ballymore and married a man by the name of Mickey. When they entered the workhouse, they had been told that the whole family had to live there to be admitted. Mick, as Sally called him, would only be given two hours per day to look for work and then he had to report back to the workhouse. Winfred didn't have the heart to tell her that her son was on his way to America to find work and would be sending for them. Sally's two small children had been sent to the children's ward.

"It's breakin' my heart to be separated from my children and husband. This is no way to live," Sally wept softly as she spoke.

Winfred felt so sorry for her. Did she really have a hope of ever getting out of the Shillelagh Workhouse or would her fate be to die within the walls of this prison?

Shortly before 5:00, a bell chimed and everyone reported to a small room outside the sleeping area where a meager amount of food was placed on a long table. Their meal consisted of twelve ounces of brown bread and one and one-half pints of soup. Dinner was basically the same thing and breakfast consisted of seven ounces of Indian meal or sometimes oatmeal and a half pint of milk. Occasionally, they received meat but there was a rumor that the meat had to be delivered at night to disguise its poor quality and evade an inspection.

The two weeks spent in the probationary ward were pretty mundane. Thomas had a similar experience in the west wing. He waited for his probationary period to be over to join the rest of the men and hopefully see Daniel or Willie and some other friendly faces.

After a long and monotonous two weeks, the medical examiner gave them a check mark showing that they bore no illness, had not exhibited signs of insanity and appeared capable to work. The workhouse received a stipend of oats, wheat, barley and flax, potatoes and vegetables and Thomas discovered that he would be working in the garden. He felt very relieved to be working outside with other farmers. He knew that whatever he learned would benefit John and the rest of his family once they moved to America. Once a week, he stood guard over the garden from 8:00 p.m. to 6:00 a.m. vigilant against marauders who might attempt to steal the vegetables. The male guard watching over the men told them that if they fell asleep while on guard duty, they would be placed in the basement in a cell for one week's time, no windows, no toilet facilities except a bucket and very little food. Thomas thought that he would rather die than fall asleep and get sent to "the cage," as it was nicknamed. The punishment sounded worse than the prison they were already experiencing.

The female matron instructed Winfred that her

responsibility was baking bread and putting together meals for the inmates. Winfred felt comfortable with that. When she baked or prepared meals, she thought of nothing else except for the task at hand. That's what she needed right now: constant tedious work.

Bridget was told she'd be working with the children. She almost squealed with delight. She loved children and wanted to have a lot of them. How she remembered many a night when Willie and she would talk about having a family someday. She hoped for three girls and at least two boys. This made her think about Joey and Rose who she missed terribly. It would be so difficult to be separated from him now had he lived.

Catherine was the last to be given her job assignment. The matron instructed her that she would be delivering food to the insane asylum ward. The color left Catherine's face. How could that be? Working around the insane? Catherine fell on her bed and sobbed. Her new job started in the morning. All of their days would begin at 8:00 in the morning after breakfast and end at 8:00 in the evening.

"Lights out at 9:00 p.m. – no talking or noise of any kind," the matron instructed sternly. The matron shared one bit of good news, however, "You will all be taught how to read and write." Winfred was overjoyed at the news because if John could find a way to communicate with her somehow, she needed to know how to read and write. Literacy offered a link across the distance that nothing else could bridge.

Their lessons would be for one-hour after the noon meal was cleaned up. Thomas could already read and write small amounts along with John something they picked up on their own working with Sam Castleford. Their proficiency was minimal but they could get by. Winfred was very upset about Catherine's new job that left Catherine mired in depression all evening. Working with the insane, missing Daniel, missing John, missing her house, how could she handle it all? She had always been such an anxious child, sweet and quiet but always overcome with worry.

Winfred asked about Catholic service for Sunday. She could give up a lot but would not give up her Catholic religion her source of strength. It was as much a part of her as one of her limbs. The workhouse provided a non-denominational service but there was a visiting priest that would provide a Sunday service and sacraments since so many living in the workhouse were Irish Catholics. Each night, Winfred lay in the dark and prayed as she clutched her mother's rosary, a ritual that had become a great source of comfort to her.

Winfred and the girls went to bed early since their new way of life would begin the next morning. As much as Winfred and Bridget tried to comfort Catherine, it did nothing to lessen her fears and she cried herself to sleep.

The bells sounded early much to Winfred and her daughters' dismay but they all got up and dressed. Catherine looked terrible with puffy eyes and a red nose. Hilda appeared in their room to line them all up in the hallway. "Before you eat your morning meal, you will be learning about misdemeanors and consequences. Follow me please," she instructed.

They marched after her in a single line; all dressed the same, like baby chicks following the mother goose. Hilda led them into a large room with chairs lined up one right after the other. She asked them to sit and she cleared her throat, held her clipboard firmly in front of her massive chest and read, "Inmates' misdemeanors are divided into disorderly and refractory. The former consists of refusing to keep silent, using four letter or threatening language, refusing to work or wash, keeping an illness quiet, playing cards, misbehaving at prayers, entering an out of bounds part of the workhouse, dawdling on an errand outside or disobeying a workhouse officer. If the disorderly behavior is repeated or if the inmate smuggles in alcohol or tobacco, attempts to assault anyone, is drunk or indecent, disturbs a religious service, damages or tries to steal workhouse property or tries to leave by climbing over the workhouse wall, she is considered refractory. Disorderly behavior is punished by extra work and loss of one's milk-allowance. Those considered refractory will result in confinement in the punishment cell, which is in the basement and known as the black hole for up to twenty-four hours. Are there any questions and have I made myself perfectly clear?" barked Hilda.

No one dared to raise a hand or ask any questions. Winfred just wanted her cup of tea and to be left to bake.

Thomas' two weeks had been nothing but eye-opening. One of the first people that he met was a scruffy lad named Red McGrath because of the bright red of his hair and his red freckles. Thomas had a feeling about Red as soon as he met him. As everyone would come to find out, Red liked to fight. He had hopes of becoming a boxer before his family landed in the workhouse. He was one of twelve children, all of who looked alike and all of who shared Red's pugnacious temperament.

One night before the probation period came to an end, Red decided to teach a few of the boys how to play cards. Thomas found the game particularly exciting and it alleviated the boredom when all of a sudden, in walked a warden.

"Card playin' is against the rules boys. That's a misdemeanor – give me the cards," shouted Mackey McClain.

Well, Red wasn't about to turn the cards over that easily, but he was ready to throw the first punch. Actually, Red threw the last punch. McClain had him in a headlock before you could blink and proceeded to beat the life out of him. After that, Red spent a week in the cage.

Thomas couldn't for the life of him figure out why he had not received time in the basement. He figured that the fight took the attention off of him and shifted it directly to Red. Thomas decided to keep his distance from Red and came to the conclusion that cards were not worth a week in the cage. Red came up at the end of a full week and was in bad shape having lost a lot more than expected, like his eyesight for the better of two weeks.

Catherine reported to work the next morning very weary since she hadn't slept well the night before. She was told to wear a nametag that along with her name had the ward that she was working in so no one could accuse her of sneaking into another ward. *Why would anyone want to sneak into the insane ward,* Catherine thought to herself. A guard sat at the desk posted outside of the ward and asked her to sign in. After checking her name on a list, he instructed her to report to the kitchen.

"Walk through these locked doors, down the hall, turn left and you'll see the kitchen bigger than life," he said without emotion. "No one can get into this ward or out of this ward without my approval."

Catherine gave a half smile and proceeded through the door that the guard unlocked for her. As she walked down the hall, she tried to ignore the agonized screaming coming from one of the rooms. She made her way to the kitchen glancing into the rooms that she would pass. One old woman was lying on a straw mattress that fit inside a cage sobbing and yelling, "Dadai, help me! Help me!" She yelled it over and over. Catherine wondered what tortured memory was reverberating through this woman's mind.

She arrived at the kitchen to find a few other women her age waiting for instructions. They looked as worried and anxious as she felt.

"Are you Catherine?" a large woman in a white apron called to her.

"Yes, ma'am," Catherine responded.

"You'll be serving food to the women in this ward along with the infirmary. You'll work where you're needed the most. Is that clear?"

"Yes, ma'am." Then Catherine followed her directions to take warm milk and a bowl of oats to room twelve where she found a young woman about fifteen afflicted with an eye infection reportedly caused by malnutrition.

"Hello," Catherine said when she walked through her door with a small tray. "What is your name?"

"Mary Ann."

When Catherine inquired about her bandaged eye, Mary Ann shared that she had ophthalmia and she feared she might go blind. Catherine's heart broke for her so she made it a point to visit her every day. But Catherine's assignment did not include the most disadvantaged inmates. Those that had convulsions or were mentally handicapped lived in cages like the woman that she had passed on her first day. Catherine attended to many unmarried pregnant women and soon she realized she enjoyed this kind of work. She shared with Winfred and Bridget after her first day that she felt much more like a nurse or attendant than she had originally been told.

One afternoon, Catherine took food into a young girl of about twelve who would soon deliver a baby. Her face was etched with fear of the ordeal that she was about to experience. Catherine sat at her bed and listened to her story. Her name was Megan Kelly.

"I fell in love with a boy down the road named Timothy and I thought he loved me too. When I found out I was going to have a baby, Timothy refused to talk to me and my parents disowned me. Father Finnigan found me nearly starved to death living in a barn and he carried me to this workhouse. I'm afraid they'll take the baby when it's born. I don't know what I'm going to do."

As the young girl spoke, Catherine held her hand. She wanted to reassure her that everything would turn out okay but she knew better. Life would not get easier living in the workhouse, it would only get worse.

Most of her days were fairly easy working in the lunatic and infirmary wards, but Catherine saw her share of disease. She never told her mother about some of the diseases that she came in contact with and she also prayed that she wouldn't contract any of them. During the worst of the winter of 1848, she encountered one case of small pox that had everyone scared, four cases of influenza, three people died of dysentery, four of scarlatina and a baby died of whooping cough.

True to Megan's fears, the day that her baby was born, it was taken from her. After ten hours of hard labor, a beautiful baby girl was placed in her arms. Catherine ran passed the guard when she heard Megan calling for her. She ran into Megan's room just as Hilda was wrapping the crying child up in a blanket.

"Where are taking Megan's child?" Catherine asked with sincere concern.

No children in this ward, no children to unwed mothers!" and she walked out of the room.

Catherine hated that woman with everything she had. Her eyes filled with tears as she sat down on Megan's bed and held her until they had nothing left to cry.

The next morning, Thomas passed a gurney in the hallway. He glanced at the white-sheeted form and knew instantly that it was Red. He had overheard the Guard, Mackey McClain boasting that he had gone a little too far disciplining Red and accidently beat him to death. Unless Thomas wanted to be the next victim, he ignored what he heard and forgot what he saw.

As the days melted into weeks, they were all prisoners waiting anxiously for the day that they would hear from John.

Chapter Eight
Journey to the Ship

April 1848

All of our dreams can come true,
if we have the courage to pursue them.
Walt Disney

John left the workhouse and made his way back to his empty home his mind dulled with a grey despondence. He didn't have the heart to tell Winfred that since their house was made of timber, the house and barn would be torn down. Samuel and Charlotte's house was made of stone and therefore left intact. A new land manager scheduled to arrive any day would be living in the Castleford house.

Samuel had advised him to tear the house down himself to save money. Doing so seemed to add insult to injury, but John reluctantly agreed, needing the shilling or two it might save him. Patrick Donegal and Father Byrne from St. Mary's offered to help demolish his home.Samuel told him they'd be leaving early the next morning for the two-day trip to the ship. John had never traveled outside of his town and only a few times as far as Shillelagh, so he really didn't know what to expect. He felt a bit of excitement at the prospect of traveling to another part of Ireland that he had not experienced.

Long into the evening, John worked shoulder to shoulder with the two men and tirelessly tore down the house and barn. He was emotionally and physically drained when he heard singing coming up the road towards what remained of his home. He glanced over at Patrick whose expression turned from exhaustion to worry. John recognized them as they came into view. They were Loyalists from Ballynulta and they had just left John Byrne's Pub. They had a reputation of hating the Irish and the Catholics. The leader of this group was Tommy Hutchinson. It was apparent that they had been drinking as they could barely walk.

"Hey, John Doyle, yer nothing but a traitor and weak man. Leaving your family are ya? What kind of a man leaves his family in a death trap like the Shillelagh Workhouse?" Tommy slurred.

"Leave it alone, John," Father Byrne urged quietly. "They are drunk and nothing good can come from getting involved with them."

John threw down his shovel and started walking towards Tommy and his men. He was as angry as Patrick had ever seen him. Just as John was within a few feet of reaching Tommy with his fists and jaw clenched,

Samuel opened the door to his home and had his Brown Bess musket in his hands. He pointed the barrel above Tommy's head and fired one shot. The blast surprised Tommy enough that it threw him off balance. He landed in the dirt on his back with his legs in the air. His friends tried to pick him up but fearing another gun shot started running leaving Tommy stumbling to get back on his feet.

John glanced at Samuel standing in the doorway. His face was beet-red but he was relieved Samuel showed up when he did. John knew that beating a Loyalist at this time would only thwart his plans and hurt his family. Samuel nodded as if to say, "*words aren't necessary John.*"

As they finished for the night, John said goodbye to his friends and wished them the best. Standing in the yard looking at the rubble, Samuel and Charlotte offered John a bed to sleep. He accepted and found the accommodations quite comfortable but the anticipation of this journey and the confrontation with Tommy left him too stimulated to sleep.

Before the sun came up the next morning, Samuel working alongside his brother George, were in the yard loading the wagon. They would be staying in coach stop inns along the way. John hoped that the inns would not be too expensive, direly limited as he was in funds. He would only be traveling with the clothes on his back and a blanket and decided the less he had to keep an eye on, the less someone could steal.

The two men greeted each other as they had on so many other, much different mornings.

Are you ready for this trip?" asked Samuel.

"I believe so."

"How did Winfred fair yesterday when you dropped them off?"

"They'll be okay. It was a difficult decision but they'll survive this, as will I. Thomas promised me that he'll look after them."

Charlotte came out of her house, flustered but beautiful as always. "Hello John. Sam, I'm ready," Charlotte chirped.

All of her things had already been loaded in the wagon. The air felt crisp with a bright blue sky and not a cloud against the backdrop of the beautiful deep blue and a sense of promise and hope for a new future welled up inside them.

John sat in the back of the wagon and passed many strangers that had set out for the ship on foot. An old woman hobbled on the dirt road with a makeshift cane, children running to keep up, old men limping from the weight of their goods. The first town that they came to was Clonegal. The little village straddled the border of three counties, Carlow, Wicklow and Wexford. John knew that Thomas, his father had been born in County Wexford but didn't remember hearing much about it outside of the rebel stories. They drove down the center of the main street, which was bordered by the River Derry. Up above, sitting on a hill, John looked in amazement at the massive castle. He had never seen anything so magnificent.

Clonegal sat in a valley surrounded by deep green forests and the land looked rich for farming. The little village had several small shops supplying everything a traveler would need. John could smell fresh bread baking in one of the shops as they passed. What he would give to sink his teeth into a small piece slathered thick with butter and honey.

As they passed the road that went up to the Huntington Castle, Charlotte turned and said to John, "Have you heard about the Weavers Cottage here in Carlow?"

"All of the rugs in our house came from there. Isn't this a beautiful area?" Samuel chimed in.

"It certainly is," John shared as he looked at the town moving further and further into the distance wondering if he would ever he back through.

"We're traveling over the battlegrounds that were once the scene of the Battle of Bunclody, "Samuel shared. "This is where the battle of the Wexford rebels took place during the 1798 Rebellion."

"My dadai used to tell us stories of that rebellion," John shared bittersweetly.

Soon they came along a small canal that ran alongside

the road which drew water from the Clody River. They had been warned before traveling about drinking water from rivers after reports of diseases spread through contaminated water.

They next came to the town of Killanne. John's memory was jogged as they entered this little town to the story his father told him about Captain John Kelly. He was a famous rebel from Wexford County and wounded at the battle of New Ross during the 1798 Rebellion. On his capture in Wexford town, he was hanged, decapitated, and his head kicked through the streets of the town. He grimaced at the thought of a man being treated so savagely.

It was getting late in the evening and John felt weary from his day's travel as did the rest of the group. They decided to stay in Rathnure. George pulled up in front of a small white building called the Broad Stone Hotel and tied the horse up to the post out front. Samuel helped Charlotte out of the wagon.

"John, what can I get for you?" Samuel asked with concern.

"Samuel, I'm fine. I have everything I need. Thank you." John responded sincerely. John walked around back and found a small barn where feed was kept for traveling horses. He considered saving his money and sleeping in the barn but after a long day, the seeming comfort of the inn was too much to turn down. They had traveled further than they had hoped for the first day. Tomorrow, they may be seeing the ship and the sea. John experienced more in one day than he had in a lifetime. He wished his brother Thomas could have traveled with him on this journey. Thomas had a keen sense of adventure and would have loved seeing all of the towns in County Wexford.

Samuel and Charlotte went into the inn while John helped George with the horses. Caked with road dust and sweat, he was looking forward to a hot bath and to sleeping in a bed. He paid the innkeeper three shillings for a room, and then followed the little man as he took the key off of the panel behind the counter and walked John to his guestroom. The small but comfortable room had one bed, a small dresser, a chamber pot and a small washstand where the innkeeper had placed a small bowl with a pitcher of water. Down the hall he was shown another room that had a large wooden tub with a clean towel placed on a table next to the tub. The innkeeper had the water drawn and as John slipped down into the hot water, he felt the weight of the world melt away. He scrubbed his skin with a brush and soap made from potash and pearlash and wrapped himself in the clean towel. Attempting to wash out his dusty clothes, he hung them on a line in the little room and hoped they would be dry in the morning. After a cup of broth and potato bread for supper, John lay down on the cool straw mattress, pulled the blanket tight around him, and fell fast asleep.

The next morning before dawn, John dressed and walked outside to wait for George, Samuel and Charlotte. He sat by the wagon watching the stars begin to fade across the sky. He heard the birds chirping and knew this part of his journey was about to end and the next chapter of his life was about to begin. Soon, George came around with the cart and motioned for John to join him when he was ready. Samuel and Charlotte came out of the inn shortly after that. They expected another full day traveling to the ship but hoped to reach it by evening.

Finally, as evening was once again coming to an end, they saw the tall mast of the ship towering high above the roofs of the homes along the river. John marveled at the sight of the massive wooden masts, their sails flapping against the wind, and the clanging of metal rings against the ship poles.

They entered the little town of New Ross which was built on a steep hill overlooking the River Barrow. George, Samuel and Charlotte found a quaint inn to stay in for the night. The small town was crowded with people milling around waiting for the ship's departure. John agreed to stay with the wagon to avoid anything being stolen while they slept.

After another night of rest, the new morning was filled with excitement. There was a slight wind from the west as the sun was peaking above the horizon. John filled his lungs with the salt air as they all walked towards the dock. There must have been one thousand people arriving, looking worn and exhausted from their long journey from their home. Many arrived with their carts and parcels, awaiting instructions on traveling to America. Young children ran about excitedly, anxious to board the ship as old people cried softly into cotton handkerchiefs, dreading the moment they would have to say their final goodbyes, perhaps forever.

John watched everything in anticipation of boarding the ship himself and he decided to sit down next to a post coming out of the river. Sam and Charlotte chatted nearby with George saying their final goodbyes. John looked up to the sky and thought to himself that it looked like rain. Heavy, ominous clouds drifted in, brushing up against the ruddy red of the setting sun.

A tall fellow dressed in a gray flannel suit with a top hat stood on a platform about ten feet from where John sat. "Ladies and gentleman," the man began, "May I have your attention please?"

Men struggled and pushed to get to the front to hear the instructions. John felt relieved at his fortunate proximity to the man so that he did not have to struggle to hear.

"We will be boarding this ship to America in a short amount of time," the man in the gray suit yelled. "The first class passengers will form a line to my left.

Your names will be checked off and you are welcome to board. If you have a reservation for the Dunbrody, you will line up on my right. Your name as well will be checked off and then when your name is called, you are also welcome to board the ship. Your accommodations will be on the tween decks. This area can only accommodate 200 people. The rest of you will have to wait for the next ship. I would suggest getting your names on the manifest to travel since we are expecting many and only have ships to accommodate approximately 200 at a time. If someone in your family is ill or for whatever reason cannot travel, your reservation will be cancelled until all can travel at the same time. Once you board the ship, you will not be permitted to leave."

John and the large group remaining for steerage received further instructions to listen for their name and when called to line up. Once on board, they would receive further instructions on sailing, sleeping, eating and going above deck.

Running off of the ship to where the man in the gray suit was standing came a portly man dressed in dirty work clothes and carrying a large sheet of paper in his hand. His name was Henry Grandy but everyone just called him "Grandy" because of his large rotund girth, his long white beard and bushy white eyebrows. He had a very gruff voice and serious expression as he unrolled the tightly bound ledger and began reading the names: "Thomas Bain, Mary and John Popham, Thomas Beaghen and wife Mary, children John, James, Margaret, Catherine, Mary, Payne, Thomas, Andy and James' wife Mary and daughter Annie...."

The list went on and on, a seemingly endless repository of uprooted lives and desperate hopes. John finally heard "John Doyle" and he pushed ahead and got in line. Mass confusion ensued since most people couldn't hear if their names had been called or the names called were pronounced incorrectly or one of the children's names was left out. John's heart broke for some of the families being turned away even though they had a reservation due to one of the children being ill, and some perhaps were delayed getting to the ship and weren't there to hear their names called.

A large number of spectators at the dock to witness the final departure of the ship raised their hats and waved white handkerchiefs and shouted long farewells to the friends and family destined for freedom and a new life. Some of those passengers would not see a new life. This distant port, with its squat houses, its creaking wood, its tangy sea-salt air, would be the end of their journey.

Part II

Chapter Nine

Sailing to America

May 1848

Man cannot discover new oceans
unless he has the courage to
lose sight of the shore.
Andre Gide

Before the ship pulled out from New Ross, Samuel and Charlotte stood with George for as long as they could.

"George, we hope to see you in Camden when you're ready," Charlotte whispered.

"I don't know, I'm thinking of going back to England. I miss the family there and I know I could find work. We'll see how things go. Possibly Lord Fitzpatrick would like to find a special project for me. Plus, I could never talk Victoria into leaving." Victoria and George had been courting for a year. He planned to ask her to marry him as soon as all of this settled. George embraced his brother and took Charlotte's gloved hand and kissed it.

"Charlotte, please have a safe voyage. Write when you can," George said with sincerity.

"Of course I will." Charlotte replied.

Charlotte walked over to John who was getting ready to get in line to board.

"John, we hope to see you on the voyage. I'm sorry we can't take you with us to the first class cabins." Charlotte shared with sincerity in her voice.

"I'll be fine. I'm grateful for all that you've done for me so far."

Sam joined them after final words to his brother and said, "John, we'll see you when we arrive in America."

Samuel and Charlotte walked over to the first class passenger line. Their bags and trunks had already been delivered to their cabin.

The captain greeted all ten first class guests warmly, "Welcome, welcome. We will try to make this crossing as comfortable for you as possible. Please come this way. We'll have you sign in and we'll give you your cabin assignment. Your trunks should already be in your cabin. I can assure you that your safety and comfort are the first and foremost on our minds."

Samuel and Charlotte stood in front of a couple also boarding first class. Charlotte turned around to say hello, "Good morning, my name is Charlotte Castleford and this is my husband Samuel."

"Hello," the smart-looking man replied. He bowed

slightly to Charlotte and shook Samuel's hand. "I'm Charles Butler and this is my wife Louisa."

Louisa Butler was a tiny little thing and apparently very much with child. She wore a beautiful sky blue dress that accentuated her eyes and a very full high waist skirt that effectively hid her pregnancy. Over the dress to further hide her growing stomach was a matching ankle-length cloak with cape-collar and the new narrower sleeves. She carried an Ermine muff with attached handkerchief which she worn to keep her hands warm. She looked delicate and glowing. Charlotte liked her immediately and wanted to ask her about her upcoming baby but knew manners dictated that it not the proper thing to do.

"Are you coming from London?" Charles asked.

Samuel replied, "Actually, Wicklow, Ireland. I worked for Lord Fitzpatrick. Charlotte and I lived in Yorkshire before coming to Ireland."

"Well, well, my parents lived near Yorkshire in a little town called Stainforth. Louisa and I were born in Waterford. We're planning on purchasing land in Camden to raise horses and cattle."

"How wonderful, we're moving to Camden also. Maybe we'll be neighbors," Charlotte cried.

The line had kept moving and it was now Samuel and Charlotte's turn to check in. Their name was checked off the list and the porter asked if they needed special assistance to their cabin. Samuel and Charlotte waved goodbye to Charles and Louisa as they walked to their room.

Their room was not particularly fancy but appeared comfortable and clean. Charlotte noticed a small round window in the cabin and below that just enough room for a small three-quarter bed, a small washstand and a chamber-pot with a screen.

The porter bowing slightly and backing out of the room shared, "Your meal will be served at noon in the dining room."

Samuel thanked him, gave him a small tip and closed the door.

"Samuel, I'm very weary. I'd like to freshen up a bit and rest before we dine."

"I agree. That's a good idea. I wonder how John is faring downstairs. I hate the idea he's down there. I hoped there would be one more room available so that I could move him up. There isn't anything I can do now. I'll mention to the Captain that he's down there. Maybe he can give him some special attention of some kind," Samuel shared, almost as if he was thinking out loud.

"That would be nice. I really like Charles and Louisa. How wonderful that they are going to Camden too. And, she's going to have a baby."

"Charles seems like a nice sport. I look forward to talking with him about raising horses."

"Maybe they ride? I didn't even think to ask them," Charlotte said excitedly.

"Charlotte, if they raise horses, I'm sure they ride," Samuel said as he threw his tie and jacket on the small bed.

"True. Oh, I must close my eyes for even a second."

About three hours later they changed for dinner which was served in a small dining room. Charlotte put on a sage green silk jacquard dress. The long slim sleeves, pleated diagonal shape at the yoke/neckline and v front waist showed off Charlotte's slim waistline beautifully even if it was one of her older dresses, she looked lovely in the design and color. When they entered the dining room, they noticed Charles sitting by himself at the window.

Sam and Charlotte walked over to him and Charlotte asked, "Charles is Louisa joining us?"

"Actually, she's not feeling well. The travel just to get on the ship has taken quite a bit out of her."

"We completely understand that. We hope she's feeling better soon. Please give her our regards," Charlotte said with concern in her voice.

"I will, I will. Samuel, we have about six hours in Liverpool before we set off for America. I plan to take a quick trip to see the Aintree Racecourse near Liverpool. I don't know if you're aware of the 1840 Grand Liverpool Steeplechase? It is quite an amazing racetrack. Do you have any interest in taking a carriage with me over to see the horses? Charlotte you're welcome as well. I know Louisa would like to go if she's feeling up to it."

Charlotte eyes got big with excitement. She glanced at Samuel for his response.

"Oh, Charles, we would love to go. We love horses. We ride as often as we can," Charlotte excitedly responded.

Samuel stood smiling at her.

"Then it's a date. When we arrive in Liverpool, meet me at the gangway and I'll arrange for a carriage to meet us at the dock. We'll only be gone a few hours. Please sit and eat with me. I hate eating alone."

Samuel and Charlotte sat at the table that was draped with starched white linen and the finest silver. A server brought them a stew with beef, potatoes, corn, carrots and beans and warm biscuits. After they ate, Charlotte went to her room to work on her needlepoint and Samuel and Charles sat and talked about farms, horses and the move to Camden.

After the group traveling in steerage boarded the ship, John found space on the top deck which at this time was crawling with many people, luggage and crying children.

Grandy had his clipboard and yelled so that everyone

could hear him, "The Dunbrody will be taken out to sea to sail first to Liverpool, England. This journey across the Irish Sea will take approximately twelve to fourteen hours. We will be picking up a few additional passengers and cargo in Liverpool to be taken to America and will then continue our journey which will be five to eight weeks in duration depending upon the weather and other circumstances beyond our control. Please form a line and follow me."

The large group tried to form a single line but it looked more like a large crowd just moving in the same direction. Grandy led them down the gangway into the ship's cargo hold. John glanced back at Ireland once last time. He felt a tremendous sadness as he looked at the green hills and thought of his family staying behind. He doubted that he would ever see this sight again. Grandy bellowed another order over his shoulder to follow him down the stairs.

"Four passengers will be staying in a four-bunk area approximately six foot by six foot. Since the men, women and children will be staying all together in one area, fraternization with the opposite sex unless you are married is prohibited. If you are caught philandering with the opposite sex, you will be severely punished and possibly sent back to Ireland on the next ship."

Gasps came from the crowd along with some people yelling that they couldn't hear what was just said.

John could hear but had a difficult time seeing since it was very dark under the hull. The air downstairs had a pungent odor of fish, animal dung, and mold. As people made their way downstairs with crying children on their hip, straddling parcels and waiting for their eyes to adjust to the darkness, the air was abuzz with tension and excitement as they all tried to find a space they could call their own.

Grandy yelled, "Each passenger will receive three quarts of water per day and seven pounds of bread, biscuit, flour, oatmeal or rice per week. Potatoes can be substituted for some of the bread. This weekly allowance will be served at convenient times, not less than twice a week."

This actually was more than John was accustomed to having and he still had a little of the oatmeal and rice that Samuel and Charlotte had shared with him. He finally found a bunk along side a dark haired young man that was busy putting his personal things away.

"Hello, my name is Patrick. Are you ready for this?"

John glanced up and noticed the nice smile Patrick had. He stuck out his hand and replied smiling, "I'm John Doyle from Coolkenno, County Wicklow and as ready as I'll ever be."

They both worked on their own personal items and tried to talk over the confusion and noise around them.

"Have you heard they're calling these ships, coffin

ships?" Patrick asked over his shoulder.

John looked puzzled. He remembered that his mother had mentioned it but he didn't know why they called them that.

"I have heard that, but why coffin ships?" John asked.

"Because if the ship goes down, we're stuck in the belly of this thing. Can you imagine 200 people trying to get up those stairs? I pray to God that we don't have to worry about that."

John continued to get settled as he watched his new bunk mate. Patrick Cavanaugh was a good looking man in his early twenties. His sea blue eyes gleamed with adventure and the vigour of his youth. A stubble of beard grew on his strong jaw and angular cheekbones. But, it was Patrick's personality that John admired the most. He had a fun-loving spirit about him which was a nice compliment to John's serious temperment.

Patrick said to John, "Where are you headed when you get to America?"

"I'm following my land manager to Camden, Canada. Have you heard of it?"

"No," Patrick replied. "I'll be looking for land to farm myself. My family and I lived in Shillelagh and rented six acres from William Leybourne to farm. Have you heard of him?"

"No, the name doesn't sound familiar."

"I'm planning to find some land to buy and bring my

family over," Patrick explained.

"That's exactly my plan as well Patrick. Is your whole family coming over?"

"My mother died of the fever two years ago. My father isn't well since her death. I have five sisters and four younger brothers that I will send for as soon as I'm settled."

"That's quite a family. I wish you well," John said with a smile.

"I'm sure we'll be seeing more of each other," Patrick said laughing.

John liked Patrick immediately. They had a lot in common and Patrick thought it would be nice to have a friend on this voyage.

John looked around and felt sorry for the women on the ship since they had no privacy to speak of. He couldn't imagine his mother and sisters sailing this way with leering and disrespectful men. He knew Thomas could handle the crossing but hoped he could afford a higher class passage for his family. John watched as people stored chests where they could be seen and some used their belongings as proprietary markers. In the dismal catacomb, the passengers did the best that they could to make the small space their own. Buckets had been interspersed between the rows of bunks for people to urinate and excrete feces. Some people made makeshift curtains to hang around the buckets for a certain amount of privacy when performing this biological function. The ship lurched forward with a start, knocking some of the poor travelers off balance followed by exuberant cheers coming from the upper deck and those remaining by the dock. John felt a sense of excitement but also trepidation. He closed his eyes and prayed to God for a safe and quick journey. He glanced around him and noticed many of the single women were sitting straight up, wide-eyed and fully clothed.

John offered to make a curtain around her bed for a young woman next to him for privacy. He took her blanket and hung it from the beams above her bunk creating as much privacy as he could. She was in her early 20's, a pretty girl and obviously alone. John thought what courage she had to make this voyage. The ship rocked and swayed. He lay on his bunk lulled by the motion and the rocking of the ship and fell fast asleep. He awoke, sometime in the middle of the night, alarmed at the sound of many vomiting. Unfortunately, many travelers not used to the rocking of the ship had already begun to get sick and the air in the dark hull became thick with the stench of vomit. John looked around and noticed the absence of sufficient buckets into which they could vomit left them in their urgency to let it spill where it would. No one could escape the misery of another so all had to suffer each other's discomfort. Those in the lower bunks were most unfortunate, forced to endure not only their own sickness but also the vomit and excrement of those above as it dribbled through the planks of the upper bunks. John wondered to himself how he would endure this misery.

One person from each small area had the responsibility of emptying their buckets twice a day when they heard a bell ring. This job would rotate to other adults so that at least once per week, you had to take the pot to the top deck and throw the contents overboard. The good thing about this job was that it enabled you to go up on the deck and get fresh air. John wasn't sure how he would survive the smell of vomit or feces for five to eight weeks so he considered volunteering to empty the buckets just so that he could clear his lungs and breathe uncontaminated air.

They had only been at sea for a short time when Grandy came down and yelled, "I have an announcement. There is a tax entering New York in America that has been approved for all passengers coming into the United States."

"A tax? What kind of a tax?" people were yelling from their bunks.

"Quiet down, quiet down and let me finish. It is thirty-one pence to enter America," Grandy explained.

People started shouting and women started crying. No one had that kind of extra money to pay a tax.

"So, what we're planning to do," Grandy shouted,

"is we're going to travel to Quebec Canada, northern America, not New York where you can avoid paying the tax. If you wish, you can continue to travel with us to New York but you'll have to pay the tax when you arrive."

John was fine with this. Samuel had mentioned to him that many of the Fitzpatrick land managers were going to a place called Camden in Ontario, Canada. John thought that they would have to travel from New York City to Canada upon arrival. He wasn't sure where Quebec was in relation to Camden but figured that Samuel and Charlotte would be arriving in Quebec also since they were on the same ship. Other people on the ship were not as enthused. Some had family or jobs waiting for them in New York City. This delay was causing a lot of anxiety and once again confusion below the decks. Patrick said to John, "I didn't have a real plan for New York so I can just as easily go to Canada."

"I think it works out better for me as well," John replied.

John wondered what Liverpool was like. Having never traveled outside his little town, he was amazed at how large the world was Wexford, Liverpool, New York City, Quebec....he felt the weight on his shoulders to conquer everything ahead of him.

During the relatively short distance that they had sailed John wished he could work as a shipmate. He couldn't imagine doing nothing for two months below the vessel. He'd gladly do anything they needed help with. Early that evening, he carried one of the buckets up to the upper deck and ran into the captain.

"Excuse me, sir," John said politely.

"Certainly," replied the ship's captain in a surly tone.

John walked past him and had a second thought "Sir, could I have a minute?"

The captain stopped and turned to look at John standing there with a bucket filled with vomit and human excretion.

"You get one minute."

"My name is John Doyle and I'd like to volunteer to work on this ship as we sail, sir. I'll do anything you ask; I'm an honest man and a hard worker. I'll do it for free."

The captain looked a little surprised and thought, *John Doyle*...he had someone in first class that had mentioned this name to him. Being short-handed and John came with a recommendation, he decided to give him a try.

"All right. I'll take you up on it. I'll have one of the first mates come down and give you some instructions. We'll give this a try."

"Thank you, sir. I won't let you down." He unloaded his bucket over the side of the ship with a smile on his face.

The first mate by the nickname of Beefy, came down shortly after John's informal meeting on the upper deck and yelled, "Is there a John Doyle down here?"

John jumped down from his bunk and replied, "I'm John Doyle."

"Are you the man that the captain said would like to volunteer?" Beefy asked quietly, not wanting to create a riot.

"I am, sir and this is my friend Patrick Cavanaugh."

Patrick looked at John with an expression of surprise as his brows rose in skepticism.

"When we arrive in a few hours into Liverpool, the captain would like you to deliver this package to the transportation office on Roe Street. If you make it back on time, you'll continue to sail with us. If ya don't, I guess you're stayin' in Liverpool." Beefy laughed, revealing a broad, toothless grin, and left the lower hull.

Patrick whispered to John, "What was that all about?"

"I volunteered us to do things around the ship."

"What?"

"I figured you'd want something to do. Do you really want to lay around for two months in this stench?" John asked.

"You're right. When do we start?"

"Obviously when we arrive in Liverpool," John said with a laugh.

Chapter Ten

Liverpool

May 1848

Courage – a perfect sensibility of the measure of danger, and a mental willingness to endure it.
William Tecumseh Sherman

The Dunbrody pulled into the harbor in Liverpool the next day just before the sun rose above the city. The hatch of the hull had been left open so that some air got into the belly of the ship but no one from the hull was permitted on deck since it would be a relatively short stay only to pick up cargo and a few more passengers. Shipmates tied the vessel up to the dock and John and Patrick hurried up the stairs. They knew they only had a short time until they had to report back. John hesitated to even leave the ship, not wanting to take any chances on missing it altogether. Patrick was a little more adventuresome.

"John, this is our only opportunity to see a big city. We'll drop off the package and we'll head back to the ship. We'll be back in plenty of time," Patrick said excitedly.

John reluctantly agreed. They walked down the gang-plank and onto a cobble stone street alongside Albert Dock. The stones glistened from an overnight rain and felt slippery under their feet. The air was heavy with fog, but the sun was just coming up over the many tall buildings dotting the cityscape. John had never seen so much activity and so many people in his life; women in fancy dresses and parasols, men in frock coats and derby hats.

John approached a man in a navy blue uniform and asked, "Excuse me sir, could you tell me where Roe Street is?"

"Up two streets and take a left and go right past the Gentleman's Emporium," the uniformed man replied.

"Thank you, sir."

John and Patrick took note of all of the warehouses along the dock.

"Did you know they sold slaves in these warehouses?" Patrick asked.

"Slaves?".

"Yeah, I heard ships would travel to Africa and force people on to the ship. They came through here on the way to America and men sold the slaves here in England and in America."

John couldn't believe that people could be forced to do labor or leave their own country, but, as he thought about it, some of the Irish had had similar experiences just under a different name.

They passed a couple of woman standing on the street. They were scantily dressed leaning against a building. "Would you like a good time?" asked one of the women. Long black hair cascaded down her back and her dress was torn and dirty.

Patrick whispered to John, "Keep walking. They want us to buy sex."

"Buy sex?"

He refused them politely without the slightest pause in his step. He felt despair for those poor souls hunched against the morning air who had no better way of earning a living than to sell their bodies. The odor from the women that John inhaled as he walked passed and their toothless grins were more repulsive than desirable. The two men stopped briefly to look in the window of the Birmingham Ladies and Gentleman's Emporium.

"You'd look like a dandy dressed like that John," Patrick smiled.

John chuckled slightly at the thought. He had no interest in looking like a dandy, that wasn't him, but, someday he hoped to see his mother and sisters in pretty dresses or his wife. He wasn't one to daydream but standing in front of the shop window looking at the beautiful clothing, things he had never seen before, it was difficult not to dream. He stared at the male model in the shop window and noted how smartly he was dressed. The model had on a grey tightly tailored tweed coat with fitted sleeves and oversized buttons with a Mansfield waistcoat and black felt top hat. The shirt was made of linen with a high straight collar and wrapped around his neck was a very wide cravat. Advertising to an apparently wealthy audience, the next model showed a woman dressed in a long pink silk evening gown with rows of ruching at the hem and lace frills at the collar and sleeves, all trimmed with ribbon bows. Her hair was smoothed over her ears and decorated with ostrich plumes. Her skirt was fully gathered with wide, flat pleats, and the pleating on her bodice was visible through the black lace. She had a poke bonnet in her right hand along with black lace gloves. Patrick laughed as he saw John and the faraway look in his eyes.

"Patrick, I feel like I'm traveling into unknown territory, where I can't get my bearings because nothing looks familiar. Do you think America will look like this?"

"Your guess is as good as mine. Let's make our delivery and then get something to eat before we head back."

They found the office that they were looking for and as John walked through the door, a bell tinkled above his head.

A man walked across the room towards him also smartly dressed and asked John, "How can I help you?"

"I'm delivering a package for you, sir from the

Captain of the Dunrody."

"Thank you, I've been expecting that," the man took the package with a cool expression.

John turned on his heal and left the shop and found Patrick waiting for him outside the door.

"Let's grab a pint and bite to eat across the street," Patrick said hungrily.

The Whitehouse Pub was a small dark building frequented by the locals. The light from the tabletop candles did little to diffuse the darkness in the room, which was dense with tobacco smoke. At the far end of the bar stood a large looking glass. A group of customers cluttered the small room around tables and chairs and the floor was strewn with sawdust. They sat down and had to yell to be heard. They noticed laughter coming from the group of people drinking dark beer and whiskey.

A young woman walked over to them and asked, "What can I get ya?"

"We'll both have a pint and some of your shepherd's pie," replied Patrick.

As she walked away to get their order Patrick and John watched the noisy band of men. The more shots of whiskey they guzzled, the more boisterous their laughter grew. It was difficult not to join in. John wasn't sharing the joke but he had a feeling of joy he hadn't felt in a long time. The world they left outside the door was reduced to a muffled rumble; all they could hear was the laughter from the next table. The food and pint was delivered and tasted better than he ever could have imagined. John wasn't sure if it was the food or because he had been eating so very little lately. He licked every morsel off his plate and every drop from his pint.

"Patrick, right now I'm a content man," John said rubbing his belly.

"As am I."

The two men paid their bill and left to walk back to the ship. They might be getting back a little early but would not take the risk of the ship leaving without them. As John and Patrick left the pub, they tried to remember the direction back but it was raining now and a fog had settled low over the city disorienting the two travelers. Nothing looked the same as it did when they first arrived. Unfortunately, they made a wrong turn on a back street and ended up in a decrepit slum. A large rat ran over Patrick's boot and he let out a scream. They had never seen a rodent so large. John started to feel a little panicky when they noticed a group of men standing by the door of another pub. The door to the pub was open and the noise and smoke from the establishment spilled out onto the street. Patrick's scream had gotten the attention of the hoodlums standing there.

"Where you blokes think you're goin?" asked one man that seemed to be the spokesman of the group.

He was a short wiry man, pencil thin but with

extremely large arms. He wore a cap over his dirty long hair and his knickers and shirt hadn't been washed in quite some time. He spit in the street and eyed them waiting for a response. John and Patrick decided to turn around and start running.

"John, they are coming after us."

Just then the fog started to lift and John noticed that down a half-block, he saw the emporium that they had stood in front of earlier. Patrick was only one step behind him but suddenly slipped on the wet cobble stones and tumbled down almost getting run over by a horse and carriage. John stopped and turned to help his friend when the group that was chasing them stopped suddenly. Walking up the street was the uniformed man that John had asked directions from earlier.

John called out to him to get his attention, "Sir, thank you for the directions earlier. We found the building that we needed."

The man responded, "You're quite welcome. Is your friend okay?"

"Yes sir, he's fine."

The group turned on their heels and decided not to pursue John and Patrick. No sense in spending a night in the slammer for two Irish micks that probably had no money on them anyway.

John and Patrick boarded the ship in plenty of time for its departure breathing a huge sigh of relief after being chased. They were permitted to stand on the upper deck and catch their breath while the remaining cargo was loaded which they watched the shipmates struggling with the heavy loads and offered to help. Once the cargo was completely loaded and stored, they heard the ring of the large bell on the ship signaling that it was time to move out and watched as the first mate raised the gangplank. John and Patrick heard screaming as the ship inched its way from the dock. There was a cluster of people running to the ship that had arrived too late for its departure. They observed in horror as men, women and children ran down the dock watching their one opportunity to a new beginning drift away. The poor forgotten souls began throwing themselves at the ship in a desparate attempt to scramble up the side. Some of the trunks were flung aboard while passengers tried climbing over the railing. A man in a rowboat was close at hand to collect the luggage or people that fell into the cold water.

"Oh my God, Patrick, I think a man just drown! That's his hat floating in the water. This is horrific!" John yelled.

Patrick looked at John and said, "I pray this isn't an indication of how the rest of the voyage will transpire."

Aintree Racetrack

When they arrived in Liverpool, James found a porter and asked him to fetch a carriage to take them to the Aintree racetrack. With the request, he slipped a few shillings into the porter's palm. The porter ran down the gangplank before permission was given to the first class passengers to disembark. Alongside the dock were numerous horse-drawn four-wheel carriages. The hackney coach had a coat of arms on the side, which was apparently an unwanted coach from some aristocratic family in Liverpool. The driver was smartly dressed in red livery typical of his profession. "Excuse me, I have four passengers that would like to travel to Aintree Racetrack. They'll be here shortly if you'd kindly wait for them," requested the porter.

"Sure, I'll wait."

The driver watched as Samuel, Charlotte, Charles and Louisa walked toward the carriage.

"About how far will we have to travel?" Charles asked as they climbed into the handsome carriage.

"Not far sir, it will take about half-hour," replied the driver.

"Very good. We'd like you to wait for us there and bring us back. Can you do that?" asked Charles.

"Of course, sir."

Charlotte and Louisa marveled at the countryside as they journeyed out of the city. It was early spring and all of the apple blossoms and roses along the dirt road were blooming and the hillside was turning a lush green.

Charlotte turned to Louisa and whispered, "I hope I'm not too brazen to congratulate you on your baby.

Have you picked out any names?"

"Thank you." "If we have a boy, he'll be named Henry after Charles' father and if we have a girl, we'll call her Isabelle."

"How wonderful for you. Do you have any other children?" Charlotte nosily asked.

"Yes, we have a little girl that just turned three. Her name is Hannah and she will be arriving once we're settled."

Charlotte daydreamed as she looked out the window about how nice it would be to have a child.

When they arrived at the racetrack, they eagerly looked for the horses. The driver dropped them by the front gate and the foursome took in all of activity at the track, which was more activity than a normal weekday at the races.

Charles stopped a handsome gent walking by that had a handful of pounds in his hand and asked, "Excuse me, sir, is there a race today?"

"Yes, thirteen horses and it starts in about ten minutes," the man said excitedly. Charlotte couldn't believe their luck. They sat down on the benches to wait for the race to start. It was a small racecourse with only thirteen horses racing. Charles had been there before and the course remained unchanged from the previous year. The thirteen horses stood in position at the opening of Shelling Road. All of a sudden the loud bang of a pistol signified the start of the race. The horses had to negotiate three small gorse topped banks before reaching Belling's Brook. All thirteen horses cleared this area without incident but at the brook, Cottondike stumbled on the landing and fell throwing the jockey into the dirt. The poor little man stood up and held his severely bloodied nose. He was carried off the track. Winningbet had established a good lead at this stage of the race. Winningbet rounded the corner with a good nose ahead of all of the other horses. The crowd got on their feet, screaming for their favorite horse to gain momentum. As Winningbet reached the second brook, the horse corkscrewed. His rider remained in the saddle and reached the finish line just a hair ahead of Ponytoride. Winningbet slowed to a canter while the crowds cheered. The rider beamed knowing he had shattered the course record by a good eight seconds.

"Oh what a wonderful race and how lucky for us to have been able to see this!" cried Charlotte.

"I'm just sorry we weren't here in time to place a few pounds on the horse." Samuel said disappointingly.

The three walked over to the riders and admired the horses for a short while until they felt that they should probably start traveling back to Liverpool. They all agreed it was a wonderful way to spend a few hours. The driver came around for them and within an hour they all rested comfortably in their cabins, never realizing the frenzy of activity that had occurred just prior to their arrival.

Chapter Eleven

Life at Sea

June 1848

Courage is not the absence of despair;
It is, rather, the capacity to move
ahead in spite of despair.
Rollo May

That evening back on the ship, someone started playing a fiddle softly. Then another brought out a flute and started to play along. Soon, the hull of the ship became alive with singing and dancing and the air hummed and swelled with music and hope. The melody in the air brought them all together and created a harmony like notes on a page. John wished he had brought his fiddle with him remembering with bittersweet fondness the music they used to make on summer nights.

Patrick asked, "John, do you play?"

"I play a little."

"Here ya go, have a try at it," a man standing by with a fiddle in his hand motioned for John to take it."

John took the fiddle and played his favorite "Mo

Ghile Mear" that his mother sang to him and everyone laughed as John sang:

He's my champion my Gallant Darling,
He's my Caesar, a Gallant Darling,
I've found neither rest nor fortune
Since my Gallant Darling went far away.
Once I was gentle maiden,
But now I'm a spent, worn-out widow,
My consort strongly plowing the waves,
Over the hills and far away.

As they all danced and clapped and tried to enjoy each other's company, John gave back the fiddle after a few songs and stood by his bunk, watching the crowd of people in the hull of the ship. Families talked, sharing stories and meeting new friends; anything to pass the hours that made up the interminable days. John noticed a dark haired character eyeing a woman that stood near him. He had a funny feeling about this fellow like he couldn't be trusted and he was determined to find out more about him.

The next day, John found out after some inquiry that the bloke's name was Jimmy McGee. Jimmy had been released from prison in Dublin on the condition that he board a ship and get out of Ireland. Determined to find out what crime he had committed, John made more inquiries.

As the day turned into evening, John and Patrick ate

their evening meal in peace and then heard the music start up. People moved their bags and personal items to make room for dancing. Everyone looked forward to this in the evening. The group clapped and sang while a funny gent by the name of Michael Flint took out a small pint of whiskey that he was hiding from the rest. He discretely gulped a swig and then stuck the bottle back in his pocket and proceeded to dance in the middle of the group.

He had everyone laughing and shouting, "More Michael Flint, more," and this only encouraged him.

Before you knew it, Michael jumped from trunk to trunk until he tripped over someone's personal bag and landed face down on the dirty wood floor.

"Was this the first day on your new feet, Michael?" someone in the crowd yelled.

The crowd roared with laughter as Michael stood up and continued to dance while rubbing his red and bleeding nose obviously feeling no pain.

As John laughed with the rest, he once again, had one eye on Jimmy McGee. Jimmy cowered in the back of the room and believing that no one was paying attention, stuck his hand in the back pocket of an oblivious Owen Foley. Jimmy quick and clever as a fox entering the chicken house, had his catch and disappeared before anyone knew the better of it. John saw the whole thing happen. He quickly shoved a few dancing people out of his way and ran over to where Jimmy was standing. The little man had an eerie expression on his face.

"Give it up Jimmy McGee!" John roared.

With that, the music stopped and all eyes stared at John and Jimmy.

"What are ya talking about?" Jimmy defensively asked.

"Give me the money you just stole from Owen!"

"I don't know what yer talking about you dirty mick," Jimmy spit.

With that John pulled his fist back and with one quick blow broke Jimmy's nose. Jimmy let out a little yell before being knocked off his feet. John steered away from confrontation whenever possible but could not tolerate men that disrespected women, liars and cheaters. Someone in the crowd grabbed John and as Jimmy began to stand to throw the next punch, a man grabbed him and held him back.

John yelled, "This man is a thief! I saw him steal money out of the pocket of Owen Foley!"

Owen immediately checked his back pocket and sure enough it was empty.

"I'll get you for this John Doyle," Jimmy said deviously, his eyes dark and full of hate.

"And, I'll be watchin you Jimmy McGee!" John shouted back.

Owen got his money back and the crowd leered at

Jimmy as he walked over to his bunk and laid down holding his broken nose.

The dancing began again and Owen walked over to John and slapped him on the back and shook his hand. "Thank you, friend," Owen said with a smile.

John's living space was directly next to a family from Tinahely. James and Mary Ann Garrett had lived at the Shillelagh Workhouse for six months before getting passage to sail to America. Mary Ann was noticeably with child her growing belly making it difficult to get comfortable in any position.

Just hearing the Irish songs made Mary Ann feel better, even though she was not up to dancing. James Garrett passed the time playing cards with a few other men and John noticed some passengers writing letters home that he desperately wished he could do.

"John," Mary Ann whispered one morning, "I learned how to read and write when I lived in the workhouse. Would you have any interest in learning?"

John looked at Mary Ann and immediately thought about his family back in Ireland living in the Shillelagh Workhouse. That's wonderful if they are learning how to read and write. "I would love to learn Mary Ann! When can we begin?"

"We can begin right now."

So Mary Ann and John spent every morning together. From under her bunk, Mary Ann brought out a small Bible and everyday she would sound out the words and help him with letters and sounds. John, a quick learner and eager to master this new skill, worked very hard at it. When he proved that he could read the verses of the Bible without much help, Mary Ann brought out a slate panel and soapstone and worked with John on writing his letters. Before he knew it, he wrote words and soon joined the words into sentences. He felt ready to write his first letter to his family.

"Mary Ann, how do I send a letter to my family?"

"When we arrive in America, I'm sure there will be a place to post a letter. Many people need to contact their loved ones back home. I'll help you with that when we arrive."

By now it had been three weeks since they left Ireland and John read as often as he could while still working on the top deck whenever they called him up. He loved having the opportunity to get out of the hull to work.

One evening, Beefy went down into the hull and asked John to come up and perform night watch. Working night duty entailed watching for any other ships at sea and reporting any emergencies that may arise. As long as John stood watch, the crew could sleep or if the night watchman became ill, John could fill in.

The captain had told John, "We'll give yer a try but if

I catch you sleepin' or stealin', I'll throw you overboard myself."

John loved sitting outside at night and looking at the stars. He would listen to the water lapping against the side of the ship and bask in the moonlight, the creak of the masts and the smell of the sea air. He would day-dream of what America would be like and how long it would take him to find land and build a house. He looked forward to getting off of this ship and starting his new life.

The captain came out one evening when John was standing watch.

"Hello John," the captain said cheerily.

"Good evening, captain."

"Nice night tonight."

"Yes, sir, it is," John said with a smile.

"We've been lucky on this voyage not to come into weather. Richard Mulvihill, the Captain of the Star had a ship full of passengers and cargo and left Liverpool a few months back. Three days into the voyage, they came into some weather, a bad storm, and capsized losing everyone on board. He was a fine captain, fine captain."

"Sorry to hear that." A sinking ship wasn't something he had really thought of. Death from disease was to him the bigger threat. He knew that if someone had the fever, how quickly it could spread. Many people felt sick on this ship and many perished, but typhoid had mercilessly still not swept through the ship.

"How many more weeks do you think, captain?"

"We have another four to six weeks, maybe a little more but it shouldn't be too much longer."

"I'd like to write a letter to my family in Ireland. Can you tell me how I go about mailing it?"

"When we arrive in Quebec, there will be volunteers that will collect your letters and will take them to the post office for a small fee. Most of them are honest. The letters are put back on a ship that's leaving for Liverpool. It makes its way back to Ireland just like you came. We have letters on board from Ireland going to New York and Canada. It takes a good two to three months for a letter to arrive. So, you can write can you?"

"Yes, sir, I learned while I was on this ship. One of the passengers lived at the workhouse and she taught me. She's going to help me write a letter before we arrive."

"That's great, John. Just about any job you get requires some skill in reading and writing."

The captain bid John a good night and went back to his office. John finished his duties and when he was relieved, he went back downstairs to get a little sleep. When he woke up late morning, it was hot and stuffy on his cot. He sat up and Mary Ann was standing nearby.

"Mary Ann, will you help me write my letter home?"

"Of course, I'd be happy to."

They sat together and worked on his letter.

Dear Mamai,

I hope this letter finds you well. I have good news. I have learned to read and write thanks to Mary Ann Garrett. You're probably hoping this is a romantic encounter, but it's not. Mary Ann and her husband, James lived at the workhouse and she shared that they teach you to read and write there and so she has taught me. I miss you all greatly. Samuel and Charlotte are in finer quarters than I have and I haven't seen them as of yet but will on our arrival in America. We have another four weeks or so aboard ship. I am told a volunteer will take my letter and put it back on a ship to you. I have so much to tell you, Mamai. I have seen so many sights to include Liverpool, England but I will save all of these stories when we can sit face to face! As you read this, I am hopeful and God willing, that I have made the final journey to our land and have begun to build a home for you. I discovered when I arrived at the ship in New Ross, that there is a special tax that travelers have to pay when they sail into America so we're going to Quebec, Canada, not New York City like we thought. Not only that, Samuel informed me that Lord Fitzpatrick has land available for us in Camden, Canada. That is where Samuel and Charlotte are headed so I believe I will follow them there. Do not despair, Mamai, we will be around other Irish farmers and there will be plenty of farmland to go around. I will write again when I arrive in Camden to let you know all is well and I will begin to plan for your journey. Mamai, please give my love to Thomas, Bridget and Catherine.

Your loving son,

John

As the ink dried on the page, John looked at his first letter with satisfaction and Mary Ann praised him for his dedication.

"John, in a little over three months' time, your family will be reading a letter from you! You must feel so proud of yourself."

"I do, thanks to you."

The final weeks slowly went by with each day seeming longer than the last. Food and water became scarce. The meat had a green sheen and the smell was so bad it was difficult to swallow. One by one, people under that hull, started to become ill. At first, John thought that people suffered from seasickness but then he realized that it could be something more.

One morning, an infant died, the son of a couple that he had met on board. Henry, David White's son, died when he was only a few months old. He had a fever and with no doctor available, they could only hold the ailing son and put cold cloths on his face. The fever got so high that evening, the baby died in its sleep, casting a pall over the passengers of the ship, and stirring fear and speculation over the nature of the illness. John thought to himself, *God help us all if it's typhoid*.

They had a small ceremony as the family sobbed and David carried the baby wrapped in a blanket up to the top deck and watched the child plunge over the side. He stood there until it disappeared into the black veil of the ocean, swallowed up like a wooden box of a casket being shut tight. He shared with John later that he had considered jumping overboard to his death but couldn't do that to his wife and other children. But, Henry was just the first of many deaths and soon the smell of death now added to the decay under the hull. At least once a week someone was carried up the stairs to the upper deck and thrown over the railing.

Conor Callaghan was the finest fiddle player John had ever heard. He played every night to a cheering crowd. He made the evenings bearable. His wife, Colleen, a soft-spoken, caring woman, shared with John her dreams for their three children. A hope of a better life in America. "A life where they don't have to fear illness, starvation or repression." Soon after Henri died, Conor and Colleen became ill and died within hours of each other. Their small three children cried at the bottom of the steps as their mother and father were carried up to join the others that had perished at sea. John wondered what would become of the three children now without parents or a place to call home.

John and Patrick quietly watched from their bunk as a body wrapped in a dirty, wet blanket was dragged up to the upper deck. The blanket slipped displaying the face and to everyone's dismay, it was Michael Flint, the passenger that brought laughter and joy to everyone he met. He was thrown overboard as the angry sea swallowed him into its abyss. Another one lost.

How many people would be alive when they landed in Quebec? How many would survive and how many would join Henry and Michael and the others that were buried in the cold depths of the ocean.

Jimmy McGee

The last couple of days on the ship proved to be the most difficult. People had not bathed in months so the spread of body lice was rampant. The remaining biscuits left to be eaten were now full of maggots and weevils. Without the proper medical attention, people had no other choice than to care for themselves and it seemed everyone came down with ship fever. John wasn't feeling good himself. He lay on his bunk and thought the rolling of the ship was going to make him heave.

Someone yelled down the stairs, "Land! Land! Land!"

As sick as John felt, he sat up on his bed and shouted to Patrick, "Oh my dear God. Thank you."

Someone yelled up the stairs, "How much longer on this coffin ship, mate?"

"We'll be pulling into port by morning."

The news instantly brightened John's weary spirits.

Patrick yelled down to John from the top bunk, "Can you believe it John? We made it!"

"We're not there yet, Patrick. I'm still praying," John replied feeling very nauseous.

The atmosphere on the ship now became filled with expectancy and renewed hope. John lay back down with a slight smile on his face. He didn't think he could fall asleep but knew that the time would pass more quickly if he did. Everyone was talking excitedly until it was so dark in the hull that it grew quiet.

John was in a light sleep when he heard a whisper in his ear, "I've been sick of ya John Doyle from the first time I saw ya. Reading and writin...who do you think you are? Volunteerin' to work above. You're not gettin off this ship alive if I have anything to say about it."

John felt a sharp object in his rib. The smell from Jimmy McGee's breath and the viciousness of his whisper would make most people tremble. John was pinned under his blanket.

"Get away from me you filthy bastard," John said under his breath.

"What are you going to do John, huh, what are you going to do?"

Jimmy plunged the knife blade into John's side and John let out an agonized scream, which woke up the entire ship. He had never felt such pain in his life. He managed to move out from under the blanket as Patrick grabbed Jimmy and kicked him so hard he fell back, hitting his head against the berth knocking himself out cold. Patrick grabbed Jimmy and tied his hands behind his back. Jimmy came to and struggled but Patrick was twice the size and weight of the little man. Someone lit a candle and John saw that he was bleeding badly. Jimmy's knife missed John's heart by only centimeters but he was losing a lot of blood.

Mary Ann yelled, "Oh my God, he's bleeding!"

John felt very light headed and he started to sweat and thought he might vomit but the pain was so bad that he blacked out.

Beefy ran down the stairs to investigate all of the commotion. He saw the blood on the side of John's berth and hearing Patrick excitedly relaying what had just happened, he took John's blanket, torn off a strip and applied pressure to the knife wound. Beefy yelled for another shipmate to drag Jimmy up the stairs where the captain waited for him. The ship was now within one hour of arriving at the dock in Quebec and the captain had a shipmate bind Jimmy's hands to await arrest when they pulled up to the dock.

"Jimmy McGee, you're a dead man. You'll probably get hung when we arrive," the mate whispered in Jimmy's ear.

Jimmy didn't respond. He just hoped John didn't live.

Patrick, Mary Ann, and James stood by John's side.

"John, hang on. We're almost to land. We'll get you

medical treatment as soon as we arrive," Patrick urgently said to John.

John was motionless. Mary Ann cried. She had grown very fond of John on this journey and couldn't imagine losing him now.

The weary travelers felt the ship lurch when it finally arrived in Quebec. The captain called everyone on deck to explain what would happen when they arrived. They would disembark on the Island of Grosse Ile.

The captain thundered, "John Doyle is in need of medical attention. He will be the first off the ship. After he is taken off the ship, the first class passengers will disembark. You all will follow. Quebec is approximately thirty miles from here. Before you will be permitted to leave for your various destinations, you must spend two weeks in quarantine."

The crowd responded with gasps and obvious disappointment. "I'm sorry, I know you all are anxious to reach your final destination but to protect those residents in Upper and Lower Canada, we must make sure no one is infected with ship fever or any other disease. You'll be fed here, be able to bathe and clean your clothes. This will be much better than what you have just experienced. So, please in an orderly fashion, collect your things and when you hear the whistle, please get in single file, walk slowly up the stairs and down the gangplank," the captain gave his final order.

John had lost so much blood that he was carried off immediately. Weak and pallid, he slipped in and out of consciousness, not even aware that they had landed.

A doctor waited for them at the bottom of the dock gate. When she was permitted to get off of the ship, Mary Ann took John's letter and went in search of a way to mail it for him. Patrick gathered John's things and followed the stretcher off the ship. After examining John, the doctor shared with Patrick that one more day on the ship and John would have died. What a terrible way to go after the arduous journey that John had endured. Jimmy McGee waited bound in the captain's closet. After everyone had disembarked the ship, a French guard dressed in military uniform and a revolver at his side came onto the ship.

The captain said to him, "This man is accused of attempted murder. Take him."

The guard grabbed Jimmy by the arm and pulled him to his feet. He took him off the ship and walked him to an area that was setup for prisoners.

"Do you have anything to say for yourself?" the guard asked.

"Nothin to you, you slimy French pig."

Without hesitation, the guard pulled out his revolver and shot Jimmy in the head.

"Maintenant, qui est le porc?

Chapter Twelve
Quebec

July 1848

Have courage for the great
sorrows in life and patience
for the small ones; and when
you have laboriously accomplished
your daily task, go to sleep in peace.
Victor Hugo

Grosse Ile was a small island that sat in the Gulf of the Saint Lawrence River. It was only one and a half miles long and one half mile wide and had been setup as a quarantine station. Many of the inhabitants of Quebec and Montreal grew fearful that people arriving from immigrant ships would be carrying diseases and they didn't want another outbreak of typhoid or any other disease coming to their shores.

The people of Canada had received news that many ships contained immigrants from England and Ireland. Dr. George Cooke, a native of England and a well-respected doctor had volunteered to run the quarantine station. Never married, he dedicated himself to his work and he became very good at it. Not only did he have a medical license, he had good business sense. He had a small staff, two nurses and a secretary that handled the paperwork. One of his nurses, Nurse Elizabeth Hatch also from England had worked closely with Dr. Cooke near London. When he asked her if she would like to join him on this voyage, she accepted without hesitation. She looked for adventure and also hoped that if she could engage Dr. Cooke in a relationship, it would make for a nice future.

Nurse Marguerite Meloche, a French Canadian nurse displayed many attributes to include long blonde hair that she worn in a tight knot under her nurse's cap. She had beautiful light blue eyes and dark lashes that she fluttered in the direction of Dr. Cooke. Miss O'Brien was the secretary, Irish descent and a no-nonsense type in her thirties. She felt comfortable with spinsterhood and planned to stay that way. She loved her job and had no intention of quitting her work for a man.

Dr. Cooke had told them to prepare themselves for multiple ships arriving. They had set up five large mobile field hospital tents with forty new cots in each tent and they could accommodate about 200 people. Dr. Cooke met the first immigrants coming off the ship.

"Welcome, welcome to Gross Ile, Canada. We are here to welcome you and take care of the ill. Please form a line here behind this small table and we'll take some information from you to determine your needs."

John had already been taken to one of the tents and now that his wound was stitched, his pain began to subside. Nurse Meloche had very gently cleaned his wound, put a fresh bandage on it and put a clean sheet over him. Patrick, one of the first in line off the ship, talked to the intake nurse about John.

"May I have your name, please?"

"Patrick Cavanaugh."

"Where are you from, Mr. Cavanaugh?"

"Wicklow, Ireland, ma'am."

"Have you had any fever in the past two weeks?"

"No, ma'am not that I'm aware."

"Are you feeling ill at this time?"

"Just weary ma'am and weak. I'm probably just hungry."

"Mr. Cavanaugh, you will be in tent two, please follow our volunteer and they will take you to an area where you can wash up and claim your cot."

"Ma'am, I am a good friend of John Doyle. He is in tent one and is being treated for a stab wound to his side. I'd like to be near him so that I can take care of him if needed.

"Why of course, Mr. Cavanaugh. Has Mr. Doyle been ill or had a fever other than the stab wound?"

"No, ma'am, not that I'm aware."

"And, is Mr. Doyle also from Wicklow, Ireland?"

"Yes, ma'am he is."

"Thank you, Mr. Cavanaugh, tent one it is."

"Next, what is your name please?"

"Thomas Foley."

"Where are you from?"

"Dublin, Ireland."

"Have you had a fever in the past two weeks?"

"Yes, ma'am I believe so. I'm freezing as we speak."

"Have you had a headache or skin rash?"

"I just got a skin rash, ma'am; could be flea bites."

"You'll be in tent four, Mr. Foley."

And so it went, passenger after passenger.

Dr. Cooke was overseeing the intake of immigrants. He put the really sick or those suspected of carrying disease in tent four. Tent five was an overflow, and tent one, two, and three he intended for the fairly healthy and surgery cases. The volunteer showed Patrick to his cot next to John where they placed a clean blanket, a clean pair of underwear, trousers and a clean shirt. They guided him to the male shower area. There he shaved for the first time in almost three months and he felt like a new man after his shower and clean clothes. He went back to his tent to check on John, who slept peacefully, so Patrick lay down on his cot and sighed in complete relief and thankfulness that he had arrived safely and relatively healthy unlike some of the others that had come off the ship.

Samuel and Charlotte along with Charles and Louisa had a much easier time disembarking from the ship. Dr. Cooke waited for them as soon as the ship arrived at the dock. Before the other passengers disembarked, the first class passengers waited in their cabins for the doctor to come around and survey them of their current health. Dr. Cooke knocked on the door of Samuel and Charlotte's cabin.

"Yes, please come in, we have been expecting you," Samuel said with a smile.

"Good morning and welcome to Canada!" Dr. Cooke said happily.

"Thank you."

"How was your journey?"

"Long, very long but we are here and glad to be leaving for our destination."

"Do you need assistance, Mr. Castleford to reach your final destination?"

"Yes, actually, we will be traveling to Camden along with the Butler's on board. I haven't checked with Charles to see if he has secured transportation. What transportation would you suggest, Dr. Cooke?"

"Mr. Castleford, you can catch a steamer over to the main dock in Quebec City. From there, you will pick up the schooner Victoria. That will take you past Montreal and into Kingston and it then travels on to Toronto. It's a new ship. I think you'll find it quite satisfactory. Once I have cleared you, you will be on your way," instructed Dr. Cooke. He proceeded to ask them questions about their health.

After a few short minutes, he said, "I wish you both the best in your new home. God bless both of you in your journeys."

"Samuel, I want to leave John a note and instructions on where to find us when he is permitted to leave. I do hope he's well." Charlotte said after Dr. Cooke left.

"Fine Charlotte, that's a good idea. While you do that, I'll go find Charles to see if he has made arrangements for transportation to Kingston. I'll be back in a few moments time."

Charlotte sat at the little table in her room where she found paper and a quill pen.

Dear John – We do hope this note finds you well. Samuel and I are released to travel to Kingston. We have been told to take a small steamer over to the main dock in Quebec. From there, you board a schooner called the Victoria. You'll take that ship past Montreal and into Kingston. That part of the journey will take approximately 24 hours. Once you arrive in Kingston, you'll be able to take a carriage to Centreville, which is very close to Camden. It's approximately a three-hour carriage ride. We'll leave instructions for you at the Stagecoach Inn in Centreville. Be safe, John. We're looking forward to seeing you in Camden.

Charlotte

When Samuel returned for Charlotte, she had the letter ready for him to ask the captain to find John Doyle in steerage and to give him the letter. Samuel noticed the captain was standing in his office getting ready to go down to talk with everyone about the disembarkation process.

"Captain, could you find John Doyle and give this to him please?"

"Of course, I'd be happy to and my best to you and your lovely wife."

The captain decided not to mention to him that John had been stabbed since he would recover and it would only delay this foursome from leaving the area. He wanted anyone that could leave the area to be on his or her way.

Alexander Buchanan, the Emigration Officer was born an Irishman from County Cork forty years earlier. His responsibility included inspecting the ships and the treatment of the immigrants once they arrived in Canada. Alexander found Dr. Cooke after all of the passengers made their way towards their assigned tents.

"Dr. Cooke, how many passengers are ill in tent two?" asked Alexander.

"Forty."

"Tent three?"

"Forty."

"Tent four?"

"Forty."

Tent five?"

"Forty."

Alexander's eyes grew wide. "Are you telling me, Doctor Cooke that 160 people are ill?"

"Yes, sir I am," replied the doctor matter-of-factly. "At this point, I can't tell you if it's ship fever or typhoid or some other disease. I have forty in tent one to include a man that had surgery after being stabbed almost to his death on the ship. The criminal that stabbed him is deceased from what I've been told. All immigrants will remain in quarantine until I give you the release."

"That's fine," Alexander said apprehensively.

"I could use some more assistance with the four tents. I only have two nurses and that's not enough."

"We have forty more ships on their way into this port, Cooke. I can't tell you how many will be ill!"

Dr. Cooke's jaw clenched and his mouth pursed. "Alexander, if there are forty more ships with approximately 200 on each ship, that's approximately 8,000 people. I can guarantee you that one doctor and two nurse's cannot handle a crowd of that magnitude. Unless Jesus himself shows up and can turn water into wine, I'd say we have an emergency on our hands. We'll need 200 more tents and I want one nurse to two tents and one doctor for every ten tents. I don't care what you have to do but make it happen!"

Panic flashed across Alexander's face. Normally tall and confident, he now stood with slumped shoulders and a furrowed brow.

"I'll get on it right away."

He walked away from Dr. Cooke perplexed at how they would get this mission accomplished. He decided that it wasn't going to be his problem. He wrote to Charles Thomas, the Governor General of the Canada's.

Honorable Governor Charles Thomas

The situation currently at Grosse Ile is tragically under-staffed. We have five tents available for incoming immigrants that have forty cots in each tent. We have 12,000 immigrants destined to arrive within the next few weeks and have nowhere to put them. Due to the deaths of some of the people either on the voyage over or after arriving, we now have children that are orphans and have nowhere to go. We need attention to this situation immediately sir, or the outcome will be dire. We need tents, medical equipment, food, clothing, medical personnel and an orphan home. If we do not have a remedy to this situation immediately, we will have to turn these immigrants and children loose. If this is your choice, please inform Quebec City, Montreal and Kingston to prepare for the reception of between 8,000 and 14,000 sick passengers. We would all hate to see another 6,000 die from a cholera outbreak as happened in 1832. A speedy reply is most wanted.

Sincerely,
Alexander Buchanan
Officer of Emigration
Grosse Ile

Alexander handed his letter to the postal volunteer and said, "Get this to the Governor immediately." The volunteer saluted smartly and rode off.

Nurse Hatch walked over to Dr. Cooke. "Doctor, you must come quickly! In tent two, there is a mother with a small child. The mother is having a convulsion!"

Dr. Cooke ran with her to the tent. When they arrived the young mother was drenched with fever and her body twitched uncontrollably. Her eyes had rolled back in her head. The baby, about one year old, looked filthy as did everyone getting off the ship. The baby cried hysterically as if it sensed something was horribly wrong. Before Dr. Cooke could get to the bedside, the woman stopped twitching and took her last gasp of air. Nurse Hatch put her hand to her mouth.

"Oh my God," she cried with tears in her eyes. "What do we do with the poor child?"

"Check and see if she came with neighbors or family. If not, we have another orphan," replied Doctor Cooke.

Doctor Cooke covered the woman with her blanket and thought to himself, *we have our first death from probably typhoid and there is bound to be others*. Nurse Hatch had taken the baby out of the tent. How many children would arrive in this new world homeless and with no one to care for them?

Chapter Thirteen

The Orphan House

July 1848

I learned that courage was not the absence of fear, but the triumph over it. The brave man is not he who does not feel afraid, but he who conquers that fear.
Nelson Mandela

In desperation, awaiting the answer from the Governor of Quebec, Alexander Buchanan had a thought. What about the nuns in the convents in Quebec and Montreal? That could be one of the answers to his prayers. He left his office and found Dr. Cooke talking with Nurse Meloche.

"Dr. Cooke, I have an idea!" Alexander said excitedly. "What about the nuns from the convents in Montreal and Quebec? Possibly they would be willing to help with the sick immigrants and the children."

Dr. Cooke looked up at Alexander and said, "That's a great idea! Father O'Malley is in tent five. He gave last rites all morning."

Alexander ran to tent five and cautiously looked inside fearful of confronting another tormented scene of the sick and dying. Father O'Malley looked up from a patient and saw Alexander standing there. The stench from the tents was overpowering, a putrid mix of mortality and illness, of failing organs and dimming hopes. Father O'Malley motioned that he would be with him momentarily. Alexander waited patiently and before too long, Father O'Malley came out of the tent.

"Father, bless you for what you do. It's retched what these people are going through," Alexander said compassionately.

Two more died in the night, eight ships filled with ill people are waiting to come in, and children are crying and parentless. It's almost too much to take," Father O'Malley lamented.

"Father, I have a thought. What about the nuns from the convents in Quebec and Montreal? Do you think they'd be willing to come in and help?"

Father O'Malley looked up with an expression of surprise.

"That's a fabulous idea, Alex! I'll send word immediately. Thank you."

Father O'Malley left the tent with a spring in his step.

The Sisters of Charity Monastery was a massive,

grand building perched atop a hill in Quebec City. Its large cross rose high about the treetops so that anyone coming into Quebec could see the monastery from miles away. A large iron fence surrounded the structure, but despite its presence, everyone and anyone felt welcome.

The Mother Superior, Marie Grant, was in her forties and devoted to the mission that the founding French woman Marguerite d'Youville founded one hundred years prior. Marguerite's husband had died at an early age in battle and left her to raise their two sons alone. Marguerite was a kind soul who did not see herself as a victim but instead, felt that she found a calling. She opened her heart and home to anyone that had a need. Along with her courage, determination and gentle spirit, she took care of countless poor souls, offering shelter and food. Despite discouraging setbacks, she carried out her charity work until her death seventy-six years prior.

Mother Superior Marie believed in that mission and never turned anyone away. She had a sign above her door that read: "*Marguerite the Mother of Universal Charity – A Model of Compassionate Love.*"

The wooden desk and floors in Marie's office had been polished to a rich shine. The smell of roses from outside her window and the soft tick tock of the clock on her mantle created a cozy welcoming atmosphere to anyone that entered. Sister Murray knocked gently at the open door to her office.

"Excuse me, Mother Superior, you have a visitor."

Marie looked up from her desk and over her glasses.

"Of course, please send them in."

"Sir, please come in," Sister Murray said timidly.

Alexander had taken off his cap when he walked into her office.

"Mother Superior, my name is Alexander Buchanan. I am the Emigration Officer at Grosse Ile. Father O'Malley has sent me to deliver a note to you."

He handed her the small envelope. She looked down with a questioning expression and opened the envelope:

Dear Mother Superior –

I am working at Grosse Ile mainly giving last rights to the dying immigrants and also holding church services on Sunday to those that can attend. The situation here is one of the worst that I have ever seen. We have hundreds of people that have fallen ill or left the ship ill and many have died or are dying. We have children that are now orphans and we have nowhere to send them. We have requested a home to be setup but are in need of assistance in running the home and taking care of these children. I am requesting through God's Grace that you consider coming to help and bringing as many Sisters of Charity as you can permit since we are so desperate. A reply is respectfully requested.

God Bless

Father Patrick O'Malley

Marie looked up from the note.

"Sir, is it as bad as Father O'Malley states?" Marie asked.

"Its worse, ma'am. You will have seen nothing as bad."

"Tell Father that we will leave by evening. I will contact the Mother Superior of the Ursuline Sisters and see how many they can bring. What about medical supplies and supplies for the children?"

"We need everything you can provide ma'am."

"We'll see you by tomorrow, Alexander. Tell Father O'Malley we're on our way."

She was already thinking of an emergency plan. With that Alexander left anxiously to tell them at Grosse Ile that help was coming.

Marie sent word to the Mother Superior of Ursuline and the Mother Superior of the Sisters of Providence. Between the three orders and much frantic packing, seventy-five nuns traveled to Grosse Ile by late afternoon. They were called to do God's work and they were ready to assist.

The Governor had received Alexander's letter and having been newly elected, he drew together his cabinet of directors and together they created a plan to get as much help as possible down to Grosse Ile. Most of this was due to the fact that it was his responsibility as governor but he also didn't want any of those people walking the streets of Montreal and Quebec City. He wanted to contain them as long as possible to protect the healthy citizens of Canada, fearful of the nightmare that would ensue if three major cities became infected. Meanwhile, as hysteria began to take root amongst some quarters of the province, people of Quebec City and Montreal were threatening to riot if sick immigrants were released into their city. They wanted them to be taken to Toronto or sent back to Ireland or wherever they came from.

"Gentleman, there is a building near the dock in Quebec City that we currently know is empty. I saw the building the last time that I was at the dock. It's a large structure, four stories high and one block from the dock. I'm taking over that building to be used as an Orphan House for the children from Grosse Ile. We'll need someone to run it. We'll also need cots set up and whatever else is determined." He looked at his clerk and ordered, "Send word to Buchanan at Grosse Ile that he can have the Adams Building on Front Street and that I have tents and supplies on their way. Ask him if he has any recommendations of who could run the Orphanage. He may already have someone in mind for that."

A note was sent to Alexander. As Alexander read the note, he gave a little squeal of joy. "That is fabulous. Mother Superior Marie can run the home; she'll be perfect for that!"

Alexander ran to inform Dr. Cooke and Father O'Malley. That evening, when the contingent of nuns arrived at the dock in Quebec City, Alex was waiting for them.

"I can't tell you how happy and relieved we are that you are here," Alex shared with sincerity.

Father O'Malley walked up to the wagons filled with the sisters and held out his hands to Marie. "I'm so grateful to you all for being here."

Marie and the other two Mother Superiors walked with Father O'Malley to hear the details of their new mission.

"Marie, we need someone to run the Orphan Home. The Governor has given us a building one block from here; it's a four-story building, for the orphans. We'll need a list of supplies that are needed to include cots, etc. We also need help in the quarantine tents; this is a dangerous job because many of the tents are holding very ill people. Anyone that works around them runs the risk of getting ill themselves."

Father O'Malley talked openly to the sisters and Marie and the rest of the women listened quietly as he spoke.

"Father, I will go with you and work with the sick," replied Mother Marie. "Mother Mary, you've had experience with orphan children. Will Mother Theresa and you work together to setup the home and then one of you come work with us in the tents?"

"Of course, Marie," replied Mother Mary.

Father O'Malley looked at Alexander and shared, "Alex, why don't you take them to see the building and we'll get their assessment and list of needed supplies. Stay with them until the list is ready. Marie, why don't you bring the rest of the sisters with us to Grosse Ile? We have a boat waiting to take us all back. We're hoping for a ship load of supplies by tomorrow or the next day at the latest," instructed Father O'Malley.

Father O'Malley gathered their gear and trunks of supplies and off they sailed. Alexander ushered the two women to the Adams Building where they found the door unlocked. Inside, the empty building felt warm and musty smelling from being closed up for so long. The sun was setting which made it more difficult to see. They walked through the main floor. The wood floors needed a polish and the windows needed to be opened to air the place out but it looked perfect so far. There were two rooms in the back. One could be setup as a kitchen to prepare food; the smaller room could be used as a sleeping room. The main room on the first floor could be set up as the dining hall. Climbing up to the second floor, they envisioned the cots to be setup for the children to sleep, girls in one room and boys in the other and the third and fourth floor rooms would be used for office space and sleeping rooms for the adults and volunteers.

"This will be perfect Alexander, just perfect," Sister Mary said with enthusiasm.

"So, how many children need a home at this moment?" asked Sister Theresa.

"We started with seven children from the ship that lost parents on the voyage. Once the ship arrived, we had eleven children total when I left a few hours ago. Four infants, three children approximately three to four years in age, a six year old little girl, her eight year old brother, a twelve year old girl and a fifteen year old boy, but we anticipate many more."

Mary took out paper and pen and wrote a list of items they would need to start their home.

The list consisted of:

Cleaning and polishing supplies

Eight adult cots

Fifty cribs

150 cots for children

Clean clothes for them to include underwear

Sheets and blankets

Medical supplies

Towels

Food and drinking water

Cooking supplies (pots, pans, dishes and silverware)

Twenty-five privies

A wood burning stove

"Alexander, here is the list to get us started. How quickly do you think you can pull these things together?" asked Mary.

"Where will you find a wood burning stove big

enough for us to cook for all of these children?" Theresa asked with concern.

"Leave it to me, ma'am. I have my sources. I'll start on it first thing tomorrow morning."

"Please bring the cleaning equipment first. While you're searching for people to donate items, Theresa and I can clean and get everything ready. We'll sleep here tonight. Can we secure the door?" asked Mary.

"Yes, of course. I'll let myself out but lock up behind me."

Mary walked Alexander to the door. She locked the front door securely and then both nuns checked all of the other doors to make sure they were locked. They also checked the windows; you couldn't be too careful these days. They took their belongings up to the fourth floor and opened the windows to let some air in.

"Mary, are we going to be able to handle this just you and me?" asked Theresa.

"Of course we will. God will help us. We'll welcome all of the children with open arms and will let God do the rest."

Early the next morning, Alexander delivered the cleaning supplies. Mary and Theresa cleaned and scrubbed until their knees felt sore and their hands raw. The place shined just like it was meant to be a home for children. Two days later, supplies started arriving and they even recruited a few women volunteers who had heard about their plight. Mary put one in charge of putting things away, another to set up cribs and beds and another to find someone to donate vegetable seed to start a garden out back. Low and behold, in came the largest six-burner wood burning stove that Mary and Theresa had ever seen. One of the deliverymen volunteered to bring chopped wood and leave it at the back door. Within three days time they would open their doors; a miracle considering the rigors of their task.

Mary sent word to Alexander, "We are up and running, bring the children."

That afternoon, Mother Superior Marie along with one of the other sisters, held the hands of the smaller children, Sister Sarah held two infants, two more children walked with the oldest and the rest followed either holding the hand of a child or carried in someone's arms. They looked dirty, tired, hungry and scared.

"Come in children, come in. You are safe now," Sister Mary said gently.

One by one, they got a bath, clean clothes and finally a warm meal. Women rocked the infants in a chair someone left just for that purpose.

"It looks like God does provide miracles."

Chapter Fourteen
The Journey Continues

August 1848

You have to accept whatever comes
and the only important thing is that
you meet it with courage and with
the best that you have to give.
Eleanor Roosevelt

Samuel and Charlotte, along with Charles and Louisa, disembarked the ship along with the other first class passengers. They boarded a small boat from Grosse Ile to the dock at Port de Quebec. Charlotte and Mary Ann felt so relieved to get away from Grosse Ile and its festering filth and disease.

Charles said to Samuel, "I'm going to inquire about the schooner traveling to Kingston. Wait here with the ladies if you would be so kind and I'll be right back."

He walked a short distance down to a building bearing *St. Lawrence Steamboat Company* in large letters where he purchased four first-class tickets to Kingston.

"We have trunks, sir. Can we leave them somewhere

while we find a place to eat?" asked Charles.

"Yes, of course. I'll have one of my men take your things to the dock where the Schooner Victoria will be docked. They will be in good hands."

Charles tipped his hat to the ticket agent and joined the group waiting for him and said enthusiastically, "We have four first class tickets to Kingston through Montreal. The ship leaves from this port in three hours. How about we get something to eat before we board?"

As they walked along the wharf looking for a restaurant, Charlotte was not the least bit impressed with Quebec City. She noticed many ships along the dock, people and workers everywhere and it just seemed like a filthy, dilapidated city. Large trees cut into lumber were stacked up and down the dock awaiting transport onto cargo ships. Walking along one of the back streets, they found a small café. It had French curtains in the window and small tables and chairs outside, as well as in. As the four entered the restaurant, they inhaled the aroma of fresh bread.

"Samuel, there is talk that there will be orphans needing homes from the ships coming in to Canada. What do you think about adopting one of those children?" Charlotte asked.

"I was waiting for you to ask that question. Why don't we discuss it in private when we're on the Victoria? It's certainly something to think about."

The four of them walked back to the dock after a delightful meal and boarded the small schooner. Charlotte was thinking the whole time about homeless children. Before she knew it, she'd be in her new home in Camden. It couldn't happen soon enough. The schooner pulled away from Quebec with ease and within a few hours, they pulled into the dock in Montreal. They wouldn't be there long so Charlotte chose not to even leave her room. Louisa was too tired to leave her cabin also. Samuel and Charles met on the deck to talk.

"Montreal is such a beautiful name for a city. I would like to come back here some day and visit. I hear it's like Paris. There is nothing like a good French Port Charles."

"I agree. We may make our way back here someday."

They stayed on deck and discussed Montreal, horses and their upcoming arrival into Camden. Tomorrow at this time, they would be in Kingston and bound for their new home.

Patrick couldn't believe the chaos that engulfed him. John was healing fairly well but he did not have the medical attention or supplies that he needed due to the focus on all of the incoming ill passengers. Patrick grew uncomfortable venturing too far from the "healthy" tent in fear of contracting a disease himself. He had come too far to get sick now. He did what he could to help and practically took care of John himself.

John asked Patrick, "How much more time do we have in this camp?"

"They say two weeks quarantine, so keep healing so we can get out of here," Patrick responded as he spoon fed John a cup of broth."

Meanwhile, the number of people dying from the fever increased every day, growing so rapidly that they couldn't get them buried quick enough. Workers from Grosse Ile dug shallow graves for the dead they brought off the ship. On the seventh day after the first ship arrived and the quarantine had been setup, it began to rain, a warm rain that came down in buckets. Soon, the tents started to leak, soaking everything - the medical supplies, blankets and the medical personnel running from one tent to another. More than fifty nuns had come in to help but they too became ill. No sooner would volunteers come in to help with the sick, they would become afflicted and many succumbed to the same untimely end as the passengers they were trying to help.

Dr. Cooke frantically tried to bring order to a situation that was rapidly spiraling out of control. Meanwhile, the rain continued for three days. The shallow graves filled up with water and pushed out the dead, which brought in the rats, thousands of them, feeding on the dead.

Patrick didn't know how much more he could

handle. He walked out of his tent to try to secure dry blankets for John and he was horrified to see a dozen or so brown rats devouring the face and body of a woman that had died only days ago, it was the most horrific thing he had ever seen. He started throwing rocks at the vermin but knew as soon as he stopped, they would just come back to finish what they had started. He had less than one week to go but wondered to himself, *would he make it without falling ill himself or lose his mind in this madness?*

On the fourteenth day, Dr. Cooke walked through his tent to inform them that as long as they felt well, they would be allowed to leave. Patrick had never heard such good news. Refusing to die there he wasn't about to tell anyone that he actually didn't feel well and decided to struggle through whatever he had to get out of Grosse Ile. He still had Charlotte's note and directions on how to get to Kingston. Alexander Buchanan was in constant contact with the Governor to get more help. Now they needed everything from grave diggers to more food and medical supplies to dry blankets and just about everything you can imagine and all the while, more ships came in with more sick and dying immigrants. John stood at the dock with Patrick waiting for the small boat to take them to the main dock in Quebec.

Away from anyone that might overhear, Patrick confessed, "Don't say a word, but I'm not feeling well. I think I have a fever. I can't stay on this island and I can't die here. Help me get to a place I can lie down."

John didn't react. He didn't want to draw attention to Patrick and have him sent back to one of the tents. They boarded the small boat that would take them to Quebec City. The waves and rocking back and forth made Patrick increasingly nauseous.

The captain looked at Patrick with a frown and said, "Are you doing okay there, man?"

"I'm fine," Patrick lied with a forced smile. I'm just a little tired of boats and sailing. I'm looking forward to getting to my new home. Thanks for asking."

The captain eyed him suspiciously.

They landed at the dock a short time later. Back on land, they shuffled away from listening ears and John said, "Let me get us a room for tonight. Maybe with some rest and broth, you'll feel better to travel."

"Sounds good. I'll sit here and wait for you to come back. I can't make a walk."

John was now growing frantic. After all they had been through to lose Patrick now would be the worst possible scenario. He walked a couple of blocks through the city. It was hot and humid and he felt filthy. He happened to come across the orphan house. Sister Mary was planting vegetables in her garden when she looked up and John stood over her.

"Oh, you startled me. What can I do for you?"

"Sister, my friend and I just left quarantine. We came in on one of the ships two weeks ago. He's weak from not eating and the crude conditions of quarantine. Could I beg of you to take us in for just one night? I'll work around the orphan house and do whatever I can. Please sister. My friend needs help."

Sister Mary stood up and whipped her hands on her apron. "Bring him here. I have a back room where we can put him. I don't want him around any of the children. Come around back and through that door. I'll be waiting."

"God bless you sister!" John wanted to hug her.

He ran the two blocks back to get Patrick who was so weak at this point that he could barely open his eyes or lift his head.

"Patrick, I'll help you but you have to walk two blocks. A nun at the orphan house said that we could stay with them tonight. She knows you're sick, but she's willing to help. If someone sees you ill, you'll be taken back to quarantine. You've got to force yourself two more blocks."

Still sore from his own wound, John helped Patrick to his feet. With all the determination he had, Patrick lifted his head and put one foot in front of the other. He never felt so sick in his life but to look at him you'd never believe it. His strength and will left an impression on John who had witnessed many such acts of determination in his life.

When they arrived, Sister Mary ushered Patrick into the back room and drew a warm bath for him. She thought to herself that she might be taking a terrible chance on infecting the entire home but she couldn't turn them away. Patrick bathed in the warm water relaxing as he lay motionless and the steam rose above his body. Sister Mary washed his clothes while he soaked. The water was brown from the dirt and filth of the past few weeks when he got out of the tub.

He lay under the clean sheets of the small bed and Sister Mary knocked gently on his door, "Patrick, I have some warm broth for you and a little bread. Are you up to it?"

Patrick told her to come in and sat up as well as he could. She gently raised a spoon to his mouth. He had never had soup that tasted so good. He felt better with every mouthful.

Sister Mary smiled angelically at him and said, "I believe that with a good night sleep and a little more food in your belly, you'll be just fine."

With that, he closed his eyes and fell into a deep sleep. John prayed for his friend's recovery. He slept on a small cot next to him and as he slept, he dreamt that he was standing on the deck of a ship and could feel the swaying motion as it rolled with each small wave. In the distance, he saw his farm that he would have some day.

In a magnificent garden, he saw his mother and kneeling next to her was a beautiful young woman. She talked casually to Winfred while putting her hands in the soil. They laughed about something spoken and all the while, the bright sun covered them with a gentle glow. He could smell the flowers and the fresh earth. He didn't want this dream to ever end. He awoke to Patrick rustling next to him. Patrick had been asleep almost twelve hours when he awoke and felt a presence in the room. He glanced over and saw John looking at him with a grin on his face.

"Patrick, you have some color in your Irish cheeks. I think you're going to make it my friend."

Patrick raised himself up on the bed still weak but energized after a long sleep. "I'm famished, but I'm ready for the journey to begin again."

Chapter Fifteen
Kingston

August 1848

It is curious that physical courage
should be so common in the world
and moral courage so rare.
Mark Twain

The two men walked the dock along the main road moving away from the city of Quebec and reading all of the signs in search of the Schooner Victoria that would take them to Kingston. The fishermen were coming in with the catch of the day; the lumber was stacked on long barges going down river, and men and women in fancy clothes traveled in regal-looking carriages. John could see the tops of Cathedrals in the distance. He found it hard to focus on one sign when so much had his attention.

Patrick said, "Look ahead, I see a booth with the word Kingston on it."

John looked down the dock and sure enough, he saw it too. For so early in the morning, people hustled and bustled everywhere.

They purchased two one-way tickets to Kingston and would arrive by tomorrow afternoon. Waiting for the Victoria, he found a comfortable spot next to a tree in a shady area by the water. Patrick sat down next to John and smiled at his friend.

"We're almost there, long journey, but we're almost there."

John told Patrick about the dream that he had had that morning.

"It felt so real. I saw my mother and the wife I'll have someday. I'm going to make that dream come."

"I have no doubt of that."

Within thirty-minutes, they saw the Victoria coming imminently closer to the dock. The waves smacked against the embankment and water splashed around the bottom of the vessel. They watched the activity of the shipmates working on the boat getting ready to grab the ropes and tie the schooner down. The sails came down and the boat finally bumped up against the dock. One very large man in a dirty cap and shirt and big bushy beard, pulled the heavy bridge down to rest against the dock and stood there to help the first class passengers off. One after another, they gathered their bags and claimed their trunks and went off on foot or had carriages waiting for them.

"All aboard for Trois-Rivieres, Montreal, Cornwall

and Kingston, all aboard!" a load booming voice called out.

The captain stood on deck thanking welcoming the passengers getting onboard. It was a fairly small boat compared to what they had just lived on for almost three months.

"Patrick, look at the cliffs over there. Aren't they magnificent?"

The boat sounded a loud ring from the bell and the mates worked diligently once again to pull the ropes in and pull the bridge back as the vessel pulled back into the water.

The next stop was Montreal. John and Patrick stood by watching the many people getting ready to disembark and listening to the languid sounds of the French language, which most of them spoke.

To John, Montreal looked like another dirty city port, pungent with the stench of horse manure and garbage, but through all of that, he could smell baked goods. It smelled like fresh bread or biscuits and it reminded him of his mother. He needed to send another letter as soon as he arrived in Camden to let them know he was alive. He prayed that Mary Ann mailed the first letter when they got off the boat. He hoped they made it out of quarantine and were on their way to their final destination.

"Mates, if you're planning on eating anything today,

now is the time to get off and purchase something. There is no other real opportunity to get food," a shipmate yelled to John and Patrick

They both realized how hungry they were after smelling the baked goods from the dock.

"We'll set sail again in an hour, you have plenty of time."

Patrick led the way walking down the bridge towards the dock area. Struggling through the large groups of people waiting for transportation, they observed laborers shoveling garbage into carts and vendors sweeping in front of their shops. The two men found the bakery that had such a magnificent aroma. They walked in and ordered their food.

"This has got to be the finest bread I've ever had. What did she call it?" asked John.

"A croissant I believe is what she said. I agree - I'm going to save half of mine for later. The broth is good too," replied Patrick with a mouth full of bread.

They finished their food without saying much savoring the buttery croissant that virtually melted in their mouth and the fresh goat cheese. Maybe, someday, John would make it back this way. It was a colorful city, the sounds of church bells in the background made him think of St. Mary's.

John was looking for his ticket in his pocket and heard, "I remember ya mates, come aboard. We're headed to the locks next. You'll like the next part of the journey," the shipmate said with a smile.

As the schooner started to squeeze between the narrowing lands on each side, it started to slow and eventually stopped in a lock chamber. The crew on land waited for the ship to come to a complete stop and safely moored when huge gates closed in behind the ship. The linesman, as John heard them being called, pulled valves from a large pulley and opened the lock and in gushed twenty million gallons of water. After ten minutes, the boat had been raised and the level reached allowed the forward gates to be opened. The lock crew sent a signal to the boat's captain and he rang a large bell from the schooner, which signaled, "Cast off" and it proceeded out of the lock. Both men looked in amazement having never seen anything like it.

The schooner continued on towards a setting sun and the bright orange of the sky marking a perfect end to another day. They had cots below deck but both men agreed that they preferred to sleep under the stars. Tomorrow they would be pulling into Kingston. They had enough of sleeping in steerage and even though they felt a chill to the air, it felt good to take in the night and count the stars.

John didn't sleep that well, all night his mind was alive with excitement over reaching Kingston and then on to Camden. He lay on his back staring at the sky wondering what lay ahead of him. Would he find the Castleford's, his own land, would he even be capable of farming on his own, how would he work out getting his family over? So many questions ran through his mind. Eventually, he closed his eyes and slept for a short time and before he knew it, the shipmates worked diligently in the pre-dawn. The sun peaked just over the horizon. John stood and looked over the railing. He blinked hard because he couldn't believe what he was seeing. The ship sailed through what appeared to be 1,000 islands. Patrick heard him and jumped up. "Patrick, come look at this. Isn't that a beautiful sight?"

The shipmate that John and Patrick had talked to on and off came over to them holding two cups of coffee.

"Beautiful area isn't it? I hear there are 1,864 islands out there but I don't know how someone could count all of them. It goes on for about fifty miles. Most are uninhabited. They're just pretty to look at. This is my favorite part of the trip."

John could see why. "How long before we reach Kingston?"

"We'll be there in an hour or so. Not much time. Where are you two headed when we arrive?"

"Camden," Patrick replied. "We're coming in from Ireland to farm."

"Lots of folks are doing that. I figured you all were from Ireland. I'm here from England across the pond from you all - Blackpool. Got here a few years ago and managed to get this job. It's a good life. I love being on the water and don't have family. I lost them all on the voyage over. This is my life. Don't want this to be the day I lose my job though, gotta get back to work." He tipped his cap to them and scurried off.

As they pulled into the dock, they heard the schooner bell and became two of the first people off the ship. Seeing a sign that said *Kingston, Canada*, John suddenly got emotional.

Patrick slapped him on the back and said, "Congratulations – you're almost home!"

John wiped his nose with his sleeve and said, "I don't know where you're headed, but I can't imagine going anywhere without you. Let's continue this journey together, unless you have better plans."

"No where else would I rather be.

Part III

Chapter Sixteen
Arrival

August 1848

Give us grace and strength
to forbear and persevere,
give us gaiety and the quiet mind,
spare to us our friends
soften to us our enemies.
Robert Louis Stevenson

Patrick took the paper out of his pocket that the captain from the Dunbrody had given to him for John seemingly ages ago, now worn and dirty but still legible.

"Patrick, look down there!"

They glanced down river and noticed shed after shed that looked very much like what they had just left in Quebec.

John said, "Excuse me," to a thin sickly looking man walking past, "What are those tents?"

The man looked at him and in a strong British accent said, "Are you crazy, man? Those are the fever sheds. You Irish are bringing the bloody fever to Kingston. If I were you, I'd get back on that boat and head back to where you came from. The General Hospital is overflowing with the kinds of you….all dying or as good as."

John's eyes flashed with anger. Seeing the reaction, Patrick grabbed his sleeve moving him away from the waterfront. They walked a few blocks toward the city center and John found a coachman sitting on a Rockaway stagecoach with two black horses. He had his reins in his hands and almost appeared as if he was waiting for them to arrive.

"Are you for hire?" John asked.

"Yep, if you got money to pay. Where are you wantin' to go?"

John looked down at the paper Patrick handed him and said, "We're headed for Centreville? There's a stagecoach inn there called the…" John was trying to find the name on the paper.

"I know, I know! There is only one stagecoach inn in Centreville and next to that is a general store. You know that inn is haunted?" asked the driver.

"Haunted?" replied Patrick.

"Yeah, ghosts. But I'll take ya there if that's where you want to go," replied the driver.

"How much and how long?" John asked.

"We'll get there by dark give or take and it will cost each of you five shillings. The ruts are really bad this time of year. Hell, they just finished the main road that goes up there. You aren't the first Irishman to travel north either. They've been coming in by the droves and I hear it's only going to get worse. You're lucky that I happened to be sitting here or you'd be walkin but since I am here and you found me, I have some rules for ya as well. Wells Fargo owns me and I have to tell you about these before you board.

- Abstinence from liquor is requested, but if you must drink share the bottle. To do otherwise makes you appear selfish and unneighborly.
- If ladies are present, gentlemen are urged to forego smoking cigars and pipes as the odor of same is repugnant to the gentler sex. Chewing tobacco is permitted, but spit with the wind, not against it.
- Gentlemen must refrain from the use of rough language in the presence of ladies and children.
- Buffalo robes are provided for your comfort in cold weather. Hogging robes will not be tolerated and the offender will be made to ride with the driver.
- Don't snore loudly while sleeping or use your fellow passenger's shoulder for a pillow; he or she may not understand and friction may result.
- Firearms may be kept on your person for use in emergencies. Do not fire them for pleasure or shoot at wild animals as the sound riles the horses.

• In the event of runaway horses remain calm. Leaping from the coach in panic will leave you injured, at the mercy of the elements, hostile Indians and hungry coyotes.

• Forbidden topics of conversation are: stagecoach robberies and Indian uprisings.

• Gents guilty of unchivalrous behavior toward lady passengers will be put off the stage. It's a long walk back. A word to the wise is sufficient."

"If you can agree to all of that, kindly hand me your money and climb aboard."

John and Patrick paid their fare, threw their things in the back and climbed into the stagecoach.

Indians? John thought. *I'll take Indians over fever sheds any day.* "Did you say, Indians? What exactly is an Indian."

The driver started to laugh and choked on tobacco he had in his lip which put him into a coughing fit.

"You've never heard of Indians?"

"No, I haven't," John replied and Patrick shrugged his shoulders.

"Indians are red folks that have lived here for a long time and think this is their land. They live in tents and ride horses and hunt. On occasion if you're living on what they think is their land, they'll sneak up quiet like a fox and kill everyone in their path. There have been a lot of fights between what they call the white man in the

United States and the Indians over this land issue. Like I said, we don't have too much of a problem around here but don't be surprised if you see one or two on horseback and sometimes with a painted face. I'm more afraid of getting robbed than I am of an Indian. They usually don't bother a lone stagecoach driver traveling up and down a road. They're more interested in towns sproutin' up and cuttin' down all the trees for the land. They like to scalp people," the driver went on.

"Scalp people? John asked.

"Oh Lord, you never heard of scalpin?"

John shook his head.

"Scalpin' is when an Indian surprises you, usually at dawn when you're not expecting it, and captures you and your family, kills you with a bow and arrow and then takes a knife and cuts the top of your head off. Some French guy said, 'they approach like foxes, fight like lions, and disappear like birds.' And that's about it."

The driver spit into the dirt.

John whispered to Patrick, "It sounds a lot like pitch capping to me."

He enjoyed seeing the countryside as they travelled. He noticed the dark green of the woods and the settlers that had built log cabins neatly placed against a backdrop of timber. The sun, high in the sky, felt good against his skin, and the fresh air of this sprawling, foreign continent was delightful. He noticed the men in the fields working and tending to their gardens. The gardens that they worked were much bigger than they had in Ireland. John wondered what they had planted – evidently, exotic vegetables, different from any he had seen before.

He yelled up to the driver, "What have these farmers planted?"

"They plant a lot of things around here. If you can get through the limestone or find a good piece of land, you can grow just about anything. There is wheat, barley, rye, peas, oats, buckwheat, corn, potatoes, turnips, carrots, beans, hay, and strawberries. Some farmers make it on maple syrup from the trees and others just have livestock. Are you two part of the Fitzpatrick group?"

"Sir?" questioned Patrick.

"Are you all part of the group that the British government has paid to leave Ireland and has promised you land to farm?" asked the driver impatiently.

"Oh, yes sir, we are."

"Well, you aren't the only ones like I mentioned before. Hope you have something in writing or you might be waiting in line for a while."

That was another issue John had not thought of. He was glad they were meeting up with the Castlefords. Hopefully, Samuel had worked all of this out since he had a head start on them.

"I suppose you were a potato farmer in Ireland."

"We were…until the famine," replied Patrick.

John's head was swimming with possibilities. He was excited to know that the bounty could be so much richer than Ireland but at the same time he had no idea what he was getting into, and a deep sense of uncertainty surrounded him. John and Patrick watched farm after farm go by, watching as farmers worked diligently with the land or with animals. They saw bulls, cows, horses, sheep and lambs, and the sight of pig farms, despite the horrific smell, was heartwarming since they had not seen animal farms in years.

"There are a lot of lumber farms if you're looking for work, you can usually get on there, even if it's just for the summer," the driver added.

Patrick nodded and said, "I wouldn't mind working on a lumber farm. I'm happy to do anything to get settled. I dream about the cabin I'm going to build."

"Really," John asked, "What have you been thinking?"

"I want a cabin with two maybe three rooms, a fireplace for cooking, a meat house in the back for salted pork and beef, a few windows to see the trees outside and a beautiful wife with lots of kids to fill up the house," Patrick said dreamily.

"Sounds like my dream too. Let's pray we both get our wish."

Just as the sun was setting in the west, the driver yelled back, "We're passing John Whelan's cabin which means we're just a few minutes out."

"Who's John Whelan?"

"He's one of the first settlers here in Centreville and built the inn I'm taking you to. It's called Whelan Corners."

They passed a log schoolhouse that looked very different than a regular log cabin. "What's that building?"

"A schoolhouse," the driver yelled back.

"A schoolhouse for who?" John yelled.

"The children that live here in this town all go to school."

"They 'all' go to school?" Patrick asked surprised.

"Sure, unless there is a reason they can't. The boys work the farm with their fathers but just about everyone wants their children to read and write," the driver said looking back at John and Patrick. "Can you read?" asked the driver.

"Yes, sir, I can. Not real well but I can get by and I can write too. Speaking of that, if I write a letter to my family in Ireland, where can I post it?" John asked.

"I'll take it for you. I also run mail between the towns.

"Can you give me a few minutes when we arrive to write a quick letter to my mother?" John asked.

"No rush, you'll need paper and something to write with. John Whelan can help you with that. I'll be back here probably tomorrow or the day after. Give it to Whelan when you're finished and I'll pick it up from him."

"Thank you," John replied with relief. "Is that a church I see in the distance?"

"That stone structure?"

"Yes."

"It's a Catholic Church. Been here since the 30's but was recently torn down and built with stone so it would last through the winters. Cold winters up here and lots of snow."

John was used to cold winters. As they came closer to the church, the church bells started to ring, sounding melodically and confidently, as if each ring signaled the promise of a new day, new city, new hope. His mood was magically lifted as they pulled up in front of the inn.

Just as John had hoped, there was a note from Samuel waiting for him.

Dear John – We hope if you are reading this letter that it indicates that you have had safe travels. We were able to locate the land and I have parceled off fifty acres for you to own. It's actually one hundred acres but you will be sharing that with a man from England by the name of Paul Booth. Nice man, you'll like him. We can work out the details when we meet. The farm that we are occupying is in Camden. You'll only have a four mile walk but when you arrive, you can stay here with us until you can get settled. Start heading east and walk around Camden Lake and about one mile on the other side of the lake, still heading east; you'll see our log cabin. If you come to the wrong one, just ask, someone will point you in the right direction. We look forward to seeing you and welcoming you to our home.

Regards,

Samuel and Charlotte Castleford

John walked back into the inn to write his letter to his family. Sitting at a small desk with paper and a quill pen he gathered his thoughts.

August 1848

Dear Mamai and Family – I pray this letter finds you well. I just arrived in Centreville, a small town in Canada. I am getting ready to meet Sam regarding the land that he has secured for us.You won't believe it Mamai, but its one hundred acres! We are sharing it with a man by the name of Paul Booth. He has fifty acres that he has already cleared and cultivated. There is so much to tell you. There is a school here for all the children to attend to learn to read and write. There is also St. Anthony's Catholic Church near by for us to attend services. The farms are overflowing with vegetables. I promise to be diligent in working and saving so that I can send for you as quickly as possible. I miss you all so much and am anxious for the day you arrive. Please write to me. If you put Samuel Castleford and my name and address it to the Castleford Farm, Camden, Canada it will reach me. I met the stagecoach driver today along with the inn keeper; John Whelan so I'm sure the letter will make its way to me. My love to you all.

John

John sealed the envelope with candle wax and wrote the address on the outside and handed it to John Whelan.

"It will be two cents to post that,"Whelan said nicely with his hand out.

"We're headed to the Castleford farm."

"Oh that's not far."

Whelan took John and Patrick outside and pointed them in the right direction. "If you don't waste any time, you'll get there while you can still see. It gets darker than the inside of a hat out there. Plus, you don't want to be walking in the dark without protection from coyotes not to mention a stray Indian."

Chapter Seventeen
The Farm

August 1848

It is only through labor and painful effort,
by grim energy and resolute courage,
that we move on to better things.
Theodore Roosevelt

Night gently spread its veil over the Canada sky as John and Patrick started their journey to the Castleford farm. The air felt warm and the crickets played their familiar music in harmony, as if part of a moonlit symphony. In the distance, an animal howled. John wasn't sure what it was but he had nothing to protect himself from a predator had one approached. They both felt very hungry and hoped Charlotte had something for them to eat even though they really weren't expected. Walking around the lake they marveled at the geese that swam lazily dipping occasionally and showing their tail to catch something below the surface of the water. It wasn't a large lake but possibly good for fishing. John would have to ask about that. He hadn't eaten fish or had the luxury of lazily sitting on a bank fishing, a sport he really enjoyed, in a really long time.

Reaching a dirt road, they walked east for about two miles away from the setting sun and into the darkness until they noticed a log cabin with smoke coming out of its chimney. It had a small front porch and was surrounded by trees. A light from one of the windows glowed in the darkness like a lighthouse guiding a ship into a port.

"I believe that's the cabin, Patrick!"

"Can you hear my stomach growl?"

"I heard something growl and hoped it was you," chuckled Patrick.

They both laughed from the excitement of almost reaching their destination and the exhaustion catching up to them on the journey they had traveled so far. On the north side of the house, John could make out a garden. He didn't see anything developing yet but there was a plow next to the garden and fruit trees alongside the dirt rows. John and Patrick walked up to the front porch and before they could knock on the door, it swung open and there stood Samuel with a huge grin on his face.

"John, my boy! Come in, come in!" cried Samuel. He gave John a warm embrace and slapped him on the back. "You've lost a little weight there haven't ya?"

"Yes, a little," John remarked, looking down at his dirty clothes that now seemed to hang on him. "Samuel, this is Patrick Cavanaugh a friend I met on the ship.

Patrick, this is Samuel Castleford.

"Patrick, good to have you here," Samuel said with a big smile.

Charlotte walked through the main room and had the brightest expression on her face. She threw her arms around John and said, "I'm so glad to see you."

"Ma'am, likewise. You look as lovely as ever. Charlotte, this is Patrick Cavanaugh."

Patrick bent and kissed her hand and said, "The pleasure is all mine, ma'am."

"Please, both of you come in. You must be starving. Ann, could you please get these two a bowl of stew and fresh bread?" Charlotte asked.

"Yes, ma'am.".

Ann was an attractive girl, about fifteen with dark eyes and dark hair that was pulled back and pinned neatly in a tight knot. She wore a plain dark blue dress with a white apron tied around her small waist. Her Irish accent gave John a tinge of homesickness and he was eager to talk with her to find out where she was from. John looked around and noticed that the house was decorated simply but tastefully. The windows were open to let in the warm night air and a gentle breeze caressed John as he waited for his meal. Samuel asked him about his journey and the two exchanged stories with Patrick chiming in. He told them about getting stabbed on the ship and staying at the orphanage in Quebec and taking the schooner to Kingston.

"I think I have a lot to learn. I hear there are Indians, beasts that will kill your livestock, fruit trees with more fruit than a man can eat, and more Irish live here than in Ireland," John joked.

Samuel laughed, "Yes, all that is true. You'll learn along the way. We can go over everything when you've had a good night sleep and I can show you around." After they ate, Samuel invited John and Patrick to sit outside with him. Charlotte had Ann put fresh linens and a blanket on each bed in the little room off of the kitchen. She had washed the linens that day and hung them outside to dry so they had a clean country smell. Ann lit a candle on a little wooden table between the two beds and placed a bowl and pitcher of clean warm water on a small table at the end of each bed if they wanted to wash up after their long journey.

The three men sat outside talking softly for an hour or so when Samuel said, "Gentlemen, I'll retire now and I'm sure you're both tired. Ann has fixed up your beds and I'll show you to your room. Is there anything I can get you before I retire for the evening?"

John said, "No" and thanked his friend for the food. "I'll repay you for everything, Samuel."

"Don't be silly, John, what are friends for?"

John entered the little room and looked around with satisfaction. It was a tiny space but it was comfortable and inviting. They cleaned themselves up and laid on the straw mattresses and fresh smelling sheets and fell fast asleep listening to the crickets outside their window and the hooting of an owl in the trees.

The next morning, they awoke to a rooster's crow, the mooing of cows, and the bright sunlight coming through the curtains. Everything about this morning smelled of summer and the excitement of a new start. John and Patrick glanced at each other when the aroma of fresh coffee drifted under the door.

As they entered the kitchen, Ann had a twinkle in her eye as she filled up their coffee mugs. Samuel walked in from outside. John wasn't sure where Charlotte was, possibly still in bed?

"Men, good morning. I hope you slept well?"

"I haven't slept that well in years."

Samuel sat down at the table and had paperwork in his hands that he put on the table.

"John, are you ready for business?"

"Yes, sir, I'm *anxious* for business."

"This is what we have," Samuel showed John his land agreement that put fifty acres of land into John Doyle's name. "This land is down the street about two miles north of here. Its good land but it has to be cleared as my own land had been cleared. Once you've cleared the land, you can use that wood to build your log cabin. I have neighbors that will help you. You can stay here until your cabin is built. You can borrow my plow when you're ready to start working your farm. I would suggest planting potatoes because you know that crop and peas, cabbage and fall wheat because it's relatively easy to grow and will survive an early frost. You'll need to work quickly because the sooner you get things planted, the sooner you'll start making a profit. In the spring, you can plant corn, oats and rye and possibly get a few livestock. You might want to purchase a heifer and a horse as soon as you can afford that. The more cows you can purchase the better. Butter and cheese are big sellers in this area. You might also want a few chickens, because the eggs you can also sell. The sooner you can get hay in the better because it will feed a farmer's dairy herd all winter. Farmers will pay a lot for that. I'll take you into town after I show you your land so that you know where everything is and you can purchase supplies. The more people you get to know the better. They can help you since so many have been through what you're going through. Word has it that a lot of Irish are headed this way. You're lucky to get this land and a new start."

John shook his head in agreement. Patrick just sat and listened. He wasn't sure what he was going to do. Maybe he could work for John as a laborer. He would approach him when the time was right. He wouldn't need a salary right away and if John would put him up for free, they could finish the work much more quickly together.

They got along well and Patrick believed John would like the idea.

After breakfast, they still had not seen Charlotte. John didn't know what to make of that. The three men walked outside putting their hats on and set out down the road. The air was fresh and the sun was just coming up over the tops of the trees. John asked Samuel questions as they walked about the townspeople, the soil, and what he had learned so far about selling crops. Samuel shared once they were out of earshot that Charlotte did not like Canada and ever since she heard about the orphans in Grosse Ile, that's all she's talked about. She wanted a child desperately but Samuel didn't think this was the time. Settling into a deep depression, she rarely left her room during the day. Samuel shared with John and Patrick that he didn't know how long they actually would be staying in Camden. Charlotte had relatives that had gone on to Australia and had been pushing Samuel to consider it. Samuel knew that once the cold came in from the north, that Charlotte would be putting more and more pressure on him to leave. Australia had mild winters and even though the cities were not as European as London, they were larger and more cultural than Canada. Patrick thought silently that possibly he could earn enough money to purchase Samuel's farm if he left.

Soon, they came upon a large oak tree and a stick that someone had planted in the ground with a white tip of paint on the top.

Samuel said, "This is the marker of your land. If you walk straight down this dirt road, you'll come to another marker and that's where your land ends. If you pace yourself and walk about one-half mile back, that's where you'll find another stick that marks the back end of your property."

John never dreamed that he would get this much land. His father only had seven acres and John was getting fifty! He felt like the wind had just been knocked out of him. Yet, as he surveyed the property, he felt slightly overwhelmed with all of the trees that would have to be cleared – tall, thick oaks and white pines, symbols of a still-pristine, largely unsettled land.

As they walked about this uncleared forest, they could see someone walking down the road towards them.

Samuel said, "Oh that's Paul Booth. You need to meet him, John. He owns the other half of this one hundred acre parcel."

Paul came into view and John noticed what a big man he was. He had dark brown eyes, a very structured jaw and wavy hair. He was quite a bit older than John or Patrick and closer in age to Samuel. John stuck out his hand and Paul grabbed it warmly.

"Welcome to Canada. I've heard many good things about you," Paul said with a sincere smile.

"How long have you been here?"

"Just since early spring. Came over from Liverpool with my wife and two children. I was able to get some crops in."

"What all have you planted?" Patrick asked.

"I have about ten acres; barley, peas, oats and potatoes, beans and hay."

"What about animals?"

"Yes, I have one horse, a new calf, and a bull."

John was surprised that he had cleared and planted all of that and had animals already. They talked and walked around and Samuel explained that there was limestone everywhere and it wasn't the easiest thing to get through.

"What trees you're not able to haul, you can burn."

"Burn, why would I want to burn my trees?" asked John bewildered.

Samuel replied, "Believe it or not John, the ashes can be sold to dealers who export potash from the wood to the British textile and glass industries. There is a small creek that flows into Camden Lake. At the end of that creek which I can show you, is a sawmill in operation which is great for you because it's so close. You won't have to haul the logs as far as some have. There is another sawmill on the Depot River at Bellrock, but its' another four miles northeast of here. It's too far to haul logs. Let's go back to the cabin, we'll get the wagon and see if Charlotte needs anything in town and then I'll show you around."

"John, I'll be happy to help you get started since we'll be neighbors. Just give a yell and I'll bring over some help," Paul said cheerfully.

"Glad to know you Paul. Looking forward to working with you."

Paul walked away and thought to himself *how young he was to be on his own and having that much land to work by himself. Well he got here! He must be a determined, hard-working man.*

Charlotte was still in her room when they got back. John and Patrick waited outside. Patrick thought it might be a good time to approach John about being a laborer for him.

"How about I work for you for nothing except a bed until you get on your feet and then we could work out a salary?"

"That's a great idea! You can see that I need the help and you're not a bad guy to have around."

Just as they were shaking hands to seal the deal, Samuel joined them. They jumped up into the wagon and Samuel showed John and Patrick where the sawmill was located. It was not far from where they had walked last night but couldn't see it in the dark. Samuel continued the ride into town which took on a different look by daylight. The roads were in terrible shape, hardly passable.

When they pulled up in front of Whelan's Corners, they saw the schoolhouse and the church that they saw the night before; they noticed a post office to mail letters. John wondered why John Whelan hadn't said anything about the post office the night before.

"The town is growing by leaps and bounds men and I've heard that government buildings will be coming to this area. You never know John, we might even see a saloon."

"Well, I have no need for a saloon, Samuel, but this general store is nice."

Samuel posted a note in the general store and post office that John Doyle would need some help clearing his land. Within hours, Paul and men from around the county showed up to start taking down trees and large rocks off of the property, enough land to build a small cabin and prepare for a small garden. Patrick and John worked tirelessly going back to Samuel and Charlotte's late at night and getting up before the sun to continue their work. John was so grateful for the friends that he made and the neighbors that helped him and welcomed him into the community. He knew that the harder he worked and the sooner he made an income, the sooner his family could join him. He sat one evening talking with Patrick and Samuel late into the evening.

"Samuel, I've been thinking. I'm a little concerned about planting too much too soon. What do you think is the safest thing to plant? I have little money to make a start and I don't want to waste any of it. The sooner I'm able to make a living, the sooner I can get my family over."

"Well John, it's up to you, but I would only clear ten acres for crops. You can have fifteen acres for pasture, a small garden, enough cleared to build your cabin. I think peas would be safe to plant, beans maybe, but I think you'd be better off purchasing animals. You can sell the butter and chicken eggs. Eventually, you can plant more, clear off more land and add barley, oats or potatoes."

"No, I'm not growing potatoes anytime soon. I've had enough potatoes to last a lifetime," John said with mild disgust.

"I understand that John, but you do know that crop."

Within a few weeks, John had cleared five of the fifty acres. He sold most of the cleared wood and didn't get as much as he had hoped, but nonetheless had more money in his pocket than he ever had. He burned another five acres and found out from Paul when the dealers would be coming in from Kingston to purchase potash. That was going to be another money maker. John had enough lumber to start building his cabin. The dreams of abundance and prosperity he kindled in Ireland, the ones he clung to during the long, difficult days at sea, were beginning to take shape.

"Patrick, I'm going to build a two story house," John

said proudly.

"What?" "You are going to build two stories and a house not a cabin?"

"Yup, I want a house my mother and family will be proud of. I don't want to build a temporary cabin like most of the people around here have done. Samuel doesn't care if we stay at his house. As a matter of fact, I think he enjoys the company. It won't take that much longer and it's permanent. I can do it with the help of neighbors and you of course."

Patrick was thrilled. He had never been in a two-story house.

John, Patrick and a few neighbors squared off a forty foot by sixty foot area that had been cleared and sat on a limestone base. They squared off each log and put notches on the top and bottom of each end. The logs were stacked and the notched ends were connected together at the corners. Chick sticks and wood chips from the sawmill filled the gaps between the logs. This took a few days but with each new day John became more and more excited that he would have his own home and a beauty at that. On the fourth day it rained, a good strong downpour that kicked up the smell of wet earth and pine trees. He needed the rain so that he could get mud from the dry dirt to fill the remaining spaces of the log house to keep the cold air and wind out during the winter. Paul knew a neighbor who was a skilled wood craftsman, a

Dutchman by the name of Derk Van Cortlandt. He came over to help build John's home and cut out a door and four windows, two in the front and two in the back. He built steps leading up to the second floor which also had two windows in the front. Most people had dirt floors but Derk took solid materials from trees and milled each board into tongue and groove lengths. While he was working on the floors, John collected large stones to build his six feet wide fireplace and chimney. After Derk finished the floors, he went to work on the door and windows. Derk put Yorkshire Sash windows in each opening. The window frame was about one inch thick, and secured into the building with squared treenails driven into round holes in the log. Derk then added the door to finish the house off. Once the walls and door were complete, a group of neighbors started working on the roof.

Meanwhile, some of the women walked up the road and called the men over for soup and Irish soda bread. They ate greedily and enjoyed sitting for a short time to catch their breath but the house was almost finished. People came from all over to see the two-story house. Now the women of the area wanted the same thing John was building. He was the envy of the neighborhood.

John walked back to Samuel's that evening and knocked on their door.

"Another day closer to having a house and home of

your own!" Samuel said proudly.

"I will repay you for your kindness. My house is finished. Patrick and I are going to stay there from now on. As soon as the barn is built, I'll have everyone over for a celebration."

"The dealers are coming into Centreville to purchase potash and I believe you have quite a bit."

"Yes, I do and I'm very anxious to sell it."

"Get in touch with Paul in the morning. He can give you the details."

The house was beautiful and more than either one could have hoped for. That night, they built a fire in the new fireplace. A skinned rabbit Patrick had caught earlier was strung over the fire, roasting slowly. They had collected some greens from outside and feasted on rabbit and wild mushrooms. Exhausted from the day's labor and warmed by the meal in their bellies, they lay near the fire even though it was a warm evening, watching it hiss and crackle, and basking in the satisfaction of hard work and progress.

Chapter Eighteen
Potash and Settling In

September 1848

Courage and perseverance have a
magical talisman, before which difficulties
disappear and obstacles vanish into air.
John Quincy Adams

The next morning, John, Patrick and Paul rode into Centreville to meet the potash representatives. The dealers walked out of the Whelan Inn as the three men approached. They looked like British dandies but John didn't care and Paul was always happy to see someone else from England. Pulling the wagon over to the side of the road, Paul got out and walked up to a conservative looking businessman dressed in a fashionable, highly starched cravat. His dark grey suit had a relatively loose cut with a pocket watch chain hanging from his pocket. The other gentleman with him was dressed the same way.

"Good morning, gentlemen," Paul smiled and held out his hand.

The two men looked surprised to hear a British accent.

"Well, what do you know, another Brit. Good to meet you. I take it you've come to sell potash?"

"Yes, sir, and my friend too."

"Well let's see what you got."

They walked to the back of the wagon.

John asked, "What do you use potash for?"

"It is needed for soap and glass primarily. We'll pay a pretty pence for it too."

As the men looked over the potash for impurities, more and more people showed up to sell what they had. John was very happy that they had been the first in line and also that Paul was British, which helped establish an instant rapport with them. The gentleman with the pocket watch said, "I'll give you $100.00 for the whole lot." John looked at Paul and tried not to gasp. Plus, it was in American currency, which John had heard was a good thing to trade in. That was $50.00 for each, which meant he could purchase a wagon, horse, seed, and maybe even a new pair of pants and shoes.

"It's a deal," and they proceeded to empty the wagon into barrels that ran along the dirt road.

It was almost October when John and Patrick walked back into town to purchase a wagon and horse and other items that they needed. John had a list of things that he wanted to purchase as he walked into Wilson's General

Store, glanced around and breathed deeply, delighting in the aroma of fresh brewed coffee. His mother was going to love this place. In one corner he noticed the rolls of fabrics lying on a table. He glanced briefly at the ribbons and yarn. He would write about this in his next letter to her.

Next to the bolts of fabric he saw men's trousers and hats, underwear, and socks. More clothes than he had seen since he looked in the window of the clothing store in Liverpool. To the right of him he noticed supplies like skillets, cookware, and tools for building and repairs. He walked down the isle of canned food and his mouth watered at all of the containers filled with things he had never heard of much less tried.

A man walked out from behind the counter and smiled at John.

"Hello, I've seen you in town but we haven't met." The older man with graying hair and gentle brown eyes held out his hand. "I'm Andrew Wilson," he smiled warmly.

"Hello, I'm John Doyle. I've come from County Wicklow, Ireland and own the farm on Dewey Lane."

"Ah, yes, near the Castleford's. "What can I do for you today?" Andrew asked.

John looked down at his list. "I need these items please."

Andrew collected seed, coffee, flour, trousers, shoes and some other needed items and placed them on the counter.

"Do you have a rifle?"

"A rifle?"

"Yep, I wouldn't live in these parts without one. We haven't had any problems from the Indians lately but you never know. You also have to think about fox, wolves and the occasional bear."

John hadn't thought about the Indians since the first night that he arrived.

"What kind of rifle do you have?"

"I have a brand new Sharp's rifle just in from the states, made in Philadelphia. It's accurate for about 500 yards, maybe 1,000."

"How much is it?"

"I'll sell you that and ammunition for $16.00."

"Okay, I'll take it. Where can I buy a horse and wagon?"

Andrew packed everything up and said, "Walk past the church and down that road traveling south, not far maybe half mile. You'll see a barn with horses and wagons on the side. Mutton owns it. He'll take care of you."

"Mutton, that's an unusual name."

"He has big mutton chop side burns. That's how he got that name. Not sure what his real name is we've called him that for so long. He's from Scotland. Honest guy."

"Thanks, I appreciate the help. I'll be seeing you

again I'm sure."

John walked out the door and Patrick was waiting outside for him.

"Patrick, I'm going over to see a man by the name of Mutton about a wagon and a horse. Do you want to stay here with our things? It shouldn't take me too long."

"Sure, I'll be right here waiting for you. You bought a rifle?" Patrick asked with amazement while he examined the sleek Sharp's rifle.

"Yeah, I keep hearing how we may need one."

John turned to walk up the road, past the church and he noticed the large brown barn as soon as he turned the corner. He walked over to the horse stalls and looked over the horses. He had never owned a horse before and wasn't quite sure what to look for.

The farmer that owned the stalls walked up to him and said, "Can I help ya?"

"Are you Mutton?"

"I am."

"I'm interested in buying a wagon and a horse," John said as he continued to examine the large beasts.

"What kind you want, racer (he chuckled), work horse, draft?"

"I need him primarily to pull the wagon and plough."

"Okay, I got a few horses for ya. Come with me. I got one that isn't as big as a draft, which is good cause they eat a lot. How much land you workin?" Mutton asked.

"Just five acres for now."

"Oh, that ain't nothin. Look at this one. Five years old, fifteen hands high. Pretty chestnut color. Good shape," he gave John a serious look.

He looked at the horse and liked it right away. "How much?"

"Twenty-five dollars."

"That's too much," John said and started to walk away.

"Okay, twenty but that's as low as I go," Mutton said with a frown across his wrinkled face, "And twenty-five for the wagon."

"Deal." John handed him the money and Mutton put a rope around the horse's neck and pulled it to the wagon.

Patrick had a big smile on his face as John pulled up. "Hey, that's quite a horse and wagon you got there."

"I'm feeling like a real cowboy. When we get back, I'm going down to see Samuel and borrow his plough."

John and Patrick worked the rest of the day turning the soil of the small area of land. He planted the seeds before the first frost, which could happen within a couple of weeks. He then placed manure from Paul and Samuel's barn over the newly turned dirt working that into the soil. The bush bean seeds were planted in rows of two feet apart and the peas less than one inch apart. He stood back and proudly looked at five acres of row upon row of peas and beans. It took six days to get the soil ready, the manure spread and the seeds planted. By spring, he would be able to sell his crop and plant more of a variety.

He stopped at the post office to see if his mother had replied to his letter. He had checked many times over the past few weeks and each day walked away a little more anxious.

He walked through the door and Mr. Timmons, the Postmaster said, "Just the man I wanted to see. I've got a letter for you."

John excitedly took the letter and walked outside. He sat on the back of the wagon and opened the letter. This was the first time he had heard from his mother in almost six months.

July 1848

My Dearest John – It was so good to hear from you. I cannot tell you how we have worried about you and your health and the voyage. We are fine but weary from worry and waiting. Catherine and Bridget send their love. They have been busy working and reading when they have free time. We don't get to see Thomas as much as we'd like since we are still kept in separate wards but we know he is well. We have lost so many friends to disease and starvation. We bury someone everyday. Do you remember the O'Malley's? The whole family came down with the fever. We buried all of them in two days. John, we are anxiously waiting to hear that you are sending for us. I want our family back together again. We pray that you have prospered and won't forget the love we have for you. We are determined to stay well so that when you send for us, we will be able to survive the journey.

Your loving Mamai

John had hoped for more information about them but it sounded like they had much to contend with. He decided to burn more wood and sell more potash. It would be spring before he could send for his family. The winter storms on the ocean could be impassable. The journey was bad enough during good weather. He also didn't want them to travel steerage like he had and hoped to make the money to send for them possibly early March. That gave him six months to raise the money. Sitting down on a bench outside of the post office he wrote her a letter back:

September 1848

Dear Mamai,

It was so good to hear from you. I miss you dearly and the rest of the family. I am working tirelessly to make enough money to send for you. I have built a house for us that you will love. You'll have a garden and soon I'll be buying a few animals for milk and cheese. You will love it here. It's hard work but there is an abundance that we never had in Ireland. The landscape is very much like Ireland though with rolling hills and lush green meadows. I bought a horse the other day and named him Chestnut. He has the same color of hair as Catherine! Tell Thomas that I'll have plenty of work for him to do. I should have enough money raised by early spring. Plan to travel in early April after the winter storms at sea. My love to you and the rest.

John

He mailed the letter and decided while he was in town to purchase chicken wire and a couple of hens. He could sell eggs until his crops came in. As he was making his way home, the sky was turning as dark as the bottom of a well. The leaves showed their underside, which he knew, was never a good sign. A storm was coming and it was going to be a doozy.

Chapter Nineteen

Challenges

October 1848

All you need is the plan, the road map,
and the courage to press on to your destination.
Earl Nightingale

John returned home and started working on a small makeshift chicken coup. He decided he would build something stronger and bigger after the storm. Patrick had already put Chestnut into the barn when he heard the first clap of thunder. He looked up at the sky and knew it was going to be a bad storm. The wind picked up and whistled through the trees and blew leaves everywhere. John made it into the house just as the first drops fell. He could hear the rain pelting at the windows and coming down the chimney. It started to rain so hard that it was pooling by the door. John and Patrick stood at the window and watched and grew increasingly anxious.

"What if it washes the seed away?" Patrick asked with concern written all over his face.

"There isn't anything I can do to stop it."

Hour after long hour it rained and John soon became disheartened. The lightening pierced the sky relentlessly – fierce, dramatic bolts from earth to clouds...over and over again. The pools in the yard became so large they bled together forming one gigantic pond.

"If we lose the crop, we start over," John said with a shake of the head.

They also worried about the barn getting hit by lightening and catching on fire. He waited and he prayed. He fell asleep to the sound of raindrops and had a dream that as he looked at his crops they grew into something like a stalk with vines that grew up to the clouds and beyond. He walked up to the stalk and looked up. It was so high he couldn't see the top of it. The big green leaves looked heavy from the beans and peas hanging off the stems. There was an abundance of beans and peas everywhere...all the way up. It started to rain peas despite the shining sun and the blue sky. Climbing and reaching for a taller limb, he slipped and started falling. He tumbled down and right before hitting the ground, he woke with a start. He sat up and it took him a few minutes to get his thoughts together. The seeds!

Desperately, he ran outside. It was still dark but the rain had stopped. Patrick followed close behind. But when they reached the field, they were devastated: it had been reduced to one big mud hole. All of that seed that they planted and all of their hard work washed right into a big puddle. It was nothing more than five acres of mud and manure. *How could this be happening*, John thought. Anxiety overcame him and then fear set in. The weeks of preparation and hard work seemed to laugh at him. In one hard rain, his dream was as useless as the mud he stared at.

Patrick slapped him on the back and said, “We did it once and we can do it again. We’ll know what we’re doing this time.”

John gathered himself, lifted his chin and said, “I’m not going to let this set me back. We’ll let this dry out for a day or two and we’ll start all over again.”

He walked to the barn to see if Chestnut weathered the storm and then checked on the hens. Two eggs! That was promising.

John and Patrick got the seed back down after all the rain, which actually helped the soil because it pushed the manure deep into the ground. The weather turned colder and John decided to cut another five acres and burn another five. He needed to plan for winter. He could fish in the lake and now that he had a rifle, he could hunt for deer, wild turkey, rabbit and possibly a quail or two. Patrick turned out to be a keen hunter and could go out in the morning and always come back with something by early afternoon. They bartered canned beans, potatoes and a few other staples from neighbors with the fish and animals that they caught and trapped. *Next year*, John thought, *I won't have to barter with another farmer. I'll have grown my own*. He cured the deer meat and hung it in the barn along with a few rabbits and squirrels. In the private moments when he wasn't working, he had recurring thoughts of finding a wife to love and cook and can and take care of the garden. He also knew he wasn't getting any younger and wanted a big family to fill up this big house. Someday, all fifty acres would be cultivated but he certainly couldn't do that on his own or with the help of just Patrick. John envisioned children that he could take for rides in the wagon and sons to help farm all of this land. He thought about Patrick and what a great friend he had been. How lucky for both of them that they found each other along with Samuel and Charlotte.

Those days, Samuel was talking about leaving for Australia since Charlotte was so unhappy. John had barely seen her since he arrived in Canada. Maybe Patrick could buy Samuel's land so he'd still be a neighbor. John was deep in thought when he heard a terrible squawking outside and then silence. His muscles tensed, and he grabbed his rifle that he had sitting by the front door. He ran out to the chicken coup, where he spotted a coyote with a face full of blood and feathers flying everywhere. *My hens!* John thought despairingly. *My hens!*

The coyote eyed him for one brief second, its hungry eyes glaring at John. It opened its mouth, which was dripping with blood and gave an expression of surprise but not fear. John aimed his rifle at the coyote and fired and hit him right between the eyes. The coyote fell back from the blast, lying still next to the dead hens. Looking down at the dead animal, he realized his hands were shaking. Cleaning up the mess, he decided to skin the animal and save the fur. He knew that it was his mistake that he hadn't built a better coup. The next day, he rode back into town for more supplies and came back and built the strongest chicken coup anyone had ever seen.

St. Anthony Padua was the Catholic Church in town. It was a small church but looked inviting. They took the wagon into town and parked it outside the church along with others wagons. The air was crisp and the leaves had changed colors. There was a sweet smell to the air when it was autumn. The sun came out and the church bells beckoned others to come in. John missed his Catholic services. The sunlight came through the stained glass windows and displayed a rainbow of colors across the wooden pews. John took off his hat and sat down in one of the back pews. He looked around at the church, which was full by now with other farmers. The Castleford's would attend the Anglican Church but this church was filled with Irish Catholics and he felt connected to them even if he didn't personally know them.

After the service, John walked up to Father Higgins

and introduced himself.

"Father, I'm John Doyle from Ireland. You'll be seeing me every Sunday from now on."

Father Higgins shook his hand warmly and said, "Welcome to St. Anthony of Padua."

"My family will be here in the spring. I'm sending for them. My mother and sisters have beautiful voices and my mother plays the accordion.

"Maybe your sisters will join the choir we're starting. And maybe your mother will play the accordion for us. We'd all like that I'm sure.

John and Patrick struggled through the high winds and cold temperatures of that early winter. On many days John would look out the window towards the woods behind the house and see the limbs of the trees bent over from the weight of ice, glistening magically. On such mornings, John would take his horse and ride through the woods hearing the crunch of new fallen snow under the hooves of his horse. He loved the peacefulness of the woods. It would be so cold he could see his breath but he didn't care about the cold. He enjoyed the solitude and knowing that he owned this land made it even better. How proud his father would have been of him.

That winter was a long winter. The wind would howl and the snow came in large drifts. John had sold another five acres of wood and enough potash to get tickets for his mother, sisters and brother and send for them in the spring. He hid the money in a special place in the floorboards of his bedroom. The house was sparsely decorated and had very little furniture and they hadn't bothered to even put curtains on the windows. John had a straw mattress on the floor and owned few clothes so he didn't need more than a hook on the wall. He had food to eat, his hens produced plenty of eggs and he felt confident that he would have a good crop in the spring. The weeks rolled by. When he could get through the snow and into town, he would check for mail at the post office and tried never to miss a Sunday service at church. Committees were formed and he was approached to be a leader at St. Anthony's. He was honored to do this and wanted to become more and more involved. He kept busy and before he knew it, the first signs of an early spring were breaking through the long winter. He saw his first robin looking for a worm and collecting nesting material in the yard. John knew it was only a matter of a few months before his family would be with him in Canada. How wonderful it would be to have them here with him. As the earth began to thaw and buds just beginning to form on the trees, John went into town and met with Father Higgins.

"Father, I want to send for my mother and two sisters and my brother, Thomas. They are living in the Shillelagh

Workhouse in Wicklow. St. Mary's Catholic Church is near the village of Coolkenno. I need your help to get the money to my family at the workhouse. Can you help me with that?"

Father Higgins thought for a second and said, "Yes, I think I can help you with that. I'll send a letter to an old friend of mine, Father John Murphy at the Parish of Ferns in Wexford. He can purchase the tickets there at the dock and send them to the priest at St. Mary's in Wicklow. We'll get your family out of the workhouse and down to the ship."

John had saved a lot of money. He knew he was taking such a risk with all of this money but if he couldn't trust a priest or three priests for that matter, who could he trust?

"Father, I'm so grateful. Do you think we can make a May departure for them?"

"Well, the sooner we send for them, the sooner they'll be here. I'm anxious to hear those voices of angels."

John handed over all of the money he had saved and then he went to the post office and sent his mother a letter.

March 1849

Dear Mamai – I have made arrangements through Father Higgins the priest here at St. Anthony of Padua to contact a friend of his, Father John Murphy, of the Parish of Ferns in

Wexford to purchase tickets for you, Catherine, Bridget and Thomas. Father Murphy will be instructed to get the tickets to Father Byrne at St. Mary's who will make arrangements for you to get to the ship in New Ross to sail to England and then on to Canada. I have good news Mamai; your tickets will be second class not steerage. I only want the best for my mamai and family. I can't wait to see you all – I'll be waiting for you in Kingston when you arrive. My love to you, Mamai and the rest of my family. Safe Travels – I'll see you in July or the beginning of August.

Love

John

John got back to the farm and surveyed the rows and rows of future crops. He knelt down and moved the soil gently and underneath his hand, just like a miracle, was the small green bud getting ready to push its way above the soil. He was going to have a successful crop, his family was coming over, he was going to find a wife and all was well with the world.

Samuel came over mid-afternoon and told John and Patrick that they had made a decision to leave Camden. It was even worse for Charlotte now that she had lived through a Canadian winter. She thought she might go mad from little to do except needlepoint. She hadn't seen much of Louisa Butler since she arrived in Canada since Louisa had a three year old and a new baby. With few other women in the area she couldn't find anyone that she had anything in common with. Charlotte needed to be in a warmer climate. She needed more to do instead of the dreariness and remoteness of Canada. As soon as the weather broke, they would be leaving the farm.

"Patrick, do you think you'd like to take over my farm? Would you be interested in purchasing it and the farm supplies?"

Patrick was ecstatic. It was exactly what he had hoped for.

Samuel had one hundred acres and had already cultivated sixty acres, twenty of which were crops. He also had ten acres of orchards and a small garden and had laborers working for him.

"I don't know if you want to keep the laborers on but I'll give you a good price for the land. You could always sell the uncultivated land or at least sell the wood on it to pay for it all," Samuel suggested.

Patrick had saved all of the money he had earned from John and since he was from Wicklow, Ireland, he too was entitled to fifty acres. He definitely wanted the farm equipment. They both did some figuring and Patrick took a small loan from Samuel and after discussing it and writing up an agreement, they shook hands. John was happy for both of them. Moreover, he was overjoyed that Patrick would remain a neighbor.

This solved a lot of problems for John. He would

need all of the room in the house for his family. Samuel's house was smaller than John's but it was the perfect size for Patrick and someday a wife. It appeared that everything in his life was falling into place.

Chapter Twenty
The Auction

April 1849

Failure is only postponed success
as long as courage 'coaches' ambition.
The habit of persistence is the habit of victory.
Herbert Kaufman

The little town of Centreville was growing by leaps and bounds from all of the immigrants moving to Canada. The general store was much larger now to carry enough supplies for all of the families moving into the area. One Saturday morning, John saddled up his horse and decided to go into town for a few items but he also wanted to explore his surroundings. He decided to investigate the towns outside of Centreville since it was a beautiful early spring morning perfect for a leisurely ride. He rode to the post office to see if a letter was waiting for him. Unfortunately, nothing had arrived so he looked around town and discovered that a new saloon was being constructed and attached to the saloon, another new stagecoach inn. This inn looked like it was going to be much larger than the one at Whelan Corners that he first saw on his arrival into Centreville months ago. He also noticed that a blacksmith had hung his shingle out and not too far from that a sign that read: "*Doctor Johnson – I can cure whatever ails you*." If he ever needed a doctor, he knew where to go.

He then rode out to Tweed. It was a small town not any bigger than Centerville. Tweed started out as a mill town but he heard that the town had flooded when they built the dam in the river to the east of the village. Able Baker, the sawmill owner, sold his land to Samuel Smith in 1821 and Smith moved the mill downstream to alleviate the flooding problems. Smith now was one of the wealthiest men in the area because once the sawmill was built he opened a store just for construction materials. This store was one of the most needed and most popular among the farmers coming into town. Smith was now the postmaster and a justice of the peace. Three of his gristmills had been destroyed by fire and some of the locals believed that someone had set the fires on purpose.

Newburgh was a quiet little village next to Camden East. The rapidly growing town would soon become one of the largest settlements in the area. Jonathan Cooke and Robert Reikart settled in Newburgh and built more sawmills and a gristmill. *This is good to know*, John was thinking because when he started growing corn and grain, he could bring it here if Centerville didn't have one up and running yet. He heard that a man by the name of Matthew Black started a tanning business tanning any hides you could take into him. He tanned mostly deer but had an occasional bear, moose, and elk. John passed an imposing two-story white building sitting back from the road on a hill and bearing a sign that read: "*Aylesworth Children's Academy*." Was this a school for children? He wondered what was taught at the academy and if it cost money to send a child there. He would love for his children to attend a school someday.

Further down the road, he came upon one of the largest manufacturing enterprises that he had ever seen. There on the side of the road was a large building with a sign that read: "*Union Flouring and Grist Mills*". It was a three story stone mill. Another addition to this large structure was in the process of being built. The sign out front read: "*Future Home of the First Woolen Mill in Canada.*" *A woolen mill,* John thought curiously. He was accustomed to seeing them in Ireland but didn't expect to see them in Canada. He was so thrilled to be living in an area that was growing and expanding and bringing in stores and merchandise from all over Europe and America. How amazed would his family be to see all of this!

As John made his way back to his farm, he stopped off at Samuel and Charlotte's house on the way. Samuel was busy packing crates to ship to Australia while Charlotte supervised with her hands on her hips. John saw Charlotte for the first time in many months. She frantically was trying to decide which gowns to pack and which gowns to leave for the smaller trunk.

"How good to see you," Charlotte said with a smile.

"You have that sparkle back in your eye," John replied hugging her.

"I'm leaving this God-forsaken place, of course I'm happy. I say that and you know that I only wish you the best but I need more. I need better weather and more people and more things to do and I so miss the parties and the horses."

"I understand. I believe you'll love Australia. Where did you say you are moving?"

"A town called Sydney and it's supposed to be lovely according to my relatives that live there. I'm so excited."

Samuel just stood there and listened enjoying the vivacity and sparkle that had returned to his beloved wife.

"John, read this letter from my cousin Sarah."

My Dear Charlotte – We are so anxious for you to join us. You will love it here. Sydney will remind you of a bustling English seaport. There are steamships that run between England and Australia. We have museums and zoos. Isn't that a funny word! In the museums are beautiful paintings by Sir Thomas Lawrence. I must have stood in front of his painting entitled "Pinkie" for hours. She reminded me of you dear Charlotte… beautiful! You will love the museum. The zoo is a place that keeps animals behind cages. They are alive and you can watch them! We saw a kangaroo, a dingo, the cutest koala bear you've ever seen, a platypus and a Tasmanian devil. There are parks here and beautiful carriages. We can visit friends and have parties and shop!! On Sundays, there are ferries that can take us on trips to the countryside. We can walk to Hyde Park...its called Lover's Walk!

They have gas lamps on the streets at night so you never have to walk in the dark. I have so much to show you. I miss you my dear cousin. Travel safely and soon.

With much love

Sarah

John smiled as he read the letter and handed it back to Charlotte.

"How could you not be excited about that? You will love it. It sounds like everything you've ever wanted."

Charlotte threw her arms around John and gave him a big hug, which was very unlike her.

"I know I will love it and someday you'll have to visit us there."

Charlotte decided to take Ann, her housemaid with her and Ann was very excited about traveling with them to Australia. The three of them would leave in the morning to take the schooner back up to Quebec and then catch a large ship that would sail to Australia. The journey would take much longer than the trip from England to Canada, up to four months, but they hoped it would be pleasant and they had so much to look forward to.

Samuel promised he would write and wanted John to know that he'd be praying for John's family to have a safe journey.

"John, you're like a son to me. I wish you success and many blessings here."

"Thank you for all that you have done for my family and me. I'm indebted to you."

John had a small tear in his eye as he turned and walked out, knowing he would probably never see Samuel or Charlotte again. The next morning after they had gone, Patrick moved his things into his new home. He looked around at the farm that he had purchased and had never been happier in his life.

By mid-May, Patrick and John both had their hands full. The crops were coming up nicely, John kept busy cultivating the rest of his land, still selling more lumber and potash and saving the money that he made. Along with the peas and beans, he planted barley, apple trees in the orchard, oats and corn. He dug holes and placed poles for the pole beans and as the weather became warmer, the beans grew up the poles lush and green.

At the end of May, John and Patrick had heard that a livestock auction near Newburgh was scheduled on a large farm just outside of the town. They rode to the farm to see what it was all about. They saw wagons lined up and down the side of the road and horses tied up to trees and more people walking towards the large red barn that sat back from the road. They tied their horses up and started walking towards the barn with the rest. They weren't sure what to expect having never been to an auction before.

As they walked through the doors, they smelled the straw that had been thrown all over the dirt floor and the pungent odor of the animals. The space filled with a chorus of animal sounds of whose origin they were unsure. In the middle of the barn stood a makeshift stage and on the stage stood a man with a big white beard and mustache. He wore brown overalls over a flannel shirt and a large white straw hat on his head. He didn't really look like he came from the area. He yelled into the crowd a language that John and Patrick didn't quite understand. It almost sounded like a foreign language but not one they had ever heard. The man spoke very fast and with a rhythm that gave it an almost musical lilt. He had a calf next to him with a rope around its neck.

"One dollar, one dollar, now two, now two, now two, will you give me three, a gentleman in the back, will you give me three and one-half, now three and one-half, I hear four, will you give me four – three and one-half once, twice, sold to the man in the back of the room with the black hat!" yelled the auctioneer.

John and Patrick looked at each other and got really excited. *This could be fun*, they both thought. The next animal that stood on stage was another calf. It was a brown and white dairy calf that appeared just a few months old. John decided to bid on this one.

"One dollar, one dollar, now two, now two, now two, will you give me three, a gentleman in the right here in the front (John raised his hand), will you give me three and one-half, now three and one-half, I hear four, will you give me four?" John raised his hand again. Four once, twice, sold to the man right here in the front!" the auctioneer looked right at John.

John started laughing. He paid a little more than the last one, but he liked the calf and he really enjoyed this. He walked over and got his calf and took it outside by the horse. He waited through the calves and horses, and then came the pigs. He waited to see how much they were going for and finally started bidding. He got beat out by a man that was starting a pig farm. John picked through the biggest and fattest pigs and decided on purchasing two. The bidding started again. John jumped in and raised his hand at two dollars. "Do I hear two and one-half? Two and one-half once, twice, both pigs sold to the man in the front."

John got a great deal. They probably came from the same litter and they were small enough to carry in his arms. He walked out with two squealing, wiggling little pigs.

Pulling his animals into the barn for the night, he looked up at the sky and a star appeared next to a big orange moon. He made a wish for safe travels for his family praying that they would arrive safely unlike so many that perished before they even reached Quebec.

Chapter Twenty-One
The Family Arrives

July 1849

It takes someone with a vision
of the possibilities to attain new
levels of experience. Someone with the
courage to live his dreams.
Les Brown

May 1849

My Dear John

We received the tickets and extra money from Father Byrne just this morning. I can't tell you how worried I was when Mrs. McCormick came to me in the kitchen as I was preparing breakfast for everyone and said that I had a visitor. I feared the worst. It was so good to see Father Byrne. He called me aside to talk privately and nosey Mrs. McCormick strained to hear what he was telling me. He whispered in my ear that he had four second class tickets to America and extra money for the voyage. I cried with relief. Father Byrne had to find me a chair I felt so faint. He said you were sending for us and Father John Murphy, the priest in Wexford, had purchased the tickets. Father Murphy in Wexford is an old family friend to your father and me, John. I don't know if you realized that. My dear son, we are so grateful and beyond excited. We will pack and leave in the morning. Father Byrne has made arrangements for us to be taken to the ship, which leaves one week from tomorrow; the sailing date May 10, 1849. So by the time you get this letter, we could be arriving in America very soon, God willing. We will be on the ship Agenora. We have been told that the journey will take about two months so we should see you sometime around the first of July. Pray to our dear Lord for our safety. Soon we will be a family again.

With Love

Your Mamai

John paid a visit to the postmaster and asked how he could find out when the Agenora was due to arrive in Quebec since he wanted to be in Kingston when they arrived on the Schooner Victoria. The postmaster suggested he leave a note with the stagecoach driver who could find out the next time he was in Kingston. John thought that was a great idea and left a note for his old friend that brought him to Centreville almost one year ago to the day. He then eagerly waited for word to arrive, knowing the stagecoach driver did the trail from Kingston to Centreville every week.

Every day he checked for an answer. Finally one week later, there was a note there for him.

Mr. Doyle, I checked the scheduled arrival for the Agenora.

It is due into Quebec sometime between the 7th of July and the 15th. That's the best they could estimate. I hope all is well with you. Please let me know if I can be of service to you.

Today's date was the 6th of July. They may be in tomorrow. He almost panicked. John made arrangements with Patrick to take care of his animals and he grabbed a few things and headed to Kingston. He was so excited he could hardly contain himself.

Winfred and the girls could barely concentrate or perform their jobs at the workhouse as they prepared to leave Ireland forever. They packed their belongings and moved around as if in a daze, filled with both excitement and trepidation. They had no idea what to expect from the journey to the ship, traveling over two to three months on the sea and hopefully finding John at the other end in America. The last thing Winfred packed was the fiddle that Thomas had given to John and she had carefully hidden. Winfred hoped it would make the last journey. Bridget had not seen Willie Quinn in a few weeks. They managed passing glances in the hallway and had created a special form of communication since it was forbidden for the males or the females to intermingle.

As Father Byrne was getting ready to leave the workhouse, Bridget called out to him, "Father Byrne, I have a special favor to ask, please?"

"Certainly," relied Father turning back.

"Willie Quinn is in the west wing with the other male residents. Could you please get word to him that John has sent for us and we're leaving? Please tell him that I don't want to leave Ireland without him."

"Bridget, I'll find him right now."

She stood wringing her hands and Winfred tried to comfort her.

"My dear, Willie will find you in America. You can write to him...."

She began to cry and through sobs said, "Willie and I have been best friends for years. I can't sail all the way to America without at least saying goodbye."

The door opened and in walked Father Byrne, Thomas and Willie. Willie ran to Bridget and wrapped his arms around her while Bridget sobbed into his chest Thomas was ecstatic about the news they were leaving and excitedly talked to his sisters and mother.

"Bridget, I've talked with Father Byrne and Winfred, with your blessing, Father Byrne can marry us right now in the chapel."

Willie got down on one knee while everyone excitedly watched in anticipation at what was happening.

"Bridget, I've loved ya from the moment I saw you years ago when I sat on my mother's knee in church. Will you make me the happiest man on this earth and be my wife?"

"I will, Willie, my love," Bridget replied throwing her arms around him and kissing him squarely on the lips.

Father Byrne escorted them to the small chapel in the workhouse with the family watching and blessed the marriage of Bridget Doyle to Willie Quinn.

John arrived in Kingston on the evening of the 6th of July. He pulled his horse and wagon close to the water so that he could watch the activity on the river. He leaned back to look at the stars. It was a clear night. He wondered what his family would think of the farm. He had accomplished so much in the past year. Suddenly, a commotion sounded from a saloon down by the water. He got out of the wagon too excited to sleep and tied up Chestnut. There wasn't anything to steal but he did grab his sack and walked down to the water. Standing on the bank above the river, he stood looking at his reflection and noticed for the first time how he had aged. He was nearly twenty-nine but the past year had given him a maturity that had occurred without him noticing. His thick brown hair could use a trim but he wasn't going to pay money for someone to cut it, knowing his mother or sisters would gladly do so. His broad shoulders and muscular build, he looked more like an athlete, tan from the Canada sun. His big blue eyes sparkled and even though he did not consider himself a good looking man he was confident and capable. That was important to him. He wasn't the least bit vain so he held his head high and hoped someday a woman would find him handsome enough to marry. He wondered what Thomas looked like now and knew he had aged as well. John walked along the riverbank until he found a pub and walked in. It was crowded but the aromas of the food being prepared reminded him that he was very hungry. Eating in a pub was a treat and he hadn't done this since traveling to Kingston a year ago. A plump woman with a white apron motioned for him to have a seat where he wanted. John took off his hat and sat at a table near a window. He had a view of his horse and wanted to keep an eye on the wagon.

"What can I get for ya, young fella?" the woman asked.

John glanced at the chalkboard at the front of the pub and asked for the beef sausage and a pint of dark beer. He didn't have to wait long for her to come back and put a steaming plate in front of him. It looked delicious and smelled even better. John took one bite, perhaps the most delectable mouthful of food he had ever tried. He would have to bring his family here on their arrival. Within minutes, he had cleaned his plate.

The woman came back and said, "I think ya liked that did ya?"

John replied, "Best meal I've ever had outside of my

mother's cooking."

She laughed. The truth was that his mother hadn't had much to cook in so many years that he could hardly remember it.

"You come back anytime," she replied as she took away his empty plate. "You can pay me when you're ready."

John sipped on his beer, feeling very content. He paid his bill and walked back to the wagon. Now he would be ready to sleep.

The next morning he woke to the warmth of the sun on his skin. He heard the activity around the dock and hoped today his family's schooner would arrive. He walked down to the water and approached a man selling tickets. The sign next to him read: "*Journey to America – See the Beautiful Thousand Islands. Travel to New York City – Travel to Toronto – The Exciting City On the Water.*" John would like to see New York City someday. That's where he thought he would be traveling originally. What kind of work would he have gotten had he not been a farmer? That was the only work that he knew."How can I help you?" the ticket agent asked, startling John from his thoughts. Do you need a ticket somewhere?"

"No, actually, I'm waiting for the Schooner Victoria to come in from Quebec. The Agenora was supposed to arrive in Quebec yesterday"

"The Agenora? That doesn't even sound familiar," the

man responded with a frown. The ticket agent walked into his little hut and checked some records. He yelled out, "Are you sure it's the Agenora coming into Quebec?"

"Yes, I'm sure," John replied with irritation in his voice.

"I don't have any record of that. Are you sure?"

"Yes, I'm sure!"

"There is a ship due in tomorrow but it's the Glenlyon," the man yelled back.

John wasn't sure what the confusion was but he was getting very angry that this man must surely not know what he's talking about. He didn't feel there was anything left he could do except to just keep coming back when a schooner arrived. Looking around the water, he decided to walk around Kingston a little bit since it was turning into a beautiful day. Walking towards Fort Fredrick, he looked behind the large gates, noticing military soldiers standing in formation. John stood watching them for a while. They looked very sharp in their red uniforms with shiny brass buttons. There was a small group near an atrium marching in formation with their weapons in hand. He liked the look of the uniform, much different than the old pair of trousers and shirt that he had on. These soldiers looked so starched and formal. Not too far from the atrium, there stood a soldier in a very tall hat with a large white plume at the top making him look even taller than he was. He looked very formal and held a shiny brass trumpet in his hand, an instrument John had never seen before. The red jacket the soldier wore, fit tightly with large brass buttons down the front, a high collar that reached up under his chin and large shoulder boards with another large four brass buttons on his wrists. He wore black pants and had shiny black shoes that looked like they had been polished for days. John bet he could see his reflection in the toes of those boots. On his left side, he carried a saber and wore a wide white sash across his chest. The soldier appeared to be practicing with this instrument. About that time, he lifted the trumpet to his lips and puffed out his cheeks and blew a golden, sonorous tone that stirred John's very soul. The soldier stood at attention and played to an audience that appeared in his imagination. He clicked his heels together and did an about-face, marching alone with the trumpet tucked protectively under his arm. He did another about-face and once again played the same tune. John watched in amazement for a while wondering who this soldier must be. He decided he better get back to feed Chestnut and check on his wagon.

As he was walking back, he glanced down river and looked again quickly. Was that a sail approaching? The vessel was too far to really see anything. The man at the hut swore that nothing was coming in that day. The sun by now was rising and very bright and John shielded his eyes trying to focus on the boat that sailed down the river as gracefully as a swan gliding across the water. His heart started to pound but he was fearful of getting his hopes up. He stood patiently as the boat came closer and closer. Finally, it came into focus and across the bow he saw in large gold letters *The Victoria*.

John ran to the dock. The vessel was still pretty far away but he was filled with elation and anticipation. There was a scurry of activity as workers came up to the dock to help bring the vessel in. Up on the deck of the schooner, people gathered to search out loved ones coming to meet them. John heard cries and saw people frantically waving. The first and second-class passengers continued to gather on the deck. John searched the crowds desperately. *What if they weren't on this boat?* He couldn't think of that now. They had to be on this one. The schooner docked and the bridge pushed out for people to disembark.

"John!" he heard a woman yell. There standing on the schooner, hanging over the side, was his sister Bridget, waving and crying.

Thomas pushed his way to the rail yelling, "We're here! We're here."

John laughed and waved through his tears of joy and relief. People came off the schooner now and moved past him hurriedly. He felt in a swirl of excitement and disbelief that his family had finally arrived. His mother walked off the boat and he ran to her. He couldn't believe how thin she was, how much she had aged and what a toll the trip had taken on her. John then saw Bridget, Thomas, Catherine and then Willie. They all hugged and cried passionately. Everyone started talking at once.

"I thank God, you're here safely! I heard The Victoria wasn't coming and didn't know how to reach you!"

Bridget said with tears in her eyes and the happiest expression on her face, "I'm married! Willie and I got married before we left Ireland."

"What? Congratulations Willie, you got a great girl."

"Come...are you hungry? There is the greatest little pub within walking distance."

"I just want to get to our home," Winfred replied. "We can eat later. I'm exhausted from this long journey."

Winfred looped her arm through John's to keep her balance. She had sea legs and felt very dizzy. The girls chattered excitedly and everyone piled in the wagon. John helped his mother in to the front next to him.

"We have a two hour trip ahead, but I have a lot to tell you and I'm anxious to hear everything about your voyage."

Winfred smiled at her oldest son. *My*, she thought, *how handsome he had become and how proud of him she felt*. John told them about his first trip to the farm with the Wells Fargo driver and Patrick. They all laughed until he mentioned the words Indian attack. John explained all of that but also mentioned that he had yet to see an Indian.

The road was very dry from little rain in the past few weeks. His poor sisters in the back of the wagon would be covered with dust by the time they arrived but he didn't think they cared since they were too busy talking and looking at the scenery.

"Do you have a girl yet?" Bridget yelled with a smile.

"No, I haven't had time to find a girl. Now that you're here, you can help me with that."

"Daniel and Catherine are getting married John," Winfred shared.

John looked at her with wide eyes. He was a little surprised that he didn't see Daniel but wasn't going to say anything until he had an opportunity to ask Winfred in private. They almost married in Ireland but decided to wait until they arrived here.

"Where is Daniel?" John asked.

"He's coming over with his family on the next ship. His mother was too ill to travel. It's nothing serious but Daniel didn't want to leave her. He's on his way."

"Thomas, are you married too?" John yelled.

"No, still looking."

Thomas was only sixteen. John hoped he wasn't married yet and thought Thomas looked good. He was very thin but handsome.

"Mamai, I think you're going to like the farm. I have a surprise for you."

"A surprise? John, I'm too old for surprises."

"You'll see. You'll like it," John was thinking of the two-story house he built.

She would be surprised.

"Well, I have a surprise for you. I brought you your father's fiddle," Winfred said with a big smile.

"The fiddle? I thought it was gone for sure."

"You're a man of little faith," Winfred teased. "I carried it all the way from Ireland through the workhouse and guarded it with my life on the ship. It's a shame a fiddle can escape the horror but not those poor people. You wouldn't believe how many people we've lost in Ireland. There are still so many waiting to get into the workhouse. Did you know Samuel Castleford's brother, George married that woman, Victoria and they are still taking care of what is left of the garden? She refuses to leave. We went past the house on the way to the ship and I noticed that our home and barn had been torn down."

"Sorry Mamai, I had to tear it down. I was hoping you wouldn't see that. Samuel and Charlotte left for Australia about two months back."

"Australia?" Winfred said, "Where is Australia?"

"Across the ocean and a long way off. I met a great friend on the crossing by the name of Patrick Cavanaugh and he helped me get on my feet when we first arrived. He ended up buying Samuel's farm and he's our next-door neighbor. You'll like him. If the girls weren't already married, they'd like the likes of him."

John and Winfred chatted about friends, memories and the crossing that for them was pretty uneventful. Their passage was nothing like steerage. Finally, John pulled up in front of the house.

Bridget asked, "Are we staying at an inn?"

"An inn? No Bridget, this is our home."

The family looked in disbelief. It was the biggest, grandest house they had ever seen. John helped Winfred out of the wagon and Willie helped his wife and sister-in-law out. They dusted off their clothes and looked around in amazement. The sun was setting but it cast a golden glow over the house and garden. Patrick rode up on his horse and jumped off and happily greeted everyone.

"Family, this is James Patrick Cavanaugh, the best friend a guy could ask for." John glanced over at Winfred and noticed how exhausted she looked.

"I know you're hungry and tired. Let's go in and I'll get something on the table and you can get some rest."

They all walked in while the sun slipped over the horizon. Winfred handed John his fiddle. Patrick was amazed watching John with this fine wooden instrument. He remembered John playing on the ship, but the sight of his own fiddle in his hands was quite spectacular. It took John a few minutes and then it was just like old times, sitting outside under the stars with the crickets in accompaniment and the girls singing with their beautiful voices. Patrick loved this family and they made him feel like one of them. He dearly missed his own family but this was a good second best. They played and sang until Winfred could no longer keep her eyes open. They would all wake early and start their new lives together none of them really knowing the twists and turns that lay ahead of them.

Chapter Twenty-Two

A New Life

1849

The best thing to do is stare it in the face and move on. We have to face our fears and plow through. I think taking chances takes a lot more courage than staying stagnant and doing what's safe and comfortable.
Terri Clark

It wasn't too long after the family arrived that Willie and Bridget found a farm in Hungerford Township not too far from John's farm and moved out. On Sunday's, they would all attend church at St. Anthony's and then go back to John's for a mid-day supper. John couldn't wait to introduce his family to Father Higgins since he was instrumental in helping them travel to Canada. Once Daniel arrived a few months later, Catherine and Daniel had a small ceremony at St. Anthony's and she moved out. The extended family was getting larger and now the only remaining people in the big house were

John, Winfred and Thomas.

"When are you going to find a wife? I want grandchildren running around this big house," Winfred would say with frustration.

"Soon, Mamai, soon."

By the fall of 1849, John had lived in Camden for a little over one year and was now twenty-eight years old. He now had a full productive farm, money saved and a comfortable life for all of them but he wasn't getting any younger and he knew he was ready to start a family. Patrick had just gotten married to a woman by the name of Nettie McCormick he had met at church. She was from Ireland and had just arrived. She had a sweet temperament and infectious smile and they expected their first child in the spring. Patrick had sent for his family in Ireland only to find out that they had all perished from the fever. It took him a long time to get over that loss. He was heartbroken that he hadn't sent for his family in time. John knew that it was only by the grace of God that he hadn't experienced the same devastation. Through patience and compassion, Nettie was able to help Patrick through his grief.

John had to run some errands in town and asked Winfred if she wanted to come along which she declined saying, "No...I'm finishing up some needlepoint pillowcases. You go on."

He rode Chestnut up to the front of Wilson's

General Store and tied him up. He walked in and his attention immediately went to the woman and young girl standing at the counter talking with Andy Wilson. They turned around when John entered. The older woman was probably in her mid-40's, much older than John. She wore a black mourning dress and had dark brown hair pulled back and tucked beneath her bonnet. When she smiled the whole room appeared to light up and her eyes sparkled.

Andy Wilson greeted John and said, "Have you met Katherine and her daughter Eliza Latimer?"

John looked from Katherine to Eliza and his breath was taken away. He did not even manage to cross the room because the loveliest girl he had ever seen stopped him in his tracks. He stood staring at her and time seemed to stop in its place. He took off his hat and somehow managed to walk over to them.

Katherine held out her hand and said, "I'm pleased to meet you. Please call me Kate."

The young girl smiled at him. She must have been about fourteen but exuded an air of confidence about her that made her seem much older. She was rather overdressed but looked elegant with a fur-trimmed coat that was a rich brown color of coffee and she carried a small fur muff to keep her delicate hands warm. The large brown felted fur hat on her head covered the rich dark hair but ringlets fell gently on her face.

Andy Wilson's voice pulled John back to reality "Mrs. Watson is considering purchasing the property next to your property. We understand that Paul is selling to move to the states?"

"Hello Kate," John managed to utter. "That's news to me. I knew that Paul was thinking about moving. He said there was more land in Michigan."

"Mrs. Watson is from Upper Canada. They are considering moving down here from outside of Ottawa."

"I see. How nice." John was so flustered that he completely forgot why he had walked into the store. It's been nice meeting you Kate, Eliza."

"John, what can I help you with?" asked Andy.

"Oh, I, I just needed some, some flour," John stuttered as he tried to speak.

"Flour? That's all you need?"

"Yep that's it." John collected his small package and looked at both women and said, "It's been a pleasure meeting you."

He tipped his hat and walked out. He was in a daze. He wasn't used to feeling like this. He rode home in a fog and decided to stop by Paul's farm and find out what was going on. Paul was in the barn when John rode up.

"I was just in town and understand you're moving to Michigan? I know you had mentioned it in the past but I didn't know it was going to happen this quickly." Well, I met William Watson not too long ago and I mentioned that I was thinking about moving and he said he might be interested in the farm. Wants to buy it and give it to his wife's son and daughter when she marries. They'd split the land of course. I have it worked over pretty well. I'd sell everything, house, livestock, the whole bit. I'm not getting any younger. I hear there is a lot of land available in Michigan and winters are not quite as cold. If I'm ever going to do this, now is the time," Paul said with a far-off look in his eye.

"I just met Katherine Watson and her daughter Eliza at Wilson's. Nice folks. They'd make nice neighbors but I'd sure hate to lose you."

Early that spring, just a few months after John had met Katherine and Eliza, Paul came to call.

"I've come to say goodbye, old friend. I'm leaving tomorrow for Michigan. It will be a long trip."

"Which way will you be traveling?"

"I'll head west towards Toronto and then on to Windsor and south across the big lake and into Michigan. I have family down there now. I'll miss you, John. If you ever want to visit, you've got a friend in Michigan."

John watched Paul's wagon disappear down the dirt road. One week later, he decided he should probably say hello to his new neighbors. He had thought so many times about the young girl in the brown coat with smoky gray eyes, but at thirteen or fourteen, she was too young for him. He walked back into the house and asked

Winfred to come with him. Winfred grabbed a fresh cherry pie that was still warm and they walked down the road to the Watson's farm. John knocked on the door and a man answered. He had an anticipatory expression on his face and looked from John to Winfred and then down to the pie.

"Hello, William Watson here and who might you be?" He had a distinct British accent and upbeat expression.

John held out his hand and replied, "John Doyle and my mother, Winfred. We're your neighbors and happy to have you here."

"Oh....come in, come in." John and Winfred walked in and walking across the wood floor as gracefully as a feline, one long stride at a time, was Kate. She held out her hand to John and then to Winfred.

"I'm Kate Watson, so nice to see you again and to meet you, Winfred. Please come in and make yourself comfortable."

They were in the process of moving in so things seemed somewhat unorganized. "Mother?" John heard from the back room. Upon hearing that voice, he immediately felt like a moth attracted to a flame. In she walked, evidently startled to see visitors.

"Hello," Eliza said with a shy smile. John stood and stared. In the same way that a seashell holds the sound of the ocean, this beautiful young girl seemed to contain within it a wild force of nature. Eliza stood there smiling and once again, life stopped. Winfred noticed John's reaction immediately.

Winfred said to John on the walk home, "My boy, I think you're smitten."

John's face grew red. Was it really so noticeable?

"She's a little young, but she's a beauty."

They walked back to the house without uttering another word. He was indeed smitten.

Later that summer, the Watson's had planned a barn dance at their farm. William and Kate sent out invitations to everyone in Camden to come to this dance. They planned to roast one of their pigs on an open pit and they asked that everyone bring their favorite dish. William heard that John played the fiddle and Winfred sang so he asked them to come prepared to play some old favorites from Ireland. William invited a few neighbors that had immigrated to Canada from Scotland and played the bagpipes.

"Bring them," William said. "We're going to have an old fashioned barn dance."

Little did William Watson know that most of the neighbors that he had invited had never been to a real barn dance, having been too poor for such frivolities or too busy working to get their farm established. But Thomas was ready for a dance. All he had done since he got to Canada was work but life in Ireland, too, was an unbroken stream of toil and labor. He was excited about this dance.

Winfred told John, “You’re going and that’s all there is to it.”

John had little interest in dancing but was getting pressure from his mother to attend.

“Catherine and Daniel are coming, Bridget and Willie are coming, Patrick and Nettie will be there and it will be great fun.”

It was two weeks away. John hoped it would rain. Winfred immediately started working on the dish she would bring. With her abundance of cherries, she thought she could make another pie. But this was special, so she decided on country rhubarb cake. The filling would be rhubarb, sugar, white of an egg and caster sugar to dust the cake. Her mouth watered just thinking of it. How grand this would be.

It wasn’t advertised but William and Katherine Watson also decided to make this Eliza’s coming out party.

The time passed quickly and on the day of the event, Eliza had never been so excited for an evening. She preferred the name Eliza rather than her birth name of Ann Elizabeth, because she thought that made her sound much older. For her coming out party, her mother and father surprised her with the most beautiful gown Eliza had ever seen. She knew they had saved for many months and holding it in front of her, she wondered how she could be so lucky.

The afternoon light filtered into her bedroom spreading a golden ray of warmth across the room. She stood before the looking glass and held the gown up to herself. It was a lovely blue silk two-piece gown with handmade ivory lace trim. Belgian lace adorned the cuffs and around the neckline and the hemline was quite different at the front with two additional rows of pleating of blue and ivory and to top it all off, a silk parasol to match. She decided to wear her hair down with blue satin ribbons and around her neck she wore the locket from her mother. As she stared at herself in the reflection, she felt pretty confident that she was becoming a beautiful young woman and knew it would forever be a day to remember. She had color in her cheeks and a sparkle in her eye. She wondered what the night would hold and she overflowed with anticipation. This was her first dance in Camden and felt different than any she had experienced in the past. Winfred insisted that John go into town and buy some decent clothes. All he had was work clothes and nicer work clothes for church. A new clothing merchant by the name of Grant's Emporium had just opened in town and they had all the latest fashions for men. John wasn't about to buy anything fancy but he reluctantly walked into the shop. There was a man adjusting suits in the shop and looked up when John walked in.

"Good afternoon, how can I help you?"

"I'm looking for something a little nicer than my

work clothes to wear to a barn dance.

The gentleman looked at John trying to judge his size and picked out a casual suit of brown wool with a pattern in the pants and a starched linen shirt complete with a cravat.

"No," John said shaking his head. "That's not me. I'm interested in a plain brown suit, with a white linen shirt."

The gentleman nodded that he understood and picked out a brown wool loose fitting frock coat with a finely patterned shawl collared vest complete with buttons down the front of the vest. The white shirt he chose had a large fold down collar over a loosely tied cravat.

"You will look very dashing."

"I'm interested in everything but the cravat."

"Very well. How about shoes or a hat?"

"I could use a new hat."

"I have just the hat. It's just in from the United States. A western hat actually."

He handed John a brown leather Antietam style hat that was a flat crowned variation of the slouch hat. John loved it instantly drawn to the smell and feel of the soft leather.

"I'll take this," he said, trying it on in front of a small looking glass the man held up for him.

John felt good about his purchases and realized they were the nicest clothes he had ever owned.

He got back to the house just in time for Winfred

and Thomas to ask in unison, "Where have you been? The dance starts in an hour!"

"I'll be ready to go in a few minutes."

He cleaned himself up and put on his new clothes. They felt good on. He topped it off with the new hat and grabbed his fiddle and walked outside where Winfred and Thomas waited for him.

Winfred had the cake in one hand but with the other hand, she grabbed her heart and said, "Praise God, you look like a wealthy farmer."

Thomas let out a whistle. "You'd think he was trying to get someone's eye, Mamai."

"You're quite the comic, Thomas," John said under his breath.

As they got closer, they could see wagons pulling up by the droves. Clearly this was going to be some event. The smell of a roasting succulent pig on a rotisserie over an open pit fire drifted all the way to John's farm.

Along with their little girl Anna, Patrick and Nettie approached Winfred, John and Thomas.

"*Yooo*!" Patrick whistled eyeing John in his new suit. "You've never looked better." John smiled and changed the subject. He gave Nettie a small hug and Anna a pat on the head. Thomas took off to go look at the food.

"John do you remember the Garrett's on the ship coming over? The same Mary Ann that taught you to read. They are coming tonight. Mary Ann gave birth to little girl named Catherine who is now five years old and they're living in Stocco. Can you believe that? It's what I call Irish Happinstance!"

John was amazed. Yes, he remembered them quite well. He was so happy to hear that they had survived quarantine and moved to the Centreville area, as well. He would have to seek them out.

Patrick asked if John had heard from the Castleford's, and John replied, "Only that they arrived safely in Australia." Thinking about the Castleford's brought back so many memories for John.

The Watsons had cleaned out the barn, putting down makeshift tables for all of the food and laying out bound bales of hay to sit on. John had never seen so much food: traditional Irish dishes, pies, cakes, soda bread and scones from Scotland. There was a large bowl in the middle of the table filled with some kind of liquid to drink.

Shortly after John arrived, Kate and William Watson came out to greet everyone and they looked stunning. William, Kate's son and Grace and Ellen, daughters John had not met talked casually with all of the guests. Just as the sun went behind the trees and people urged John to play his fiddle and Winfred to sing, in walked Eliza. Everyone turned to watch as she entered the barn looking more dazzling than a million stars in the sky. She was just breathtaking in her blue gown. William Watson walked over and took her arm as she entered and escorted her to the middle of the room. John tried not to stare but her beauty was beyond words. William danced with his stepdaughter to an Irish tune that filled the barn with the beautiful soft melody. When the music stopped, William introduced Eliza and said to the crowd, "What a better opportunity to have a coming out party."

Everyone clapped and John noticed a few whistles from the crowd. Eliza blushed but it was apparent that she enjoyed all of the attention.

As the evening went on, the air was filled with music from Ireland, Scotland and England. John was able to locate the Garrett's and greeted them warmly.

"I've thought of you so often," Mary Ann said smiling up at her old student. "This is Catherine, John. Can you believe it's been five years since we last saw each other?"

John smiled down at the little girl thinking she looked just like her mother. "No, I can't. Time has certainly flown by."

James Garrett shared with John that he had his farm up and running also and couldn't have been happier since arriving in Canada.

Feeling merry John picked up his fiddle and Winfred sang.

<u>An Immigrant's Daughter</u>

Oh please ne'er forget me though waves now lie o'er me
I was once young and pretty and my spirit ran free
But destiny tore me from country and loved ones

And from the new land I was never to see.
A poor immigrant's daughter too frightened to know
I was leaving forever the land of my soul
Amid struggle and fear my parents did pray
To place courage to leave o'er the longing to stay.
They spoke of a new land far away 'cross the sea
And of peace and good fortune for my brothers and me
So we parted from townland with much weeping and pain
'Kissed the loved ones and the friends we would ne'er see again.
The vessel was crowded with disquieted folk
The escape from past hardship sustaining their hope
But as the last glimpse of Ireland faded into the mist
Each one fought back tears and felt strangely alone.

The seas roared in anger, making desperate our plight
And a fever came o'er me that worsened next night
Then delirium possessed me and clouded my mind
And I for a moment saw that land left behind.
I could hear in the distance my dear mother's wailing
And the prayers of three brothers that I'd see no more
And I felt father's tears as he begged for forgiveness
For seeking a new life on the still distant shore.

Oh please ne'er forget me though waves now lie o'er me
I was once young and pretty and my spirit ran free
But destiny tore me from country and loved ones
And from the new land I was never to see.

When they finished playing, the crowd cheered and asked for another song. There wasn't a dry eye in the house. John decided to play something a little more lively so he played "As I Roved Out," looking over at Eliza as he played.

<u>As I Roved Out</u>

And who are you, me pretty fair maid
And who are you, me honey?
And who are you, me pretty fair maid
And who are you, me honey?
She answered me quite modestly:
I am me mother's darling.

cho:With me too-ry-ay
Fol-de-diddle-day
Di-re fol-de-diddle
Dai-rie oh.

And will you come to me mother's house,
When the sun is shining clearly
I'll open the door and I'll let you in
And divil 'o one would hear us.

So I went to her house in the middle of the night
When the moon was shining clearly
Shc opened the door and she let me in

And divil the one did hear us.

She took me horse by the bridle and the bit
And she led him to the stable
Saying "There's plenty of oats for a soldier's horse,
To eat it if he's able."

Then she took me by the lily-white hand
And she led me to the table
Saying: There's plenty of wine for a soldier boy,
To drink it if you're able.

Then I got up and made the bed
And I made it nice and aisy
Then I got up and laid her down
Saying: Lassie, are you able?

And there we lay till the break of day
And divil a one did hear us
Then I arose and put on me clothes
Saying: Lassie, I must leave you.

And when will you return again
And when will we get married
When broken shells make Christmas bells
We might well get married.

When John finished the song, he mustered all of the courage he had to walk up to Eliza and ask her to dance. Without a word, Eliza took John's hand and even though he was not a dancer, with her in his arms, they glided across the floor. Eliza stared up into his eyes as they danced and he saw only the beautiful half-smile on her lips and stars in her eyes. He had never felt so smitten before but he knew instantly he wanted to be with her forever. Their attraction was no secret; in fact it exuded such energy that everyone in the room took notice.

"You are the most beautiful woman I have ever seen."

It took a lot of courage for him to say it but it also felt so natural and her appreciation was evident on her face and in her eyes. *He didn't say girl*, she thought to herself, *he said woman*.

One week later, John walked down to the Watson farm and asked to speak with William.

"I'd like your permission to court Eliza, if she'll have me."

William looked up from his task and smiled.

"She'll have you. I'm sure of it. Yes, you have my permission. What is your intention?"

John wasn't prepared for that question. He stood with hat in hand and moved back and forth on his feet trying to figure out how to respond.

"I'd like to marry her, but I'm not quite ready to ask

you for her hand in marriage."

John started seeing Eliza on a regular basis and Thomas teasingly said, "You've got the prettiest woman in Canada."

Chapter Twenty-Three

Grand Trunk Railroad & The First Real Christmas

1850

Courage is what preserves our liberty,
safety, life, and our homes and
parents, our country and children.
Courage comprises all things.
Plautus

John and Thomas rode into town to get supplies when they saw a large poster outside Wilson's General Store that read, "*A Railway at Last.*" They read on and the poster said: "The Grand Trunk Railway System will take you from Montreal to Toronto in a matter of hours."

It bore a crude picture of a large locomotive and a sign-up sheet for anyone wanting to work on this new railway.

"Thomas, don't get any ideas," John said jokingly. "I need you on the farm."

Thomas laughed. "I'm not signing up, don't worry."

At the same time, Thomas was curious. On Friday evening at 7:00, Mr. John W. Bell, representing the Grand Trunk Railway, would talk at the town hall meeting. John along with Thomas looked forward to getting more information about this new railway. It could open up all kinds of business if they didn't have to rely on wagons and horses to transport crops, livestock and farm equipment. This sounded promising.

Friday evening came and John, Thomas and Winfred rode in for the meeting. They wanted to hear how Camden might be changing and expanding with innovation and modern transportation. They sat in the back as the room filled with curious townspeople. John noticed Patrick across the room and waved. He didn't see Nettie and assumed she had stayed home with Anna. James and Mary Ann Garrett showed up and sat next to the Doyle's. There was a lot of chatter until Mr. Bell walked in with a few other visitors. He was ushered to the front of the room where his assistant, John MacDonald, quieted the crowd.

"Ladies and gentleman, it is with great pleasure that I introduce our speaker. Mr. John W. Bell represents the new Grand Trunk Railway that is coming to Napanee. I'll let him tell you the exciting news."

John W. Bell smiled and looked over the crowd. There had been a lot of opposition to the railway coming in; not here in this little town, but in Montreal. People still worried about illness and felt that the Grand Trunk Railway could just spread disease quicker. "Ladies and gentleman," Mr. Bell bellowed out, "the railroad will revolutionize how we travel, how we do business and how towns will thrive and prosper. Imagine going from Montreal to Toronto all 333 miles in a mere ten-hours. You could travel there on one day and return on the next. The communities without a train station on the Grand Trunk line will wither and those with a station on the line will thrive. You'll be able to ship lumber and farm goods to towns that you couldn't reach by a mere horse and wagon. Imagine selling your lumber and it traveling on rail all the way to Western Canada. Imagine selling your cattle and the cattle traveling all the way to the United States. You will no longer have to haul your merchandise to Napanee. We'll haul it for you."

Mr. Bell looked around with enthusiasm as the room became very excited. He heard a flurry of chatter from the crowd.

One man yelled, "Are we getting a stop here in Camden?"

"If you want it here, you'll have to fight for it. We only want to build where we feel there is going to be a profit made. We're building a station in Napanee and Brockville and we're headed northeast. Our goal, ladies and gentlemen, is to construct a railway that will run the whole length of this province."

William Watson walked up to John and whispered, "This is being financed by a bank in Britain."

John had wondered who was paying for this incredible venture.

Mr. Bell clapped his hands to get everyone's attention and yelled out, "The line will start in Napanee and the first stop will be Brockville, as I said before. From there they are building tracks right now and need strong men to help lay the tracks. The pay is good but the work is hard. The station stops being considered are Newburgh, Centreville, Thompson Mills, Camden, Moscow, Enterprise, Tamworth and Stocco."

John and Thomas looked at each other. This could be good. This could be very good.

"How many would like to see a station here in Centreville or Camden?"

Just about everyone raised his or her hand.

"Okay," Mr. Bell nodded. "I'm going to send around a petition. If you want a station here, I need you to sign the petition as long as you're a resident of Centreville or Camden. Is that clear?"

Mr. MacDonald gathered his paper and writing utensils and passed the papers around for residents to sign. There was another flurry of activity as people got their names on the list. If they couldn't write, there was a neighbor there to help. They ended up with 162 names on the list just from the people that showed up. They would circulate the petition and hopefully get all 1,500 or so farm owners to sign it.

Mr. Bell called out to the crowd, "I have another sheet for anyone to sign that is interested in working for the railway. Please put your name and address and we will post a sign in Wilson's store window for further instructions."

Quite a few of the men came up to sign that sheet. Among them were men who had tried their hand at farming and struggled or failed, others who simply preferred to earn their keep by labor rather than working the land. The prospect of working on the railroad seemed to be an exciting adventure.

"I thank you all for your attention and am hopeful that you will see a station here in Centreville or Camden in the very near future."

Mr. Bell left the stage and walked over to Mr. MacDonald, who conversed in private. Winfred didn't say much on the way home. She liked the idea that this railway could help John and Thomas prosper further with lumber, crops or farm animals. Plus she thought to herself, *maybe me and my girls could take the train to Toronto, the city on the lake for a day*. She daydreamed all the way back to the farm while John and Thomas planned ways to possibly make more money.

The leaves started to change colors on the trees and

the days got shorter. John would visit Eliza as often as he could. With Winfred's coaching, he would take her small bouquets of wild flowers Winfred had grown in the garden. He had bunches of Creeping Mayflower with their beautiful white petals and Indian Mallow with their velvet golden leaves. Eliza loved the attention and Winfred had her hopes on grandchildren. On most Sundays after church, John and Eliza escorted by either Thomas or Winfred or both would take the wagon out and visit surrounding towns. Most Sundays, Catherine, Daniel, Bridget and Willie would come over for a big meal and Eliza would help Winfred and the girls in the kitchen where they cooked oxtail soup and corned beef and cabbage that came right out of the garden. For desert, Winfred would make bread pudding with rum sauce and raisins. After the feast, just like the old times, they would sit outside and the girls would sing and John would play the fiddle. Eliza was shy at first but she had a beautiful voice and once she learned the songs, she would join in as well. Once the wind began to blow and they knew fall was ending and the long cold winters would begin, the Sunday dinners became shorter and everyone retreated back to their own farms. Eliza would stay until John took her back in the wagon.

He would kiss her hand as he walked her to the door and whisper, "Until next time my beautiful, Eliza."

He wanted so much to kiss her beautiful lips and to

touch her hair. She would look up at him expectantly but knew that he respected her enough not to do anything that would tarnish her reputation. John was a man of values as difficult as his passion for her was to resist.

Early in December, Winfred said, "John, I want a real Christmas. This year, I want a tree with candles and we'll have a special Christmas dinner."

Thomas said, "A tree? We've haven't had a tree for so many years I'd almost forgotten about a tree. That would be wonderful to have a tree again."

"That's what we'll have then. Mamai, I'm going to talk to William about marrying Eliza."

Winfred stopped mid-sentence. Thomas stated whooping and hollering.

"It's about time brother!"

John ignored him.

Winfred misty-eyed replied, "Praise be to the saints in Heaven. It's about time."

John just smiled. "So, I take it you would be okay to have Eliza as a daughter-in-law?"

"Okay with it?" Winfred exclaimed. "I would love it. She's a beautiful girl, John. You couldn't do better than her and what beautiful children you'll have. When do you plan to have this blessed event?"

"I'm hoping next month."

"In January?" Winfred asked a little startled.

"I'm ready for a wedding. This could be the best Christmas yet!" Thomas said with a smile.

Later that day, John walked through the snow and felt the cold Canadian air on his skin as he knocked on the Watson's door.

Kate answered and said, "Come in and get out of the cold."

"Thank you, ma'am," John said as he kicked the snow off of his shoes and walked into the warm room.

Eliza ran up to John and greeted him with a big smile.

"Is William available?" John asked smiling down at Eliza.

Kate and Eliza looked at each other expectantly.

"Yes, I'll call him. William, can you come out here please? John wants to have a word with you."

William came out from the back room. "Hello there. What can I do for you?"

"Could we talk privately, sir?"

"Of course."

Kate and Eliza excused themselves.

"Sir, I'd like your permission to ask Eliza to marry me? I have a producing farm; a large house and I can take care of her and protect her. I love her with all my heart and would like to ask for her hand in marriage."

John was a little nervous. He wasn't sure why; he knew William was aware of his intention all along, but to actually ask made him nervous.

Nevertheless, with great enthusiasm William slapped him on the back and said, "I'd be honored to have you as a son-in-law. Yes, of course, you can ask Eliza."

Kate and Eliza were in the other room with their ears pressed against the door and Kate started crying and Eliza started jumping up and down but trying to do it quietly so the men wouldn't know they had eavesdropped. Plus, Eliza didn't want to ruin the surprise when John asked her.

Kate whispered, "Shush Eliza, they'll hear you."

John said goodbye to William with a smile on his face and said, "Please say goodnight to Kate and Eliza for me. I'd like to get back before it gets too dark."

He walked home in the snow and wind but felt warm with the thought that soon Eliza would be his wife. He would have her with him all the time, without escorts. He was so engrossed with his thoughts he didn't even remember the walk back.

The day before Christmas, John went into town to get a few presents for his family. He went into the general store and saw his old friend Mr. Wilson.

"I'm here to buy presents, Andrew."

He bought Thomas a pocketknife with a silver handle and a leather case. John knew it would probably be the most extravagant thing Thomas had ever owned. For Winfred, John picked out a new bonnet lined with black silk and a ruffle of brown silk attached at the base, along with a large black and brown bow she could tie underneath her chin. For Eliza he found a beautiful vanity set. It was an oval shaped hand-held looking glass that was decorated with a spray of pink and sterling lavender roses on a crisp white background. It had a matching brush for her hair that had a polished brass frame and handle embossed with roses. He picked up Christmas candles for the tree and a few other little things for his sisters and their husbands. With the railroad coming closer to Camden, Mr. Wilson was able to get more items in and planned to expand his store in the spring to hold all of the merchandise that was arriving.

When John got back to the farm, he went out to the backfield and found the biggest most beautiful evergreen he could find. He put it in the back of the wagon and brought it back to the barn inhaling the smell of evergreen. Chopping off the bottom of the tree and shaking off the snow, he filled the wooden bucket with water from the well and placed the Christmas tree in the bucket. That night after Winfred went to bed, Thomas and John snuck out to the barn and brought in the tree. They covered it with candles and stood back to see the result. Winfred would be so happy. John was sure that she thought he had forgotten about the tree with a wedding on his mind. After Thomas went to bed, John snuck back out and wrapped their gifts in old mail order catalogs he got from Mr. Wilson. He placed the wrapped gifts under the tree and went to bed feeling quite satisfied.

The next morning, John got up early and lit a fire in the fireplace. The wet wood crackled and popped but the heat from the fire warmed John's hands and soon the scent of evergreen and burning wood filled the home. Thomas came out while John was lighting the candles on the tree. Winfred heard them whispering and came out in her nightgown, wrap and bed cap. She looked at the tree and started to cry.

"I thought you forgot about the tree?"

"Don't cry, Mamai." John walked over to her and put his arms around her and gave her a big hug. "It's a beautiful tree isn't it?"

"It is, John," she said, her voice cracking with emotion. " I wish your father was here to see this. He would have loved it."

"He's looking over us, Mamai, I promise, along with Rose and Joseph." Thomas lovingly replied.

They opened their gifts and sat by the warm fire looking at the tree. Winfred loved her new bonnet and said she was wearing it to church that morning. Thomas instantly took to his pocketknife and sat sharpening it on a leather razor strop. John opened a few little gifts from them and they got ready to leave for church. John was meeting Eliza and her family at church and then Eliza would come back with John, Thomas and Winfred. After a beautiful Christmas Mass, they returned to the farm and Eliza opened her gift.

"Oh John, it's the most beautiful vanity set I've ever seen and my very own looking glass!"

John beamed with pride as he gazed adoringly at the love of his life.

John, then got down on one knee and held Eliza's hand in his and said, "Eliza, I've loved you since the first time I saw you. Will you do me the great honor and become my wife? I will love, protect and cherish you all the days of your life."

With tears in her eyes, Eliza nodded and said, "Yes, I will."

He kissed her lightly on the lips and was so moved that he had a difficult time standing up. They had a wonderful first Christmas together and later that day, John took Eliza home and they shared the news with Kate and William and Eliza's siblings. The women chattered excitedly and Eliza began planning her wedding.

Chapter Twenty-Four

The Wedding

1851

Being deeply loved by someone
gives you strength, while loving
someone deeply gives you courage.
Lao Tzu

Kate, Grace, Ellen and Eliza sat by the fire talking and planning the wedding and Kate reminded Eliza of the old poem:

Marry on Monday for health,
Tuesday for wealth,
Wednesday the best day of all,
Thursday for crosses,
Friday for losses, and
Saturday for no luck at all.

"Well Mother, Wednesday it is. I'm glad John didn't pick Friday or Saturday."

They all laughed. The wedding was only a couple of weeks away and there was still much to accomplish.

The date was set for Wednesday the 16th of January. Eliza asked Elizabeth Whelan to be her witness. They had been friends for some time and knew each other from church. John asked James McKeone, a farmer that he knew from St. Anthony's and they had worked together on a few committees. Father Bernard J. Higgins would perform the ceremony.

"Eliza, I think we should invite Winfred to go with us to Napanee for your dress," Kate suggested.

Eliza agreed and Winfred declined saying that she had too many things to do. In reality, Winfred felt that this was something between a mother and her daughters. Kate, Eliza, Ellen and Grace left soon after Christmas for the trip into Napanee. Kate wanted to purchase a wedding dress that wouldn't be available in the small towns of Camden or Centreville. William, Eliza's brother agreed to take them in the carriage. It shouldn't take more than an hour to get there if they didn't run into high snow drifts and ruts in the ice. It was very cold the morning that they set off and they could see their own breath but the sun was bright and glistened on the snow to where they had to shield their eyes from the reflection. They wrapped themselves in Canadian beaver pelts for the trip into Napanee and huddled together to keep warm.

The women talked excitedly as the horse pulled the carriage down the snow-covered road past John's farm.

It was going to be a very small wedding, limited to intimate family and friends. When they arrived in Napanee, they rode along the main street into town and turned left onto East Street passing the striking town hall in neo-classical Greek style, that had just been completed this past fall. The women loved being in the city and its abundance of things to see and do.

It felt even colder in Napanee and they could feel the wind off of the river that ran along the city and it made them wrap their pelts even closer. *Poor William*, Eliza thought. *He must be freezing up there.* They turned right at the new railway station.

"Oh!" Eliza said to her mother. "Look Mother, the railway station! Isn't it exciting? Maybe we can start taking the train down here next time."

William turned right onto Isabella Street and pulled in front of a little shop that looked like a French boutique.

"Oh, we're here!" Eliza exclaimed excitedly.

William got down and opened the carriage door and held out his hand for his mother and sisters.

"Be careful, it's slippery," William warned.

The four women walked through the door of the little shop.

William said, "I'll wait for you in the gentleman's pub down the street. I'll be back shortly after I warm up."

The shop was decorated in a rich cream and French

provincial blue with two pair of Louis XVI blue silk chairs by the fireplace. The ornate gold fireplace mantle was beautiful with a candelabrum on each end. Near the fireplace sat a large oval looking glass that also had gold around the frame. Eliza had never seen a looking glass so big. She glanced at herself in the mirror and tucked a loose strand of her hair back in her bonnet. They stood warming their hands by the fire.

"Bonjour, Madame and Mademoiselles," a petite French woman said as she came out of the back.

The four women smiled at her.

"My name is Marguerite. How may I help you today?"

Kate said, "Eliza is getting married in two weeks and we'd like to try on wedding dresses."

"Oh, how wonderful for you. My best wishes to you and your betrothed."

"Thank you," Eliza replied sweetly.

Marguerite was only about 4'5" tall with dark black hair pulled back off of her face and tied in a beautiful French twist. She looked very stylish with a long dark blue velvet dress covering her petite body. The bodice of the dress had a low neckline and exposed her small shoulders. The skirt of her dress was knife pleated which made the skirt look very full. It was especially beautiful with her dark hair. She measured Eliza and went to the back of the store. She brought back with her a dove colored wedding gown that was quite fancy complete with a very large hoop skirt and short cap sleeves.

Eliza whispered to her mother, “Mother, I would like to dress very simply. I know John will not be dressed like royalty.”

“I agree. Marguerite, we would like to go with a simple wedding dress.”

“Oh yes,” Marguerite replied as she went back into the back room to retrieve another gown.

She came back out this time with a deep champagne colored gown that had a fitted bodice that narrowed at the waist and dipped into a narrow V shape. The skirt was full but not nearly as full as the last gown and it had three wide flounces and then seven narrow ones and came with three petticoats for the fullness instead of the large hoop. Its delicate silk reflected the light from the fireplace like the glow of a warm candlelit evening. It had an overlay of fine Belgian lace, whose color matched the dress and tied up the back with a silk ribbon. The decoration around the neckline was made of tulle with a high collar that was also made of lace. The lace veil was very long with the top of the veil displaying a small coronet of flowers. As Kate and Eliza examined the dress, Marguerite brought out small white gloves and a hanky embroidered with small flowers that matched the ones on the veil. She also provided silk stockings that had embroidery up the front and flat champagne-colored shoes decorated with the same ribbons that went up the back of the dress. It was simple but exquisite.

Kate looked at Eliza and said, "Do you know how beautiful you will look in this gown?"

Grace added, "Eliza, it's the most beautiful gown I have ever seen."

Eliza's eyes welled up with tears.

"It's beautiful, isn't it? Do you think it's too fancy?"

"Eliza, it's so simple but elegant. John will love it," Ellen replied.

Marguerite took Eliza in the back to try on the dress. Kate assisted as Eliza's sisters looked on and Eliza walked up to the large looking glass and felt overwhelmed.

"This is the dress, Mother. I love it!"

Kate agreed.

Marguerite said, "It appears that this dress was made for you. I also have a warm wrap for you if you're interested. You might be cold without something."

She brought out a wrap made of lamb's wool that was luxurious to the touch.

"We'll take it all," Kate announced.

Marguerite helped Eliza off with the dress and they sat on the blue French chairs while she wrapped everything up. What an exciting day and the big event was only a few weeks off. William walked in just at the right time. He had drank a pint or two to warm himself and stood at the fireplace with his hands out preparing himself for the cold ride back.

"So, little sister, did you find what you wanted?"

Kate interjected, "Wait until you see her, William. She'll be the prettiest bride to ever wed."

William winked at his sister. "I have no doubt about that. My little sister, all grown up."

On the ride back to Camden, Kate said, "Eliza, you know you have to have something old, something new, something borrowed and something blue? I have your grandmother's locket that you can wear on your dress. That would be your something old. Your gloves and veil would be considered something new. We'll have to find something borrowed and something blue."

Grace said, "I have a small handbag you could borrow. That would be perfect for something borrowed."

Ellen added, "You could add a small sprig of blue flowers to the ones already in the veil and that would be your something blue."

"How does that sound?" asked Kate.

"That sounds perfect," replied Eliza.

They chattered the rest of the way about the wedding not even feeling the cold until they arrived home.

John and Thomas sat in the house waiting for Winfred to put their supper on the table. Thomas said, "I've been looking at a small farm in Stocco. Mamai and I are going to move so that you and Eliza can have your own home without us getting in the way."

"What?" replied John "I won't have it."

"No, you need to have your own place."

Winfred said, "John, I want lots of babies running around and if I'm here, that might not happen."

They all laughed and Thomas told John all about the house and farm that he had found. He had a nice room for his mother and they wouldn't be that far away.

"Will you be attending St. Anthony's?" asked John.

"No, there is a small church there by the name of St. Edmunds. We can attend church there. We can still get together every Sunday. It's not like we're headed back to Ireland."

John had a far away look in his eyes. "I'm anxious to see your farm. I'll have to hire someone to help me in the spring."

"You need sons – lots of them," replied Winfred. They chuckled merrily.

John decided he couldn't have his beautiful bride riding in an old farm wagon so before the wedding, he went into town to see Mutton about buying a new carriage.

Mutton came out when John rode up on his horse and said, "Good to see you. I hear you're getting married next week to Eliza Latimer?"

John got off his horse and said, "I am Mutton. Can

you believe it?"

"You're a lucky man. She's a real beaut."

"I know I am Mutton."

"What can I do for you?"

"I'd like to buy a new carriage something a little nicer than my wagon. What can you do for me?"

"Well, I have a Calash from Quebec in the back. Do you want to see that? You want an enclosed carriage right?"

"Yes."

"Let me show you this one."

Mutton took John to the back of the barn and sitting there as shiny as a new penny was a black Calash.

"Let me tell you about this buggy. It's a light carriage with small wheels, inside seats for four passengers, a separate driver's seat and a folding Calash top and a body hung on leather straps or thorough braces, usually drawn by one horse; you can use one horse or two to pull this. It's set up right now for one. The inside is horsehair."

John opened the door and looked in. It was the finest carriage he had ever seen.

"How much Mutton?" John asked knowing that it would be very expensive.

"Its $900, but for you, I'll sell it to you at cost. That's $750."

"That's a lot of money. I'll have to think about it," John was turning to walk away.

"I might be able to find a used one for you. It might be a little rough around the edges but less expensive. Let me see what I can find. Stop back at the end of the week."

"Okay, I'll do that. Thanks," John said, feeling a little discouraged.

The day of the wedding began with a bright, flawless morning, despite the chill. The sun was rising over the trees as John got up. It was so cold in the house that he could see his breath. As he prepared the fire, excitement welled inside him, though he felt nervous too. John had never been with a woman. He really didn't know what was expected on this wedding night and Eliza would be sleeping in his bed tonight. His mouth went dry but other parts stirred just thinking about it. Winfred and Thomas had moved out over the past weekend and he missed having them around. Winfred had cleaned up the house before she left so John went out to the barn to look at his new Calash. It was going to be a surprise for everyone. Mutton had found a good deal on a carriage that was older and a little worn but it worked the same and he really liked it. It was fitting for the woman he was about to marry. John took care of the animals and went back in to heat some water over the fireplace. He poured the hot water into the large round wooden tub and stripped himself of all of his farm clothes, sliding down into the water, enjoying the warmth on his skin. Thomas had helped him pick out a three-piece Jarvis suit in gray wool with five cloth-covered buttons fastening up the front. The buttoned cuffs and many pockets were now all the rage even though John was not one to give into fashion, but he wanted to look nice for his bride. He pulled on a matching waistcoat and pair of trousers made with a fine hand in haberdashery, two pockets on the outside, fully lined on the inside and a matching satin back with belt adjuster. The pleated, pants zipped up the front. He was glad the wool had a lining so he wouldn't itch himself to death, and he nostalgically recalled the many times when he was young trying not to itch when he sat in church.

Glancing at his timepiece, he thought he better get to the church; he didn't want to be late. Taking out the new carriage, he placed a beaver wrap next to him on the seat. Luckily it hadn't snowed so the ground was hard making it easy for Chestnut to pull the new carriage on the dirt road. He arrived in front of St. Anthony Padua and his heart was beating so fast, he was afraid he'd die right there on the spot. A few carriages had already arrived. He walked in the back of the church and was greeted by his sisters, Bridget and Catherine.

"Oh John, look at ya. What a handsome man you are!" Bridget cried.

John blushed and the girls kissed him on the cheek.

He saw his mother and Thomas, Daniel and Willie. Father Higgins was standing up by the alter looking over the ceremony. Patrick was there with Nettie. All eyes fell on John that made him very uncomfortable. He didn't like the attention. Patrick sensed John's anxiety.

"You'll be fine. You're marrying a wonderful girl. You just have wedding jitters."

"I know, I just have a little bit of the groom's nerves."

Mrs. O'Mally began to play softly on the small reed organ the church recently acquired, her fingers moving carefully in recollection of her memorized songs. The bells in the steeple started ringing and their strong tone echoed throughout the church. They heard some talking and laughter right outside and John looked towards the doors. In walked Kate, William, Grace and Ellen. Eliza had asked her stepfather, William Watson to walk her down the isle. Father Higgins asked everyone to get in place. James McKeone felt for the gold ring in his pocket. He had been worried all morning about leaving it behind or losing it. He stood at the front of the church with Father Higgins and John. They faced the back of the church. The door opened and in walked William holding the door open for Eliza. John smiled when he saw her. Everyone stood and looked back at Eliza as she walked through the door. You could hear the gasps from the family and friends in the church. She was the most elegant, beautiful bride they had ever seen. She smiled and it was like a gust of energy that swirled and the whole room lite up. John felt very emotional and teared-up just watching her. How lucky he was. William walked her down the small isle and Father Higgins started the ceremony. James handed John the gold band and Elizabeth handed Eliza the wedding band for John. After the short ceremony, Father Higgins said, "You may now kiss your bride."

John looked down into Eliza's face and putting one hand gently against her cheek warmly said, "I love you so dearly," and gently kissed her lips.

The room erupted into exuberant applause and laughter and all the women cried, so happy as they were for the new couple. John and Eliza walked out of the church and her new carriage was waiting. "John, you didn't?"

"I couldn't have you traveling in an old farm wagon on your wedding day!"

He lifted her up into the carriage and put the warm blanket over her and they rode off to the Watson's for a wedding breakfast that turned out to be a feast. When they arrived and went inside, Kate had prepared all of her favorite dishes and music filled the house with fiddle playing and even Father Higgins had a port. By late afternoon just before the sun started to set, John and Eliza left for their home as husband and wife.

John warmed up the cabin as Eliza changed her clothes. After John got out of his suit, they lay on top of the beaver pelts in each other's arms in front of the fire and reminisced about the day. Everything had been so perfect. John kissed Eliza and she got up and gently took him by the hand. She led him into the bedroom and he laid down on the bed and put his arms out for her. She undressed in front of him. Though normally, very shy, at that moment her timidity melted away, a testament to the depth of her love. As John watched her undress, his nervousness was overcome by the urge to watch her. The normal male reaction took over and he felt like he had done this a million times. He loved seeing her naked body that was as soft and as white as the snow gently falling outside. She fell into his arms and they made love all night long.

It was a great relief to everyone, especially the farmers that spring came early that year. John had hired a young man by the name of Kevin McTavish, who had come over from Ireland losing his whole family on the ship coming over. He was a hard worker and John kept him busy. Part of the wedding purse that John had received from Kate and William Watson was another one hundred acres of land. John and Kevin cleared another twenty-five acres and spent the spring planting more crops. John's tireless effort was paying off and with the train now coming into Centreville in the summer; he would be able to sell more crops than he had in the past. He could also sell the lumber that he had cleared for planting. He had purchased more farm animals and was really doing very well. Eliza and John continued to be very involved in the church and other community activities and watched as Camden and the other towns in the area grew and prospered.

They appeared to be living the perfect life but they would soon find out that life is not perfect.

Chapter Twenty-Five

A New Family and War

1853-1861

Where there is love there is life.
Mahatma Gandhi

In the middle of September of 1853, Eliza was visiting with her mother and mentioned that she hadn't had her monthly.

Kate looked up from her needlepoint and said, "Are you with child?"

"I don't know, Mother; I just didn't have a monthly which is unusual for me and I'm very tired."

Kate put her needlepoint down and walked over to her oldest daughter and hugged her gently and said, "Have you told John?"

"No, I want to wait until I'm sure."

October came and Eliza still hadn't said anything to John. She didn't feel ill, just very tired, but she was still able to keep up with her daily chores. Finally at the beginning of November, after they had eaten their evening meal, Eliza said, "I have something to tell you."

John looked at her expectantly but with a worried expression on his face.

"What is it?"

"I'm with child."

John was stunned. The gravity of the joyful news left him speechless, so he just grabbed her and hugged her.

"Are you sure?"

"Yes, I'm sure."

"When do you think our baby will be born?"

"I'm thinking sometime in June. Mother and I paid a visit to Hannah Dunn's."

"Hannah, the midwife?"

"Yes and based on what she told me, she's thinking the middle of June."

John couldn't wait to tell his family. Winfred would be so excited for them. She had teased him that she didn't think that John would ever give her a daughter-in-law, much less a grandchild.

John and Eliza went through the cold winter and he showered her with attention. Winfred, as expected, was beside herself with joy. The spring crops were planted and on a warm day in June, as he worked in the field, he heard Eliza calling for him by the way of ringing a large bell in the yard. At the sound of the bell, John took off running. He got to her and she was holding her large belly.

"Are you okay? Is it time?"

"Go get Hannah. Tell her I'm about to give birth. Tell her to hurry."

John ran to the barn and jumped on Chestnut bareback and took off towards Hannah's while Kevin ran to get Kate. John was back in under an hour with Hannah following right behind him. Kate had just arrived with Kevin and was ready to assist. "I'm going to need you to bring clean towels or sheets and boil some water," Hannah instructed. "How long have you been in pain, Eliza?"

"About two hours."

Hannah thought to herself that since this was Eliza's first, she could be there a while. She walked Eliza back to her bed and all of a sudden there was a big splash of water.

"Oh my God, what just happened?" Eliza asked anxiously.

"It's okay, this is normal. It just means the baby is on its way."

Kate found old towels and cleaned up the fluid. Hannah held Eliza's arm and helped her get into the bed. John was frantic trying to boil water and running in with sheets.

Eliza felt very aware of the terrible pressure she had and the pains started coming more and more consistently. Hannah put her hands under Eliza's bottom and felt the head right away. She put clean sheets under her and dried off her legs. Eliza gripped the top of the bed, wide-eyed and frightened as the next contraction came on strong. Kate wiped Eliza's brow and Hannah told her to try not to push because she was afraid that she might tear. Meanwhile, John stood in the other room with Kevin and William, anxiously pacing back and forth waiting for more instructions from the midwife.

Hannah checked Eliza again and saw a puff of little brown hair crowning. She grabbed a towel and told her to start pushing. She let out a scream and pushed as hard as she could. The head turned and emerged between Hannah's hands, first the forehead, then the pink chubby cheeks, then the chin and finally the shoulders. She continued to pant and push and out slid a little girl right into Hannah's waiting arms. The new baby let out a little cry as she took her first breath. Hannah wrapped the baby in the towel and placed the pink little girl into Eliza's arms. The women started to cry and the new mother gasped because she could not believe the new little life staring up at her squinting her eyes and pursing her small rosebud lips. Hannah walked out to get the hot water from John to sterilize the knife to cut the cord.

"You can go in and see your wife. You have a beautiful little girl," Hannah said proudly.

Kate left the bedroom as John walked in wanting to leave the new parents alone and gave him a hug as she passed him. John looked at Eliza lying there holding this beautiful miracle. He took his handkerchief and wiped Eliza's damp forehead as he kissed her and looked at the child she held.

"I love you so much."

"And I love you. What shall we name her, John?"

"I'd like to name her after my sister that I lost in Ireland. Do you like the name Roseanna?"

"That's a beautiful name and it fits her. I'll call her Rose for short."

Hannah finished up and said she'd be back to check on Eliza and Roseanna. She instructed her on how to nurse the new baby and then she left so that the new family could become acquainted. As soon as Hannah left, John laid down on the bed with his new family. He had never felt so content in his life. He had a surprise for Eliza. He had been building a new cradle in the barn. He said he'd be right back and came back a few minutes later with a maple cradle that rocked, much to Eliza's surprise.

"I didn't know you were a skilled carpenter!"

"I didn't either. Kevin helped me a little but I did most of it. Do you really like it?"

"It's the most beautiful cradle I've ever seen."

Winfred came over as much as she could get away with. She cried when they told her that they had decided to name the new baby after Roseanna. Bridget and Catherine had children now of their own so Winfred was a busy grandmother, which is exactly what she had hoped for.

Three more years passed before John and Eliza had another child. John was hoping for a son. He needed the help on the farm but dreamed of having a little boy that would follow him as he did his chores. But in February of 1857, Eliza delivered another little girl; Margaret Elizabeth Doyle had chestnut hair like her mother. This delivery came as quickly as the first and Hannah just barely got there in time.

A few years later, John picked up Rose in his arms and asked her if she wanted to go for a carriage ride. She loved going places with her father. John worked such long hours trying to get ready for the winter months that it had been awhile since the two could sneak away. Margaret was getting all of the attention now so John bundled Rose up and lifted her into the wagon and she proudly sat next to her father.

John was amazed how much Newburgh had grown, now a busy little town of nearly 1,000 residents. As they rode down the main street, John looked at all of the new merchants, blacksmiths, carriage-makers, shoe-makers, an ashery, cabinet-makers, a cooper, millers, harness-makers, a tinsmith, a foundry, tanners, one carding mill, one baker, two doctors, druggists, merchants and tailors. He couldn't believe it. Newburgh had grown to almost the size of Napanee. He also noticed the Newburgh Academy where he wanted his children to attend, the same one he laid eyes on many years ago, when it was still an object of curiosity, and he was still naïve about many things in this new world.

A group of farmers sitting outside the store by an unplayed draught board looked up when John and Rose walked up.

"The war has started in America and they want men to sign up to fight for the Union Army!"

John walked up and tipped his hat, "Gentlemen, what's this about a war?"

"Haven't you heard? America needs men. The north of America and the south of America are fighting. The Confederate states, that is the south, want to keep their independence from the north and they want to keep slavery legal."

"Slavery?"

"Black slaves coming over from Africa and other countries. They have them working on their plantations picking cotton and planting rice. They don't get paid and we hear are treated pretty poorly, beaten, separated from their families, sold at auctions."

John was stunned that this could be happening just

south of the Canadian border. He recalled the day long ago in Liverpool when Patrick mentioned slavery to him then.

"Britain is neutral but if they had to take a side, it would be with the north. Do you know Joseph Edmonds?" the old farmer asked John.

"I don't know him well, but I know who he is."

"Well, rumor has it that his cousin is Sarah Emma Edmonds and she came over from England, moved down to Michigan and is part of the Union Army."

"What?" John kind of laughed.

"Charlie tell him the story," the old farmer said to Charlie sitting around the table.

"Well, Sarah had always been an adventurous kind of child and when she was a little tike like your little girl there, she read a story about Fanny Campbell. Fanny dressed like a man so that she could get on a pirate ship. So, she wants to be in the Union Army and remembers the story about Fanny Campbell and decides to dress like a man and enlists in the Michigan Infantry. Her name now is Franklin Flint Thompson. She felt just because she was a woman that it shouldn't keep her from serving in the Army!"

"She's an infantryman?"

"No, she's a field nurse dressed as a man."

John couldn't believe what he was hearing. What woman would want to be in the Army?

"The new Grand Trunk Railway is putting together a military brigade because there have been concerns over the safety of passengers. It's an all volunteer militia. This unit of the Canadian Volunteer Militia recruited amongst railway employees had infantry and artillery companies deployed along the railway lines in Canada east and Canada west."

"Well, gentleman, this is a lot to think over."

"Can I get you something?" asked the storekeeper.

"Yeah, I need a hammer and some barn nails."

"Sure thing," the storekeeper said as he got up and collected the things John requested. John was thinking about this war and the woman dressing like a man to be a part of it. He paid for his items, tipped his hat to the men sitting and talking and walked out with Rose hand-in-hand.

Eliza was pregnant again and due in the early spring. On March 10, 1862, a boy was born and John was ecstatic and thought *I finally have a son*. He loved his girls but he had waited a very long time for a son. It was easily agreed that he would be named Thomas after John's father. Then, two years later, John and Eliza had their fourth child, another boy. He was baptized John but they decided to call him William after Eliza's father.

As the war raged in America, John would hear

stories from time to time. He saw the militia armed on the Grand Truck Railway. Patrick told him about men volunteering to go fight with the Union Army and he recently read in the Picton Gazette of others volunteering to fight with the south.

James McKeone, the best man at his wedding had started a committee to help run-away slaves through an underground railroad. At great risk to themselves, through a secret network of routes and safe houses, many of them became guides to aid people in finding their way to the next stop along the way. John had only seen a few Negroes in his whole life and not any living in Camden or Centreville. James told him in confidence that the group from church that helped these slaves used railroad terms as code words. The people that helped slaves move from place to place called themselves 'conductors' and the people running from slavery called themselves 'passengers or cargo.' The 'stations' were homes volunteers offered as safe places for the passengers to rest. Different places along the secret routes had names also, Detroit was known as 'midnight' and the Detroit River was known as 'Jordan,' a biblical reference to the river that led to the Promised Land. The end of the journey was coded 'dawn.' He had overheard people in town using these code names but didn't think much of it. "Tell them to take the railroad from midnight to dawn," he would hear. He learned that most runaway slaves went to Windsor and the western part of Ontario.

Indeed, it was a turbulent time that made him think back to the bloodshed and the injustice that had plagued Ireland for so long. Was the world getting better? Was humanity really making progress? He thought long and hard as he rode home in the wagon unable to imagine keeping a man or woman against his or her will. Just like Britain, if he had to choose, he hoped the north would win the war.

Chapter Twenty-Six

Newburgh Academy

1863

Education is the key to
unlock the golden door of freedom.
George Washington Carver

John and Eliza enrolled Roseanna and Margaret in the Newburgh Academy.

Miss Anna Wesley, a rather homely woman in her thirties, had come from England and had wanted to teach as long as she could remember. She wore a long black skirt and a very starched white linen blouse with a cameo at her neck. Her long brown hair was pulled back and tied in a knot at the base of her neck and she wore thick glasses on her rather long pointed nose. Even thought she was a tad homely, she was very sweet and her love of children shone through in her demeanor.

"They are just like my own," she would always say.

This schoolhouse similar to the others in the area, was a log shanty thirty feet by twenty-two feet long. The chimney was made of lath covered with plaster and served for heating, ventilating and lighting the structure. There was one small window on each side and the furniture was as simple as the rest of the building. Holes were bored into the wall made of logs about four feet above the floor and pieces were driven into the logs. Rough planks about three inches thick were placed upon these pieces to create desks for the children.

Miss Wesley and the other administrators at Newburgh Academy felt luckier than most because they had books and supplies that many of the other small schools didn't have. Fifteen students between five and fourteen years of age were enrolled and started school at the same time as Roseanna and Margaret. All students would be given a quill pen, ink that was made from water stained with maple bark, a book entitled *A Concise Introduction to Practical Arithmetic for the Use of Schools*, written by John Strachan, the *Upper Canada Spelling Book,* written by Alexander Davidson, a reader, a geography book, history book and one grammar book. Miss Wesley was trying to get the Irish National School Books since these graded series of books did not favor any particular religious denomination and she had a mixture of students favoring the Catholic religion to the Church of England. Also, these books were less expensive than anything else she had seen. She taught all eight grades starting in September and ending in May. The boys had permission to help with farm chores but each child was instructed to come back when the chores were finished. Soon after school began, the children had gone outside to play and eat their lunch and Miss Wesley prepared for the afternoon lessons when she heard a ruckus outside. She looked out the window and noticed Johnnie Young running zigzag from Eddie Jones.

"I'll get you, Johnnie!" Eddie yelled and flung a rock so swiftly and accurately that it hit Johnnie square in the back of the head, and down he went. Miss Wesley ran out the door and ran up to Johnnie who was rubbing the back of his head, which was now covered in blood.

"Oh my, we need to get you to Doctor Johnson."

"Nah, I'll be okay Miss Wesley, it's just a cut.

She took him in and bandaged his head as best as she could. Afterward, she went back outside and grabbed Eddie by the ear and dragged him back into the classroom. Eddie found himself standing in the corner with his nose pressed against the wall for the rest of the day.

Roseanna and Margaret would come home from school and excitedly tell John and Eliza what they had learned that day and share stories about people like Johnnie and Eddie and listening to their stories, John felt very proud that they attended school. Winfred was a little surprised when she heard about the girls going to the Newburgh Academy but knew that this was a different time, very different than living in Ireland.

As the boys got older but still too young for school,

William spent countless hours playing in the barn, feeling at home around the animals and he loved to climb up into the hayloft. He had an imaginary friend and he would pretend that they sailed on a ship and discovered lands from far away. At his young age, his curiosity was sparked by stories about America, and he longed to travel and discover places no one had ever been to.

Eliza read the children stories at night to help them sleep and William's favorite story was *Gulliver's Travels*. In his imagination, he would travel on the ship with Lemuel Gulliver to remote places in the world. He was a surgeon one night and a ship captain the next. When the sailing ship *Adventure* was blown off course by storms and forced to dock for want of fresh water, Gulliver was abandoned by his companions and found by a farmer who was 72 feet tall. William wanted so badly to be on that ship. One afternoon he went out to the barn to play. He pulled back the barn door and watched the setting sun illume the inside of the barn. He breathed deeply the smell of fresh hay and animal dung. He climbed up the stairs up to the loft and almost fell backwards at what he saw. His eyes grew as big as saucers as he looked at the blackest person he had ever seen.

"Please master – please don't holla!" the Negro begged. "I won't hurt you."

William just stared.

"Who are you?" William asked. He didn't feel afraid

just curious.

"My name is Soloman and I'm traveling west of here. Have you ever heard of a place called Windsor?"

"No, I haven't but why are you so black?"

"That's just the color of my skin."

William was intrigued. This man wore ragged clothes and no shoes, and had a head of black course curly hair. Not only was he the blackest man he had ever seen, he was the biggest. His hands were bigger than the supper plate in the kitchen. He must have stood at least seven feet tall. William wanted to touch his hair to see what it felt like.

"Where are you from? I've never seen you before." William asked.

"Have you ever heard of America?"

Will's eyes got big again, "America? You remind me of Gulliver from *Gulliver's Travels*. Have you traveled all over the world?"

William was still standing on the top rung of the ladder.

"No, I haven't traveled all over the world, but I did come from Africa. I was taken from Africa and my family and I was forced to work on a farm in South Carolina. It was a rice farm. Have you ever had rice?"

Will shook his head no.

"It's hard work."

William became very brave and climbed the rest of

the way up and sat looking at the man. "Soloman, how did you get here?"

"I've had friends help me along the way. I was taken from my family in Africa when I was a little bigger than you."

"Why didn't you run away?"

"I couldn't. They chained us up on the ship so we couldn't leave." William's eyes got big again.

"We landed in Charleston, South Carolina and I was sold at an auction to a plantation owner named Middleton. There I worked with other slaves until I found friends that helped me get away."

"Why did you want to get away?"

"Because they weren't very nice to us. They would beat us with whips and if we had a wife or children, they would sell them to other owners so that we couldn't see them."

William was deeply saddened. He had never heard of such cruelty. He liked Soloman and he felt sorry for him.

"You can't tell anyone that I'm here. Can I trust you with that?" Soloman pleaded.

"Sure. I won't tell."

William wasn't sure how his mother or father would react but he didn't want this man to get in trouble and he didn't want to get in trouble either. William heard the outside bell ring.

"That's my mother. She's calling me to supper."

"What's your name, little one?"

"My name's William."

"Could you bring me back a biscuit or anything to eat without being seen? I'm mighty hungry."

"Sure, I'll do my best."

William climbed down the ladder feeling pretty special that he had met this stranger. He cleaned his plate but when no one was looking, he put a fresh biscuit under his shirt.

He managed to get back to the barn where he found Soloman crouching in the back corner.

"It's just me Soloman, William."

"Master William, God bless ya."

The next morning after his chores, he went out to the barn and climbed up the stairs but Soloman was gone. He had left the night before as soon as the sun went down. William was sorry he was gone. He liked Soloman and prayed he got to Windsor safely, wherever that was.

John's boys grew so quickly and unlike William, Thomas took to farming but William didn't seem too interested. He would rather play in the barn or torment his sisters. Life was very good for John and Eliza and their four children until the year of 1871, when things took an unexpected turn for the worse.

Chapter Twenty-Seven
Eliza

1871

There is nothing in the world
so much admired as a man
who knows how to bear
unhappiness with courage.
Lucius Annaeus Seneca

It was early May of 1871 and all four children left the farm to walk to school. Eliza got up to get the children off and John had already left the house to ride out to the back of the property line. When he came back in for lunch, Eliza had laid down. She had mentioned not feeling well the night before which was unlike her and John had noticed a cough that Eliza had had for a few months. The only time John had ever seen her feeling a little under-the-weather or extremely tired was when she was pregnant. John thought to himself, maybe she's with child again but that wouldn't explain the cough. He walked into the bedroom and sat on the bed next to his wife.

"What's wrong?"

"I don't know, I just don't feel well. I'm sure I'll be okay with some rest."

"I'm going to go get your mother."

Eliza didn't object, which made John all the more concerned. He heard her cough as he left the house. He rode down to the Watson's and found Kate in the kitchen. Kate looked up alarmed to see John so early.

"It's Eliza. Can you come back with me and see what you think? I'm not sure what's wrong."

Kate went back to the house with John and walked into her daughter's bedroom.

Eliza could barely open her eyes they ached so. She also felt very cold.

"I'm freezing, could I have another blanket please?"

Kate looked at John and without saying a word feeling the same concern.

"John, why don't you go into town and see if Doctor Johnson can come back to the house?" Kate suggested.

"That's a good idea. I'll leave right now."

Kate felt Eliza's head and it was very hot. She put a cold rag soaked in spring water on her forehead and Eliza just moaned. John rode to Doc Johnson's and had to wait since the doctor was in with another patient. He paced as he waited for him to come out of the examination room. Finally, after a period of time that seemed an eternity, Doc Johnson walked out and noticed John standing there.

"John Doyle, what can I do for you?"

"Doc, it's Eliza. She has a fever and aches all over and she's been coughing. Can you come out and take a look?"

"Sure, I'll finish up a few things here and I'll meet you out there."

When John returned to the farm, Kate talked to him quietly outside the bedroom.

"I'm worried about her. I've never seen her so sick and so quickly. She seemed fine two days ago."

"She was fine. The cough started a few months ago but all of a sudden she said she didn't feel well and she's getting worse. Doc Johnson is on his way."

He waited anxiously for the doctor to arrive watching for him out the window. Finally, he pulled up to the farmhouse in his wagon, grabbed his black bag and jumped down. John opened the door for him and beckoned him in.

"Eliza, it's Doc Johnson. I'm here to examine you."

By then, Eliza could barely open her eyes and her face was pallid and glistening with sickly sweat.

"She's burning with fever," Kate said sullenly.

He looked at Kate and John and said, "We need to fill a cold bath and get her in it."

Kate filled the tub with cold water as John carried Eliza in her nightdress and laid her in the cold water. She flinched at the shock, and John noticed with worry that she was taking on an ashen color to her skin. She didn't seem to have the strength to even hold herself up. *My God, I can't lose her,* he thought. *She's the love of my life. She's everything to me.*

Doc Johnson gave John Dover's Powder to help counteract the symptoms of influenza by increasing perspiration and by acting as a sedative.

"Just keep her comfortable. I'll stop by in the morning to see how she's doing. What we don't want to see is bleeding from the nose or from the ears. I can't say this is nothing. For her illness to come on so quickly with such a high fever, this isn't a good sign."

John felt lightheaded upon hearing those words.

When the children came home from school a somberness descended over the home. Kate and the girls prepared supper in silence but John had no appetite. Kate put them to bed and told John she would stay with the children. She didn't want to leave. She got them in bed early and John lay down with Eliza. He put his arms around her and wept. She didn't move. He didn't know how he would cope if he lost her. He dozed on and off during the night. The window was open slightly and he heard a barn owl hoot in the night. The full moon outside gave light to illuminate his sleeping wife.

Sometime during the night, Eliza's breathing became very labored almost as if she was choking. John woke up and lit a candle next to the bed. He immediately noticed the trickle of blood that ran out of Eliza's nose. Panicked, he wiped her face and as he moved her head, he noticed the blood on the pillow that was draining from her ear. He got on his knees and prayed to God that he would spare his wife. He held her hand up to his lips.

"I love you, Eliza," John cried.

And with that, she was gone.

When he walked out of the bedroom that morning, his expression was a picture of devastation and grief. Kate didn't have to ask. She ran into the bedroom and wept holding her oldest daughter. She loved her dearly and couldn't believe she was gone at such a young age. John felt like he was in a daze. Doc Johnson rode up on his horse early that morning and knew by the look on John's face that Eliza had died.

"I'm so sorry. I wish there was something that I could have done."

Kate walked out and somberly greeted Doc Johnson.

"John, I'll take Margaret back with me. Rose can stay here with you. You'll need her. Thomas and William can help you here also."

John couldn't even respond.

He walked back to the bedroom and closed the door behind him. There lay his beautiful wife with her lips slightly parted. John buried his head in her hair and wept. He inhaled the fragrance of lavender and the scent of her skin. He got a bowl of warm water and washed her body lovingly as tears of grief dripped down on to the sheets. John took out her wedding dress that she had only worn a few years back and gently dressed her in the dove-colored gown. She looked as angelic as she did the day he married her, and his heart and mind recoiled at the idea of putting her in the ground and walking away. John left the house and went towards the barn. He saddled up his horse and rode to St. Anthony's church as tears ran down his face and stung his eyes. Though normally stoic and strong, he didn't know how he would learn to move forward. He made his way to Father Higgins's house, tied up his horse and knocked on the door as he removed his hat. Father Higgins answered the door and was shocked to see a tear streaked John Doyle standing there on his doorstep.

"What's happened?"

"Eliza died in the night. Doc Johnson isn't sure what it was but he suspects influenza and possibly consumption.

John sat with Father Higgins and sobbed. They made arrangements for a small Mass and burial. John explained to Father Higgins that Eliza would be buried next to her brother who had died at the age of eight, and her father, William Latimore, in the Latimore cemetery. After he made the arrangements, he made his way into the small church. The smell of the church comforted him. He knelt in prayer and only wanted to be alone in his grief.

Three days later, as the birds sang from the tree tops

and the sun came up in the east, as if nothing had happened out of the ordinary, John and the rest of the family wept as Eliza's wooden casket was lowered into the ground. Winfred stood close to John. She felt so sad for them all, John, the children, and Kate. She had been through the same kind of loss but the experience did not help her with her own grief. She offered to stay with John until he was back on his feet.

"That would be great, Mamai. Margaret is going to stay with Kate but I could use your help with the boys."

Winfred moved back in with John and helped where she could. She showed Rose how to cook and take care of the house. It was going to be a long summer. John stayed as busy as he could with farming and did anything to keep his mind off of his misery, but Eliza's death plunged him into a deep, black, despairing depression.

Five months later, Winfred and John sat at the kitchen table.

"I know you are still grieving but I'd like you to think about finding a wife."

John looked up at her as if she had lost her mind. He started to say something but Winfred interrupted, "I know what you're thinking but the boys need a mother and you need a wife to take care of you and the house. There is someone I want you to consider. Catherine

Garrett is a lovely woman. She's beautiful, comes from a good family and has a wonderful sense of humor. As a matter of fact, you came over on the same ship with her parents coming over from Ireland."

He knew Catherine from church and she was good friends with Patrick and Nettie next door and had visited them frequently. She was a beautiful woman.

"There is a social after church this Sunday. The Garrett's will be there and I'd like you to be there also."

"Okay, Mamai. I'll consider it."

That Sunday, Winfred got the children ready for church and John walked out of the bedroom and he was all cleaned up. He had a clean shirt on that Winfred had pressed and new trousers and shined shoes. Winfred had baked a pie for the social, which was cooling in the kitchen. She didn't say much to John but was wondering what he was thinking about the social and meeting up with the Garrett's.

After Mass, everyone went outside. The air was still warm even though it was October and the leaves had turned from green to orange, red and gold. The air carried the distinct smell of early fall, with gourds and pumpkins of all sizes ready to be picked and made into pies. Women scurried to collect the food that they had brought and place it on a long table that had been draped with a white cloth. Children ran around the grass with parents yelling at them not to get dirty. John sat with his brother Thomas and best friend Patrick and talked about farming and the upcoming winter.

"Hello, John."

John turned in his seat and there before him stood Catherine Garrett, looking lovely in her church clothes, a blue cotton dress with matching bonnet. She had striking blue eyes that sparkled beneath her black lashes.

John stood and said, "Hello, Catherine. It's been sometime since we've spoken."

Patrick said, "Hi there, Kate."

Catherine smiled at Patrick. She had known him for a long time. John walked away from the table and Catherine walked next to him.

"How are you? I know this has been a difficult time."

"I'm getting by. As well as can be expected."

Winfred watched from a distance and was excited to see them talking. She walked over to Catherine's mother Mary Ann and said, "I'm so happy to see them talking together. I think they make a fine looking couple."

Mary Ann smiled as she watched the two. Catherine was known for her good sense of humor and had John laughing in no time.

Winfred remarked, "That's the first time I've heard him laugh in months. Catherine is good for him."

John left Catherine asking if he could call on her, a proposition she welcomed eagerly.

The following June after courting Catherine for eight months, they married in St. Anthony's church on a Wednesday morning. It was a very small wedding with a minimum of fanfare. Catherine dressed simply in a peach-colored wedding gown with buttons up the front and lace around the collar, a peplum and long sleeves. Her beautiful dark hair was pulled back with a tiny orange blossom at the top of her twist. John wore the same suit he had for his first marriage, stirring bittersweet memories, but he was in love again and excited at starting a new life.

The bridal party and family went back to James and Mary Ann's after the service. Catherine was a joy to be around. She wanted many children, was a hard worker, and dedicated to her faith and family. John believed they would be very happy together.

Rose was fifteen at the time of the wedding and looking forward to a wedding of her own someday. She had decided to become a teacher at the Newburgh Academy and with Catherine's encouragement, Rose began teaching the younger children, grades one through three. Margaret was growing into a beautiful girl and continued to live with her grandmother, Kate. Thomas was now ten and loved farming with his father. He became John's shadow learning as much as he could about crops, the animals and running a large farm. William, only eight wasn't much interested in his new mother or farming.

He grieved for his mother, Eliza. He stayed to himself and spent as much time alone as he could get away with. In his heart, he believed his dead mother would visit him when he was alone. She spoke to him and he felt the warm embrace of her arms.

Two years after John and Catherine married, on September 1, 1874, they delivered a beautiful healthy boy and named him James. James got all of the attention, mostly because he demanded it. William liked the idea of having a new baby around. He was ten years old and bored and James gave him an outlet for his pent-up frustration and idleness. Robert was born two years later on February 8, 1876. He was sickly at birth (suffering from undeveloped lungs) and to Catherine and John's great sorrow, Robert died when he was less than one month old. Catherine grieved for the tiny infant, whom they knew from his birth that, tragically, it was only a matter of time that they would lose him.

During the next ten years, John continued to build his farm and bolster his reputation in the community and Catherine was loved by all who met her. She always had a smile on her face and handled any challenge with ease. Her love for John was unwavering and she took care of her family with grace and elegance and a strength that people relied on but John and Catherine also endured more hardship. They lost two more daughters within five years of each other, Winopher was only three when she succumbed to influenza and Winnefred died of a congenital heart defect at the age of one and one-half. By 1881, Catherine and John had eight children, Roseanna, Margaret, Thomas, William, James, John, Michael and Patrick. John had worked through his grief with each dying child helping Catherine cope with each challenge and the children took care of each other…all except William.

Chapter Twenty-Eight
William

1882

Hope is the thing with feathers
that perches in the soul –
and sings the tunes without the words –
and never stops at all.
Emily Dickinson

It was difficult for John not to favor his oldest son Thomas, who was agreeable and hardworking, the opposite of his younger brother. When William turned seventeen, John asked him to leave. The arguments that ensued between John and William caused tension between John and Catherine along with the rest of their children. William packed his things and left. The Grand Trunk Railway now ran up to Stocco where his Uncle Thomas and Aunt Ellen lived. He asked them if he could stay with them for a short time until he found a job and a place to live. They reluctantly allowed him to move in knowing he had no place else to go but fearing that it would anger John. Stocco had been a small town with one small church but it was quickly becoming one of the most bustling villages in the area, with four general stores, two hotels, two carriage-making shops, two blacksmiths, a shoe-repair, harness shop and a resident physician. Stocco also boasted a saloon that was about to open called the Keilty Saloon. William walked to town one August morning to find work.

A sign in the front of the saloon window advertised "*Help Wanted*." William thought to himself, *I might just be in luck*. The door was locked, but he peered through the window as his breath made a circle on the glass. Inside was an ornate bar along one side with a large mirror behind it. Bar stools lined the front of the bar and along the backside was bottle after bottle of alcohol. He had never been in a saloon before, and the sight intrigued him, a curiosity made all the more appealing by John and Catherine's adamant opposition to such places. A player piano sat in one corner with sheet music on the stand. Ten small tables were placed in the middle of the room with four chairs around each. Above the cash register was a sign that read "*No Spitting on the Floor*," in large black letters. He wondered what kind of work was available and when they would open and decided he'd come back later.

Picking up the Stocco newspaper, he spotted a notice in the back that read, "*Lodging Room Available. Must be Respectable. Signed Margaret Temple.*" William walked the three blocks and stood in front of the house. It was a small log style house with flowers along the walkway and overflowing in the window boxes. He walked up to the door and took off his cap and knocked. A young woman about the age of twenty-three answered the door.

"Can I help you?"

She wasn't a homely girl but William couldn't really consider her nice looking either. On top of her head was very curly brown hair that seemed quite out of control even though she had it pulled back in a wrap. Her brown eyes looked kind but they were hidden behind large framed, thick glasses. She was friendly though and had a nice smile.

"I'm inquiring about the room."

"My name is Adeline and my mother is renting the room. Please come in."

William stepped into the house and stood on a small handmade rug that was in front of the door. The girl looked at William and hoped her mother would like him enough to allow him to rent the room. A large woman walked into the room wiping her hands on a dishtowel and looked like she had already put in a full day.

"This is my mother, Margaret Temple," Adeline said politely.

William at seventeen was blond and tall nearly 5'11, with a slight wave to his hair and piercing blue eyes. He held his hand out to shake Mrs. Temple's hand.

"Hello, my name is William Doyle and I'm interested in renting your room."

"Are ya now?" replied Mrs. Temple, looking him over carefully. "Are you a respectable young man? I won't have any carousing going on in my house. And what religion are you?

"I have been raised Catholic, ma'am."

"Oh well that's a shame…but I won't hold that against you. Come see the room." Margaret turned to show William the way.

They walked to the back of the house and Mrs. Temple opened the door. It was a small room but cozy with a single bed on which lay a handmade quilt, a small chair and bedside table with an oil lamp on it and a dresser for his clothes. As she stood there watching William she noticed his good looks. Mrs. Temple then began to ramble on about how they were all members of the Free Church. William wasn't sure what kind of congregation that was but he didn't much care. He claimed to be Catholic but wasn't that interested in going to church or being a part of any religion, which was another sore point with John and Catherine.

"Have you got a job, Mr. Doyle?" asked Margaret with her hands on her rather large hips. "Well, actually I'm applying for one in town today."

"Well, if you get the job, you can have the room."

Adeline overheard this and was overjoyed.

"How much is the room?" William asked.

"Its $2.00 per week and that includes meals."

William thought that sounded reasonable.

"Okay, sounds great. I'll be back this afternoon."

"Well, I have six other lodgers here. We all get along and my son George lives here with us. Like I said, I won't have any funny business in my house. George makes sure of that," Margaret said with authority.

William assured her he would be on his best behavior and smiled as he walked out of the house. He walked back to the saloon and sat on a bench outside the building deciding to just wait for someone to come by. He liked the room he just saw and thought Mrs. Temple would be easy enough to get along with. She had a coarseness to her disposition but William believed it was all show. About that time, a man came around the corner whistling with a newspaper in his hand. He was in his 40's, a short man with brown hair, a big mustache and a cigar hanging out of his mouth. Casually dressed, he stopped short when he saw William.

"Hello there young man, are you waiting for me?"

"I am. Are you the owner of this saloon?"

"Yes, I'm Michael Keilty, the owner."

"I'm inquiring about your sign."

"Oh, sure, come on in," Mr. Keilty responded as he unlocked the door.

William looked around and liked the smell of the

freshly oiled mahogany bar.

"We're opening this Friday. Have a seat. So, what kind of experience do you have?"

"Well sir, I'm talented at a lot of things."

Michael thought this was very funny.

"Well, William, I'm looking for a carpenter and someone that can do repairs around here, help behind the bar if needed, that sort of thing."

William didn't have much experience fixing things but was determined to get this job.

"I've lived on a farm all my life and can fix just about anything. I'm not very familiar with mixing drinks but I'm sure I can learn," William said confidently.

Michael liked the looks of this boy and liked his enthusiasm.

"Can you start this Friday at 4:00?"

"I certainly can!"

"Well, I'll pay you $5.00 per week and we'll see how you do."

$5.00 per week! William felt like that was a fortune.

"You won't be sorry, sir. Okay, I'll see you Friday at 4:00 sharp."

"Welcome aboard."

He left Keilty's Saloon with a spring in his step. He walked back over to Mrs. Temple's house and gave them the news that he had in fact secured a job and would be moving in within the hour.

"That's nice," replied Mrs. Temple. "Welcome to the family."

Adeline smiled but didn't say a word. She was really delighted at the thought of staring at him over the supper table. William went home and packed, gave his aunt and uncle a hug and walked out.

Thomas said to Ellen after William had left, "When John finds out that William is working in a saloon, that will be the end of him."

The first night at Keilty's Saloon, William arrived apprehensively. He didn't have any real skills as a carpenter and worried that he might lose his job on the first night when Michael asked him to fix something. William seemed to Michael a pleasant but aloof young man who guarded his private matters closely. That was okay with Michael, he really didn't want an employee that got involved in everyone's affairs.

William noticed a few employees rushing around for their opening night and a young man with red hair and green eyes stood behind the mahogany bar wiping off bar glasses and checking the inventory of the bottles of alcohol.

"Hello," the young man said to William as stood in the middle of the saloon. "Can I help you? We don't open for a few hours."

"I'm here to start work. My name is Will Doyle. Is Mr. Keilty here?"

"He's in the back, he'll be right out. My name is Dan, Dan O'Rourke."

"It's nice to meet you," William said with a smile. William walked up to the bar and shook hands with Dan. They felt wet from the water and William wiped his hands on his pants.

"Sorry," Dan sheepishly remarked.

"No problem."

Mr. Keilty walked into the room and said, "William, welcome!"

He took William around and introduced him to the few people that worked there. Walking in from the back room came a woman with a black and burgundy corset on trimmed in black lace appliqué and short lace sleeves. The corset scandalously revealed her bare legs and she had more cleavage than William knew a woman could display. Her black-heeled shoes that tied up the front made a clicking sound as they sauntered across the wood floor. She wore red silk stockings, a headdress with feathers, gloves and black neckband. As she walked, William noticed a garter on her left thigh. She was gorgeous with black hair and green eyes that went right through him as she glanced at him under long black eyelashes. Brazenly, she walked right up to William and put her dainty gloved hand in his view to be kissed. William obliged her but couldn't talk and worried that his manly parts exposed themselves. He had never seen anything like her, but the ravishing sight of this seductive-looking creature stirred in him a kind of excitement he never before experienced. Her name was Blanch Beauchene.

When he finally got his voice he said, "The pleasure is all mine."

"Blanch will be asking our guests if they'd like drinks from the bar and she has a voice like nobody's business," Michael informed William.

All this time, the piano player, Paul Proud, was practicing his songs for the evening. Paul came from New York City and knew all the current songs. He set in to a ragtime number that had a real kick. Paul glanced up and smiled at William. Blanch was off getting the small tables prepared and Michael handed William a list of things to get started on. William read the list to himself: light the oil lamps, fix a creek in the door, help get the bar ready, etc., etc. William had no problem making his way down the list and performed each task with ease. So far, the first night was a glowing success.

With each night after that, William grew more confident. He loved his job at the Keilty Saloon and eventually worked his way up to assistant manager of sorts. The people in the saloon changed every night and he truly enjoyed the variety. Some appeared a little rough around the edges and most drank too much but every night was a surprise waiting to happen. This was much different than the farm life he could have settled for but abhorred.

He also liked his room with Mrs. Temple but he longed for his own place maybe with a little piece of land.

But most of all he adored Blanch. On slow nights, they'd talk at the bar and she'd tell him stories. She was born in Montreal and wanted out of the big city and away from her sister. Her mother and father had both died in a tragic accident when Blanch was small, victims of a sudden fire that engulfed their farmhouse while they slept. Blanch and her sister Nelly made it out but her mother and father perished. Nelly still lived in Montreal but they hadn't talked in years.

Still, her ebullience masked the tragedy that she had endured as a girl. Blanch was a fun loving, high spirited girl and didn't want to be bothered with all of the shoulds and shouldn'ts of her time. Her sister was the older of the two and felt compelled to parent Blanch. Nelly felt responsible for her and disapproved of her ways.

Like William, Blanch also loved working in the saloon and flirting with all of the men that came in. But she never left with any of them and Mr. Keilty always made sure she got home safely, not far from where William lived.

"What about you?" Blanch asked.

"My story isn't that interesting. I grew up on a farm not far from here. My mother died when I was seven. My father remarried and wanted me to run the farm with him and I hate farm work. See...it's pretty boring,"

William said with a shrug of his shoulders.

"I'm sorry about your mother."

"Thanks, that's okay, I'm over it."

He changed the subject, secretly hoping that his relationship with Blanch would go further than just talking at the bar. Little did he know that Blanch was thinking the exact same thing.

Chapter Twenty-Nine

The Keilty Saloon

1882

Death is no more than passing
from one room into another.
But there's a difference
for me, you know. Because
in that other room I shall be able to see.
Helen Keller

During a warm day in July, Thomas stopped by to see John to break the news to him about William. He dreaded having to tell his brother where William was now employed but he didn't want him hearing it on the street. He noticed as he pulled the wagon up to the front of John's house that he was building an addition to his home.

"I'm sorry to have to tell you this but William left my house, has a job and is living as a lodger."

"That's great news. Why would you feel bad to tell me that?"

"Well, he is working at the Keilty Saloon."

"Well, that's his decision. Is he attending St. Edmunds on Sunday?"

Thomas wasn't going to lie to him. "Um, no not that I've seen."

"Well, he's no son of mine. How's Mamai?"

Thomas knew that the discussion about William was over.

"She's doing well for being 94 years old," Thomas said with a laugh.

"Tell her I'll be over to see her after church on Sunday."

"She's not going to be able to attend church much longer," Thomas shared. "I talked with Father Murphy and he said he'd be happy to bring her Holy Communion on Sunday if she couldn't make it in."

"That doesn't surprise me. Let me know if I can do anything."

"Ellen loves her and takes good care of her just like she did her own father."

"I'm sure she does," John said with a smile.

At that moment, the barn door opened again and four year old John Jr. came into the barn and greeted his uncle.

"Hi, Uncle Thomas."

"Hi there, Nephew. Hey, what's the construction I see going on?"

"Yeah, its great isn't it? We're building more

bedrooms and I think I should have my own room."

John and Thomas just laughed.

"Catherine says she's going to keep having children until she has a girl. I figured we would need more room," John informed him with a laugh.

"Well, I better get back to my own work. I'll see you Sunday," Thomas said with a wave.

One year later, Catherine delivered another boy. Patrick Henry Doyle was born on a chilly spring morning in March of 1883. When Patrick was only a few days old, he had black hair that was so long Catherine joked that he needed a haircut. Four year old Michael asked, "Momma, why is Patrick so hairy?" And from then on Patrick was nicknamed, Harry. John was relieved that he had built more rooms onto the house. Besides his two older daughters, he had a house filled with rowdy boys but Catherine managed the children and the house exceptionally well. Just after Patrick's birth, John went to see his mother and realized just how frail she was. She was now ninety-six years old and unable to travel even to church anymore.

"John, thanks to you for getting us out of Ireland when you did, I've had a long life. You've been a wonderful son. Can you believe it's been almost forty years since I've seen my Thomas and my dear Rose and baby Joseph?" Winfred shared with misty eyes.

John would just sit and listen to her reminisce about

the old days and her deceased husband and children. He loved his mother but knew it was a matter of time when he would be burying her too. On Wednesday, September 24, 1883 just three days after John had sat with his beloved mother, Thomas came over to inform him that she had died in her sleep. Thomas and John wept together and openly. They both knew her death was imminent but it was difficult to say goodbye to her. They would miss her strength, her courage and her dry sense of humor. William showed up at the funeral but stayed in the back of the church and only talked with James his younger brother. William's presence only exacerbated John's hurt, and William himself seemed indifferent.

Three years later, Catherine delivered another boy, Joseph on June 12, 1886 and then tragedy struck again. Margaret Elizabeth, John's youngest daughter died November 1, 1888 at the age of twenty-eight of influenza. On April 7, 1890, just seventeen months after Margaret's death, Roseanna died and was buried alongside her sister in St. Anthony's cemetery. John was consumed with grief in losing his daughters. And then, adding to his despair, only four months after that, John's son, Thomas died on August 24, 1890 of consumption. John had been inseparable from his son and the loss crushed his spirits like no other. He had planned on Thomas taking over the farm someday. John was now sixty-nine years old and starting to show his age. The deaths of his first wife and children had taken a toll on him. The loss of William also weighed heavily on his spirit, even though he refused to share with anyone to include Catherine that he still cared about William, who was still his son. It was almost unbearable the loss he felt.

Finally, as if the cloud over him had lifted, on July 8, 1890, Catherine delivered a beautiful little girl that they named Mary Ann after Catherine's mother. Annie was the pride and joy of the family and quickly became everything in the world to John. Catherine finally had her girl and she was surrounded by five big brothers; James, John, Michael, Patrick (Harry), and Joseph.

* * *

For ten years, William worked at the Keilty Saloon and grew so knowledgeable about the saloon business that he could take over when Michael Keilty was out of town. When some of the more rowdy customers came in and had too much to drink, William would step in and escort them outside. A few times voices got too loud and the police came to subdue the crowd, quiet the noise or stop the fights. As William's little brother, James got older he started visiting William at the saloon unbeknownst to their father John. James liked the Keilty Saloon too.

"William, I want to work here with you. I hate farm work," James confessed.

He looked up to his brother and missed William not being around at home. James was a stocky guy, about

5'8" with brown wavy hair, blue eyes and big dreams of being a boxer. He had an engaging personality and loved telling stories which he did with a lot of flair. "Big Jim," as he was affectionately nicknamed, drew the attention of townspeople who relished in his tales and always encouraged him to tell a joke or a story or two. Most people couldn't tell if the story was true or heavily embellished but he was so entertaining, no one cared.

One evening there was a rather large crowd in the saloon and William was needed behind the bar.

Mr. Keilty looked at James and said, "Big Jim, how about I hire you to be my peacekeeper? You can practice your boxing skills and take care of anyone that gets out of line or causes trouble. I would prefer that you be the peacemaker though. Don't go startin' any fights."

James accepted on the spot, and when he told his brother, William replied with a grin, "Great, James. You'll need a place to live though because your father will never let you back in the house working here."

"I'll find a room just like you did," James replied.

James found a room to rent the next day.

Yes, much to John Doyle's dismay, he lost another son to a saloon. John also thought boxing was a waste of time and a dishonorable profession and discouraged James from participating in those events. However, after James insisted that he wanted nothing to do with farming, John finally realized that James was a free spirit just like William.

One day, William found Blanch staring at him when he was working. He'd look at her and she'd quickly look the other way. Between them blossomed a chemistry that William couldn't quite describe and he found himself thinking about her all the time. He wanted her like he had never wanted a woman. Blanch meanwhile, thought William was one of the most handsome men she had ever seen. His blue eyes seemed to undress her when he looked at her. There was a hot passion between the two that could be felt across the room.

When Blanch was ready to leave work late in the evening or usually early in the morning, Mr. Keilty always made sure that she arrived home without an incident. One evening, Keilty asked William to make sure Blanch got home because he had to leave early that night for a trip to Kingston.

"Sure, I can do that," William replied, his mind racing.

William had never been alone with her and he wasn't sure he could trust himself. Keilty had already left, the bartender was cleaning up, the piano player was long gone and Blanch went to the room in the back of the saloon to change her clothes. She came out a few minutes later wearing a conservative blue dress with a matching small bonnet she wore over her long hair that she had pinned up. She looked more like a schoolteacher than a saloon girl, but William thought she was prettier than ever.

Blanch, too, felt a nervous excitement course through her. She felt different around him but they always had people around but walking into the evening, so late at night, this felt thrilling. She shivered as she walked into the night air pulling her wrap even tighter. The full moon appeared high against a cloudless sky and cast a bright light over the street. It seemed eerie to have it so quiet but so light out. A solitary owl hooted in the distance. William put his arm around her to keep her warm. She walked with her head down not wanting to slip on the damp stones.

As they arrived at her home, William asked coyly, “Blanch, can I kiss you?”

She stopped and looked up into his eyes. She didn’t have to murmur a response, her body responded and she kissed him passionately.

“I want you like I’ve never wanted a woman before.”

“I want you too,” she replied fervently.

“Will you come back to my house with me? We’re only a short distance away.”

William took her hand and they walked the few short blocks to his home. The house was dark and William knew everyone would be asleep. That was a good thing because Mrs. Temple forbade anyone bringing a guest after hours into the house especially someone of the opposite sex. William unlocked the door and very quietly motioned to Blanch to follow him. She slipped off her shoes so as not to wake anyone. They tiptoed to the back of the house and William unlocked his door. He felt relieved that he had cleaned up his room before he left for work earlier that day. On most days, one could find his clothes strewn all over the floor.

He closed the door behind them and he stood there and looked at her, unable to believe that within a short amount of time, she would be in his bed. Then he helped her off with her wrap and put his hands around the back of her hair and gently kissed her lips. She responded by lifting her head and kissing him back. Neither said a word; no words were needed. He kissed her neck and she reached up and pulled the pin out of her hair to let her beautiful long hair drape down her back. She became wet with anticipation. William was not the first man she had been with, but he stirred something in her that she had never felt. He was gentle and caressing but appeared to know how to please a woman. She wondered how many women he had slept with.

He lay back on the bed and watched her unbutton her dress until it slipped off and pooled around her feet. Then she unbuttoned her white cotton slip and bodice. She watched John all the while removing her clothes. As her slip fell away, she exposed the largest breasts that William had only imagined. His man part was so erect that he ached. She removed her white undergarments, which were already wet from lustful longing. Slowly, walking over to him, she leaned down and undid his suspenders as he unbuttoned his shirt. Falling back on the bed he kissed her with all of the hunger he had stored for her for so long. She tasted so sweet and he inhaled the smell of her hair, which was a combination of tobacco smoke and lily of the valley soap. He made love to her all night until she could take no more.

Completely spent, they curled up together and their wet bodies glistened in the little bit of moonlight that crept across the room. It had been difficult to keep quiet but he knew that if anyone heard them, he ran the risk of getting thrown out not to mention ruining her reputation. He awoke just before sunrise and kissed her softly on the neck. She moaned and moved towards him thinking he wanted her again.

"Blanch, we have to go," William whispered. "I'll walk you home but we have to go before anyone wakes up."

Blanch opened her eyes, suddenly remembering where she was. She kissed him and smiled. They got up quickly and quietly dressed. William did not want this night to end but hoped there would be more nights with her. They tiptoed down the hall and left the house just as Mrs. Temple got up and moved around her room. William put his arm around Blanch to warm her from the morning air. A few songbirds chirped away as the sun came up just over the horizon.

When they arrived at Blanch's door, William asked, "When can I see you again Blanch?"

"Please don't get attached to me. I had fun with you, you are a nice man, but I'm not the commitment type."

William looked stunned. "Okay, I'll respect that."

He kissed her on the cheek and turned and walked away. In less than twenty-four hours, his heart had soared to the highest heights and then been crushed.

Chapter Thirty

The Boxing Match William's Departure

1884

Valor is stability, not of legs and arms,
but of courage and the soul.
Michel de Montaigne

One evening, a man came into the saloon. He drew attention because of his massive size and shiny baldhead. He had an enormous nose that appeared to have been broken many times. On top of his head, he wore a brown felt hat and had a cigar hanging out of his mouth. Dressed like a gentleman, it was difficult to determine his occupation. He said he was passing through and stopped at the saloon to get a few drinks before traveling on to Toronto. William struck up a conversation with him and found out that he was a boxing trainer and promoter employed by the Canadian Amateur Boxing Association. He introduced himself as George Griffin originally from County Cork, Ireland. He mentioned to

William that the Association was always looking for new men to join to promote this relatively new sport.

"You need to meet my brother James," William remarked.

"Is he a boxer?" asked George.

"He wants to be. I think he has it in him to be. You passed him when you came in to the Saloon," replied William. "Big Jim, come over and meet George Griffin!"

George was 6'2" and weighed 200 pounds of solid muscle. He had a thick Irish accent and exuded the unmistakable look of an all-around athlete. Jim walked over and shook his hand. George towered over him.

"So, Big Jim, you want to be a boxer, yea?" George asked.

"Yeah, I sure would."

"You think you got what it takes?"

"Well," Jim stammered a little, "I'm quick and throw a mean punch."

Jim hadn't had much experience with boxing, just squabbles with his brothers and some of the neighbor boys.

"I'll be around for a few days. Why don't you show up at McCully's Warehouse in Newburgh tomorrow morning and we'll see what you got," George said with a grin.

"Sure, I'll do that. Thanks Mr. Griffin. I'll see you in the morning."

Jim went back to his post outside and William said, "Thanks. We'll see if he has what it takes."

George stood and talked to William for some time. William shared with George that he would like to get out of Stocco. He knew that there was a whole world to see and he wasn't seeing it. He still worked around Blanch and they acted like they always had around each other but William was not about to show her he cared one way or another. If she wanted him again, she would have to ask him. In fact, he wanted to get away from Blanch especially now that he knew he could never really have her, away from Stocco, away from his father and away from all of the reminders of his family that had died. He couldn't handle any more funerals. He was just tired of everything.

"William," George asked, "have you ever been out west?"

"Out west of where?" William replied.

"West, Montana, Idaho, Colorado?"

"No, why do you ask?"

"The railroad is headed west and there is silver and gold in the mountains. Mountains so high there is snow on the top," George replied with enthusiasm.

"Really?" William asked with interest. "Tell me more."

"You can catch a train and take that to South Junction, Manitoba, and then head south into Minnesota. Or, you could go west all the way to Kingsgate and south into Idaho. You'll find more land there than you can imagine and towns are springing up all over the place. Just across the border from Kingsgate, is a little town in Idaho called Sandpoint. You'll find the most beautiful lake and mountains bigger than anything you've ever seen. You'll see Indians too but most are very friendly. I just think you'd like it," George said sincerely.

"I've been thinking about moving on and I'll give this some serious thought," William said with a look of deep contemplation.

The next morning, George Griffin and Jim met to discuss boxing and training. George told him that he had a trainer in the area by the name of Ralph Dixon and George would arrange for Jim to work with him to get in shape for his first boxing match. Jim couldn't believe his luck. They worked out a schedule and made a plan for Jim to meet with Ralph Dixon every morning for two hours. If Ralph thought that Jim had it in him to win a fight, Ralph would let George know and they would schedule the first fight for him. When Jim met Ralph a few days later, he couldn't believe how small this man was or his color. Ralph's nickname was "Chocolate Drop." Little for his size, he was only 5'3" tall and weighed only eighty-five pounds soaking wet and had the color of skin that looked just like a chocolate drop. Jim had never seen a Negro before. Dixon was born in Toronto and traveled all over Canada as the first and best professional boxer, earning an incredible record: 163 total fights, 71 wins, 37 wins by KO, 30 losses, 56 draws and 6 no contests.

Jim watched him move around the ring and couldn't believe how fast he was and incredibly light on his feet. Despite his size, he pushed and bullied Jim constantly working on his strength as well as his agility. Jim sweated through every session, hoping that he would soon be ready for his first match.

After six months of intense workouts and hard conditioning, Ralph told Jim he thought he was ready for his first fight. Ralph contacted George and George contacted the agent of Cal McCarthy, one of the finest new boxers in Canada, not yet professional but he had a strong reputation of being one of the next great boxers. He scheduled Big Jim's first match to be held on October 6, of 1891 at the Napanee Arena. George circulated flyers around to advertise the bout. Jim, meanwhile, was excited but his nerves were rising. He had dreamed of becoming a boxer and according to Ralph he was going to be a pretty good one, if not professional, at least amateur. In the back of his mind, he thought of his father and how much he would disapprove of boxing much like he disapproved of him working at the Keilty Saloon.

Two weeks before the fight, Michael Keilty

advertised at the saloon that Big Jim was going to fight Cal McCarthy. The customers excitedly talked about it and placed bets on who would win. In fact, there was so much interest in the fight that Michael decided to close the saloon, and everyone made plans to attend to include William and Blanch, one of the few of her sex to take an interest in such an event.

The night of the fight, the arena was buzzing with anticipation. Ralph worked with Big Jim and gave him last minute tips. William went back to see Jim when he arrived to wish him luck and pat him on the back. George Griffin had come in for the event and sat in the locker room talking with Ralph. A lot of money was at stake for this fight. If Big Jim won, he'd have $500 in his pocket. He thought of all of the things he could do with $500. They heard the announcer telling everyone to take their seats and George yelled, "It's show time!"

Under the dazzle of lights and the flicker of daguerreotypes, Big Jim walked out to the ring with a white towel around his neck and donning green boxing shorts. He held his fists up in the air as the crowd cheered wildly.

"Ladies and gentlemen, welcome to the Napanee Arena. It is now time for the main event," the announcer yelled. "Introducing first, on my left in the blue corner wearing the burgundy trunks with white trim, weighing in at a fit and ready 185 pounds, with an outstanding record of 19 wins, including 6 knockouts, against only two losses, fighting out of Toronto Canada, the undisputed middleweight champion of Canada, "Cavalier and Courageous" Cal McCarthy! On my right, in the red corner wearing green trunks with black trim, weighting in at a right and ready 180 pounds with a promise to be a middle weight champion, Big Jim Doyle!"

Cheers went up for both boxers. Big Jim met Courageous Cal in the center of the ring and they tapped fists. Dancing and pumping their fists in the air, they waited eagerly for the first bell. *Bing*, there it went, and instantly Courageous Cal jumped in and back and ducked just as Big Jim threw the first punch and missed. Cal quickly moved around Big Jim and swung a punch just as Jim danced back and danced forward swinging another punch. Jim jabbed at Cal clipping his jaw as Cal moved back and quickly advanced toward his opponent throwing a punch so quick Big Jim didn't have time to react. Jim took Cal's fist to the face and landed on his back. Cheers erupted while Jim tried to get to his feet. Blood dribbled down his chin and he looked dazed but he was back on his feet and able to swing a fist into Cal's rib cage, knocking the wind out of his opponent. Jim danced and pranced around the ring as Cal doubled over trying to catch his breath. Believing he had the advantage, without thinking he dropped his guard for a split second just as Cal delivered a right upper cut to the jaw and a quick jab to his gut, sending Big Jim flying towards the ropes. He bounced off and fell to the floor face down in a pool of blood. The roar of the crowd drowned the referee's count out. Big Jim was out cold. The ref grabbed Cal's arm and lifting it in the air, declared Courageous Cal the winner of the match at the second bell.

William waited for Jim after the fight.

William took one look at Jim and said, "Wow, little brother. I guess boxing wasn't what you had hoped for."

Jim was in too much pain to respond. William helped him home and told him to take a few days off to heal. It wasn't long after that boxing match that William decided to take George Griffin's suggestion and head west. He waited for the right moment to approach Michael Keilty. They had finished shutting down the saloon and Michael had reached for his key to lock the door.

"Michael, I'm thinking about heading west."

"Michael stopped and turned to look at William with surprise.

"Really William, where out west?"

"I'm going to Minnesota. If that doesn't suit me, I'll go further west, maybe Idaho or Washington. I want to see what else is out there besides Stocco," William shared.

"I can understand that. When do you think you'll leave?" Michael asked with concern. He had grown close to William, as close as anyone could get. He thought of him like a son.

"I'll get my ticket by the end of the week and probably leave by the beginning of next week. I have a few things to take care of before I go."

Michael gave William a fatherly hug and told him he'd miss him and assured him that he could always come back to the saloon if things didn't work out west. Michael threw a big going away party for William at the saloon on Saturday night. All of the old customers came by and James begged William to take him with him but William refused. This was something he had to do on his own. William promised James that once he was settled, he could visit. The saloon's customers bought William shot after shot so by the end of the evening, his head was swimming in a cloud of alcoholic intoxication.

Emboldened by drink, he walked up to Blanch and said, "Blanch, go with me. We'll get out of this God forsaken town and see what else is out there."

An expression of interest flashed across her face.

"Let me think about it. I'll let you know by the end of the weekend."

Michael helped William home that evening and Mrs. Temple woke up because William was talking and laughing too loud.

"William, I'm ashamed of you. It's a good thing you're leaving because if you weren't, I'd throw you out myself."

She walked back into her room with a look of disgust.

She was sorry William was leaving, and Adeline who had long maintained a crush on him even though she had married a few years back, also lamented his departure. They had grown rather fond of William.

Before he left, he went by the farm when he knew his father would not be home. He wanted to say goodbye to Catherine, and his brother's and four year old Annie. Catherine was aware of the relationship that William had with John and understood why he wanted to leave. He would never be a farmer and Catherine accepted that but knew John never would. It probably was best for William that he find the life that he wanted to live.

William anxiously awaited Blanch's answer. But he also knew that if she did decide to go with him, at any moment, she might leave for something better or decide she wanted another path. They had not slept together since that first time but for William, the passion for her he had in the beginning still burned. He knew she had feelings for him too; she just wouldn't commit.

When Sunday evening came and went, he assumed that Blanch had decided not to go with him. Early Monday morning, alone, he walked to the train station in downtown Stocco and sat on the bench to wait for his train. Daydreaming about what the future would hold, he thought he might like to own a saloon like Michael. He was very comfortable in that environment and it seemed to suit him. Just then, the train came into view with a belch of smoke and a piercing whistle.

Suddenly, William heard, "Hey handsome, want some company?"

He turned and standing there smiling with her small trunk beside her was Blanch, waving a ticket at him. William wasn't sure what to expect but the lovers got on the train together, and he never returned to Canada.

Jim took over William's place as bartender and bouncer but abandoned his boxing dreams. It took sometime for the saloon customers to stop heckling Big Jim every time they saw him.

"Hey, Big Jim, how about a Big Knockout?" they would joke, then dance around him like they were in the boxing ring. Jim ignored them for the most part, knowing he could send them to the floor with one left hook. He had a few brawls of his own from time to time but they always happened outside the saloon and usually because someone had pushed him past his breaking point.

Chapter Thirty-One

Joseph and Mary Francis

1909

I have found the paradox,
that if you love until it hurts,
there can be no more hurt, only more love.
Mother Teresa

Joseph grew up to be the fair-haired boy of the family. He was one of the younger boys and wasn't much of a farmer but was cooperative and easy to get along with. Even though he didn't have the charisma that William and James had, he was very handsome and had a quiet charm that drew people to him. He was 5'8" with blonde-brown wavy hair and the most sparkling blue eyes that twinkled like a cloudless starry night. His angelic good looks made it almost impossible to refuse him anything.

Joseph got along with everyone and felt especially close to his mother. When Joseph was twenty-three years old, they had a Christmas party at the farm. Catherine loved entertaining and took every opportunity to invite people to her beautiful home. John loved having everyone together. He wasn't able to do much anymore but could now rely on his sons to take care of everything. Michael had turned out to love farming as well as John Jr. and John felt proud of them for taking care of everything so well. On this particular occasion, they had decided to invite people from St. Anthony Padua and a nearby Catholic church in Sheffield, The Church of the Assumption of the Blessed Virgin Mary. John now eighty-eight years old had Michael and John Jr. go to the back of the property and find the largest evergreen tree they could find. Annie, now nineteen along with her cousin Mary Ellen Garrett decorated the barn. Catherine and her children painstakingly put small candles all over the tree. The smell of fresh pine filled the barn and imbued the place with a festive air. Annie informed everyone that she would be in charge of the tree and would keep an eye on it to make sure nothing caught fire. They built a fire in a pit outside under the stars so people could stay warm throughout the evening and threw fresh straw on the floor of the barn. Along one wall were tables that would soon be piled high with food. They planned on dancing, singing Christmas carols and providing sleigh rides for the guests. Michael had prepared a pig to roast and everyone would be bringing his or her favorite dish.

This event was talked about for months. In an effort to reach out to the community, the members from the small church in Erinsville had been invited for the first time. Mary Francis Fox looked forward to going to the party. Her sisters had all moved to Montreal and she was one of the last in her family to marry. She became increasingly worried that marriage might not be in the cards for her. Mary Francis was twenty-three years old and starting to feel like a spinster. Her father had died a few years back but her brother, Michael now in charge was very strict and the only parties she was permitted to attend were parties that had something to do with the church. Mary Francis had so few opportunities to meet young men that she counted the days to this dance. Her best friend Ann Fournier had called on her a couple of weeks before the dance.

"Mary Francis, you are going to the Doyle dance aren't you?"

"I want to go. I can't imagine not going," Mary Francis replied.

"We'll go together! It's going to be so much fun."

Petite, Mary Francis was only 4'8" with dark auburn hair and dark eyes. Her father came from Ireland but her mother had been born in Kingston. She inherited her dark hair and eyes from her father's side. Mary decided on a dark green simple dress with a white collar and cuffs and little pearl buttons down the front. She loved the dress and with her dark eyes, she was a real beauty. She also had a sweet disposition and was somewhat soft spoken. Had she lived in an area with a larger pool of prospective bachelors, she would have been picked quickly for her sweetness and good looks. Michael Fox insisted on taking the girls and dropping them off, cautioning them that he would be picking them up by 10:00 and not a minute later. Mary Francis and Ann Fournier arrived at the party just as the sun went down. Many people had already arrived and a large field had been designated just for parking the horses, wagons and carriages. The evening felt crisp but not unbearably cold. Both girls wrapped themselves in horsehair blankets and commented on how nice the night was. Mary Francis looked up into the sky and reflected on the clear tranquil night. They could smell the wood burning in the pit and see the smoke from the fire. They could hear the music coming from the barn and smell the food, which made the girls' stomachs growl. People laughed and danced inside the barn, helping themselves to plates of food.

John had picked up his fiddle and was playing a delightful song while Annie and Mary Ellen kicked up their heels, giggling and dancing in a circle. The two girls were first cousins and had been born only four months apart and remained best friends and inseparable from birth. Annie's mother Catherine and Mary Ellen's father Thomas were brother and sister so the two girls had much in common. They even looked quite similar and many thought they were sisters, not just cousins. Just the previous week St. Anthony's Church had their Christmas party that Annie and Mary Ellen had every intention of attending. When Annie inquired who else from the family was going, no one volunteered. They all said they had something they had to do. Annie couldn't believe it. She knew she was not permitted to attend a party without a chaperon so she knew she had to convince someone in her family to go.

"How can we not go? Everyone will be there," she pleaded.

"Annie, the answer is no!" Catherine replied. "We have too much to do around here to get ready for our own Christmas party next week. In addition, I have made an appointment to visit Mr. Richardson, the photographer in Napanee the same morning as the church party. It's too much."

Annie loved going to Richardson's for pictures. They had to force John to go but Catherine and Annie always made a day of it taking the train in, a photography session and then shopping.

Annie said to Mary Ellen, "El, why don't you spend the night and maybe we can talk someone into going with us."

Mary Ellen and Annie spent the afternoon trying to convince her brothers to go with her but when everyone refused, they decided to take matters into their own hands. "El, we're going to that dance!" Annie whispered determinedly to Mary Ellen.

That evening, John and Catherine had retired to the parlor and Annie told them they were going to bed early since Annie was tired from her day with the photographer. Her brothers had either stepped out or stayed in their rooms. Annie and Mary Ellen as quiet as church mice crept down the stairs and oh so quietly left the house out the front door. They had taken off their shoes and were now tiptoeing on snow to get to the barn. Annie decided if they went to the dance for a short while, they could get back before anyone noticed. The two girls got into the barn and attached the brown mare to the carriage and managed to get down to the road before breaking out into relieved laughter. They couldn't believe their good fortune and success at sneaking away. Annie basked in her rebellious pride, while Mary Ellen just prayed they wouldn't get caught. When they arrived at the church, they could hear the music flowing into the cold air and couldn't wait to get in to the rectory to warm up; their feet were wet and freezing. Annie and Mary Ellen had just entered the dance and stood quietly, heads together murmuring and sharing a nervous, self-conscious giggle at the success of this feat. They had not been there more than five minutes when Annie looked up to see John walking towards them.

"Oh my God!" she whispered to Mary Ellen.

Annie began to sweat and felt like she was on the

verge of crying. If there was a way to escape, she would run. She knew what she was up against and there was nowhere to turn except to face John and what was to come. Annie knew she couldn't cry; not in front of everyone watching. Forcing down her feelings only made her feel worse and more self-conscious. Her breathing became more rapid and she started biting her nails, which only made her more embarrassed, but she couldn't stop. If only Patrick Cavanaugh and his friends weren't watching. Everyone was watching.

"Girls, it's time to go home," John said.

The expression on his face said everything. Brother Michael was waiting outside in the wagon when John, Mary Ellen and Annie walked out.

"Michael, I'll take the girls home in the carriage, you go on back with the wagon," John said with a commanding voice. "Girls, I have nothing to say except that I'm ashamed you would go out after being told no."

Annie and Mary Ellen embarrassed from the evening said nothing all the way back to the house except, "I'm sorry."

"Apology accepted," John replied grinning slightly as he looked away to hide his amusement.

The girls hoped that everyone had forgotten about their embarrassing moment from the previous week and the Doyle Christmas party this evening promised to be more fun with much less grief than the previous week. Annie and Mary Ellen both glanced up at the same time and who was looking in their direction but Patrick Cavanaugh, James Patrick's son who lived next door to the Doyle farm.

Annie whispered with a self-conscious giggle, "Mary Ellen, do you see who's here?" Mary Ellen glanced up and then quickly down to her high buttoned shoes. Patrick stood there with his locks of dark wavy hair and deep brown eyes. He was tall, well built from hard work on the farm and incredibly handsome. Annie, the more outgoing of the two grabbed Mary Ellen by the arm and dragged her over to where Patrick stood. Annie stared up into Patrick's eyes but Patrick was looking and smiling at Mary Ellen. Mary Ellen still had her head down.

"Patrick, you know my cousin Mary Ellen Garrett, don't you?"

Patrick replied without even looking in Annie's direction, "No, but I would certainly like to. I noticed you two last week at the St. Anthony party but you didn't stay long enough for me to come over to say hello," Patrick said with a laugh.

Annie pursed her lips thinking the whole time, "He doesn't even know I exist and now he's teasing us about last week and Mary Ellen couldn't care less."

Surely, there is a way to get his attention. What an

awkward situation and the longer they stood there the more frustrated she became. She had four brothers and a doting father and was used to getting all of the attention. She glanced at Mary Ellen with a look of exasperation.

Joseph stood with Harry and greeted the guests along with Catherine. They actually wanted to scrutinize the cute girls that were arriving.

"Welcome," Catherine said to Mary Francis and Ann as they arrived. "Please come in and get warm. There is hot cider on the table, Joseph go and get the girls a cup."

"Sure," Joseph replied as he ran off to get two steaming cups of hot cider.

The two girls chatted briefly with Catherine about how they attended the Assumption church. Catherine was in her element, greeting the guests warmly and making them feel comfortable. Joseph came back with the two cups of cider and handed one to Ann Fournier and when he handed Mary Francis her cup he looked into her eyes and touched her hands as she reached for the cup.

"Hello, Mary Francis, my name is Joseph."

Mary Francis, suddenly tongue-tied just smiled. Harry called Joseph at that moment.

Joseph said, "I'll be right back."

Ann looked at Mary Francis and said brightly, "Mary F, I think he's gorgeous. Did you see the way he looked at you?"

Mary felt very nervous and replied, "He is handsome isn't he?"

A few minutes later, Joseph came back and asked if they'd like a seat and walked them over to some chairs that had been put out for the guests. Ann was asked to dance shortly thereafter and Mary Francis spent the rest of the evening with Joseph, talking and dancing a little. She couldn't have felt more comfortable than to sit with him and talk. They shared family stories, with Joseph telling her about William moving to Minnesota and Mary Francis telling him about her sisters in Montreal.

"Why haven't you gone to Montreal?" Joseph asked.

"Well, my sisters moved there a few years ago and my father and sister Mary Ann died last year so my mother and brother would be all alone. I hate to leave them alone but would love to move somewhere else," Mary said sweetly.

An adoration for her was quickly building within Joseph. She appeared to be a good listener and her beauty was undeniable.

Ann Fournier came over and said, "Mary F, your brother is outside we have to go."

"Okay," Mary grabbed her wrap and said to Joseph, "Thank you for the nice party."

"I want to see you again, can I call on you?" Joseph asked.

"Sure," replied Mary. "I'd like that."

She walked out with her friend and glanced back over her shoulder. Joseph watched her leave with a warm smile on his face.

Soon after Christmas, Joseph appeared on the Fox family doorstep. He became a regular caller visiting for short periods of time since she wasn't allowed to be alone with a boy. He came on occasion to supper with her family and then invited her over to his house. Joseph picked Mary Francis up in the carriage and wrapped her up in blankets to keep her warm. Once they were out of sight of the Fox home, Joseph reached over and kissed her. "I've missed you Mary F."

Mary just looked at him and smiled in such a way that made his heart melt. They had a delightful supper with the rest of the Doyle family when Catherine fixed a pot roast with vegetables and a homemade apple pie. After supper Mary felt very full but very happy. Joseph asked her if she'd like to see the new horse they purchased that afternoon. They walked out into the fresh air and Joseph took her hand as they walked out to the barn. The snow felt hard under their feet and Joseph put his arm around her to keep her from slipping. He pulled the barn door back and lit an oil lamp that hung just inside the barn door. The horse whinnied as they approached.

"Oh, it's beautiful!" Mary said with delight.

She inhaled the smell of the barn and looked around at the animals. The Fox family didn't have any horses, just one cow and one pig, so this was a real treat. Joseph put his hand on her back and pulled her close to him. He looked at her and seemed to be studying her eyes when he kissed her deeply. Mary Francis felt her legs go weak. She kissed him back with all the passion that had been building inside her. He was so charming and so handsome. She let his tongue explore her lips and her mouth and she grew afraid, but even more afraid to say no. Then he took her hand and he told her to climb up into the loft. She did as he asked and he held the ladder for her and then followed her up. Once inside the loft, it became magical. The light from the oil lamp below cast warm shadows all over the barn. Joseph lay on top of her and smelling his scent, she felt outside of herself, as if the moment had transcended into an out of body experience. She had never known such passion or exhilaration. It hurt for a second as he entered her but all she could think of was the love she had for him. All he could think of was the lust he had for her. Shortly after he came inside her, they could hear someone coming. They hurriedly put themselves back together and climbed down the ladder just as Michael opened the barn door.

"Where have you been?" Michael asked with irritation in his voice.

"Just showing Mary Francis around the barn," Joseph replied.

"What were you looking at, the ceiling? You'd better get the straw out of your hair before mother or father sees that," Michael said walking away. "Father wants you inside."

Joseph rolled his eyes, picked the straw out of Mary Francis' hair and the two walked back towards the house.

After that evening, Francis saw less and less of Joseph. With each day of silence from him, she grew more and more anxious. The days became short and cold and she felt unusually tired. At the beginning of February, she realized that she hadn't had her monthly and she panicked. What could that mean? She couldn't tell her mother or brother anything so she confided in Ann Fournier.

"Ann, what will I do?"

"Did you have relations with Joseph?" Ann asked with sincere concern.

"Yes," Mary broke down in sobs. "It only happened once. What will I do if I'm pregnant? My mother will be so ashamed of me. Ann, I love him. Why hasn't he called on me?"

Ann shook her head. She felt afraid for her friend. The beginning of March came and Mary Francis was more than sure that she was with child.

"You need to see Joseph and tell him Mary Francis. If he knows you're pregnant, surely he'll marry you," Ann pleaded with her.

"Do you think so?" Mary asked with tears in her eyes.

"Yes. Go see him," Ann begged.

By mid-March, late one morning, Mary Francis took the carriage and called on Joseph. An early spring was evident all over the farm with small buds on the trees and the grass was starting to turn green. Mary knocked on the door and Annie answered and looked surprised to see Mary Francis standing there.

"Hi, Mary Francis. What a pleasant surprise. Come in please," Annie said warmly.

"Thank you, Annie. I need to talk to Joseph."

"Oh, I think he's in the barn. Go on out and see him," Annie replied pleasantly.

Annie wondered what that was all about. Mary F didn't look herself. Mary Francis felt very nervous as she walked from the house to the barn. Her heart was beating so hard she could hear it. Joseph was putting some rope away when she walked in. The door was open to let the spring air in and he looked up with a stunned look on his face.

"Mary F, what a surprise," he said as he continued to wrap the rope around his arm in a circular motion. "How are you?"

"Joseph, I'm not good. I'm pregnant," Mary said with sadness.

Joseph stopped and looked up at her. "Hum..I'm sorry to hear that. Who's the father?"

Mary Francis began to cry.

"Who's the father? Is that all you can say? It's your child I'm having!" Mary said quietly.

Joseph walked over to her and put his hand on her arm.

"Mary Francis, I'm sorry…I don't know what to say. I hope you're not thinking I'll marry you because I'm not ready to be married," Joseph said with a shrug of his shoulders.

"I love you, Joseph. How can you do this to me?"

"I'm sorry. I care about you too but I'm not ready to get married."

Mary Francis felt like the wind had been knocked out of her and without thinking she turned and ran to the carriage sobbing. She cried all the way home, in disbelief over Joseph's heartlessness. What was she going to do?

Joseph went back to his rope and didn't realize that Annie had walked out after Mary Francis and was standing outside the barn and heard the whole thing, disgusted by Joseph's reaction. Fearful of what her parents would do, she decided not to tell them. She decided to tell Mary Ellen hoping she'd know how to handle this mess. That evening after supper, she walked over to Mary Ellen's house and confided in her about the pregnancy.

Mary Ellen whispered to Annie, "You have to tell someone."

"If only my brother Jim was here. I know I could

confide in him and he would know what to do," Annie shared with concern.

Mary Francis went home and decided to tell her mother and brother that evening.

"How could you disgrace the family this way Mary Francis? If Joseph isn't willing to marry you, you will have a bastard for a child and no man will ever want you."

Mary Francis was devastated. As the weeks turned into months, she became withdrawn and wasn't interested in seeing anyone to include Ann Fournier. She sulked around the house as her shape changed and she could no longer hide her pregnancy. Despite her sullenness, and the weight of the situation on her, she loved this baby knowing it was Joseph's and she continued to have feelings for him, hoping that he would change his mind. She remained hopeful that the birth of the baby, the sight of his child, would change his sentiments.

John and Catherine didn't know about the pregnancy. John was now eighty-nine years old and this kind of news would devastate him. If John had known, he would have made Joseph do the honorable thing and marry Mary Francis. Jim did come to the house that summer and Annie pulled him aside when he was there and told him she had to talk to him. She told Jim about Mary Francis and the pregnancy and Joseph's response. Jim became furious and went to find Joseph.

"Joseph you low life son-of-a-bitch! Is it true that you got Mary Francis pregnant and aren't marrying her?" Jim asked.

"Mind you own god-damn business," Joseph shouted.

Though his boxing days were long behind him, Jim still had a bit of a temper, and furious, he punched Joseph in the face as hard as he could knocking Joseph on his back.

Joseph held his face and yelled, "Get the hell out of here, Jim!"

Joseph's nose was gushing blood, down all over his front. Jim was afraid he'd kill him if he stayed, so he left. Annie knew what was going on but decided to stay out of it. Catherine just thought it was sibling rivalry once again. Why Jim and William couldn't get along with the other children was beyond her.

Early that fall, Mary Francis delivered a baby girl on September 25, 1910. She had Joseph's blue eyes and blonde hair and Mary Francis named her Margaret. She was baptized at the Assumption Church but the church records read, "Parents Unknown," since Mary Francis was an unwed mother. There was no more shame than that.

Mary Francis hung on to the hope that Joseph would come for her. She watched Margaret grow into a beautiful little girl even as Joseph continued to ignore and avoid her. Year after year went by with her mother and brother trying to convince her to send Margaret to live with one of her sisters in Montreal but Mary Francis couldn't bear the thought of being separated from her daughter. One day it would come to that. Mary Francis' mother and brother made arrangements behind Mary's back for Margaret to live with her sister Catherine in Montreal. Catherine could not have children and was alone most of the time since her husband worked for the railroad and worked long hours. No one would question Catherine taking in a small child and possibly with the child out of the picture, Mary Francis could find a husband. When Margaret turned three, she was taken to Montreal and Mary Francis was beside herself with grief. She fell into a deep depression with no life to speak of, no husband and now no child.

Chapter Thirty-Two

John

1918

In three words I can sum
up everything I've learned
about life: it goes on.
Robert Frost

Catherine felt forlorn looking at John through the kitchen window as he walked back from the barn. He had not felt well the last few months and she noticed how frail he had become. How life would change for all of them when he died. Despite the passage of time, Catherine loved him with all of her heart and couldn't imagine waking up without him next to her.

In the late spring of 1918, the evenings grew warmer. Spring had always been John's favorite time of year. He loved the green of Canada, which reminded him of Ireland. He had such bittersweet memories of his distant homeland.

As he walked from the barn to the house, he heard the sweet call of a bird sitting in one of his fruit trees, he breathed deeply the smell of the fresh cut grass that Michael had mowed earlier that day and he reflected on his life. He thought of the people that had made such a significant difference to him over the years, Samuel and Charlotte Castleford and Patrick and Nettie Cavanaugh, his dear sisters, Bridget and Catherine and brother Thomas that had all died years ago. He thought of his father and mother who he missed so much. He knew his father, Thomas would be proud of the things he had accomplished as he looked around the land that he owned, the big red barn that he built now filled with livestock of all kinds along with the seven bedroom house that everyone talked about when it was first built. He recalled the loves of his life, the beauty of Eliza, and the intense, pure love they shared, and his wonderful and witty wife Catherine his greatest joy and his beautiful daughter Annie so smart and so devoted to him. He felt pain at the disappointments, his son William whom he had not talked to nor heard from in years. And he thought of the children that he had lost and the children that had survived and would now be heirs to everything he worked so hard for. He had come a long way since all of those days in Ireland. But rarely did he let himself reflect on his life. At that moment, he felt very weary and looked up at the evening sky as the sun was getting ready to set with a warm feeling in his heart that he had lived well and prospered, had triumphed over hardship, had done what he had been put on this earth to do. On that early summer evening on the 30th of May, just eleven days before his 97th birthday, John walked into the house and told Catherine that he felt very tired and wanted to lie down. When Catherine went in to check on him a short time later, he slept soundly but his breathing had become labored.

"Michael, go get Father McCarthy from church. I want John blessed in case his time is near," Catherine said with sadness.

Father McCarthy returned with Michael within a few hours and entered John's bedroom and gave him the last rites with Catherine and the children by his bedside. Catherine leaned down and kissed John on the forehead. As the children closed the door behind them they did not realize that it would be the last time they would see him alive. John died of heart failure that early morning on the June 1, 1918. Catherine kept watch over him all night and when he took his final breath, she was by his side and wept openly. She did not want John to think that even in death the two would ever be separate. She recognized that she had not been his first love but she was his last and she knew he had adored her and the life they had made together. She quietly got up from the bed and undressed and bathed him. He lay so still, a slight smile on his face as if he had recognized someone or something that brought love to his heart. Inhaling the smell of him she knew that she would often reach out for his arms to find nothing there but memories. She now would have to begin the joy of remembering.

John's obituary read:

A gloom was cast over this community on
Saturday, June 1, 1918
When death claimed as its victim an old and
respected resident in the name of John Doyle.
He had been in failing health for some
time and all that medical aid and loving hands
could do was of no avail.

He was visited on Tuesday by Father McCarthy and received the last sad rites of the church. Born in Wicklow, Ireland in 1821 he came to Canada in 1847 and settled in Camden where he spent the rest of his life as a true friend and a kind and obliging neighbor. The funeral was largely attended on Monday morning at the church of St. Anthony of Padua, Centreville, all vying with each other without distinction of creed to pay their last tribute to one so favorably known. He leaves to mourn his loss a loving wife, six sons and one daughter. William of Idaho, James of Stocco, John of Moscow, Michael, Harry, Joseph and Annie at home. The bereaved family has the deepest sympathy of the community in their sorrow.

Annie

Life around the farm was not the same after my father died. I was twenty-eight years old when he took his last breath. I know that his last wish was to see me married with a large family but I never found a man that measured up to him or was as great as I thought my father to be. I loved him for his strength, his courage and his determination. He also had a gentleness that not many people saw.

William didn't come back from Idaho for the funeral even though he had been sent a telegram of our father's death. Jim had moved to Windsor and was working as a laborer for one of the automobile companies in Detroit glad to be out of rural Canada. He came home for Father's funeral and was a comfort to us all.

Just five years after Father died, in the early part of February of 1923, Mother and Joseph came down with the flu and pneumonia and died within one week of each other. Joseph was so sick that Michael had to carry him downstairs to attend Mother's funeral. Joseph never married and took his guilt to his grave about how he had treated Mary Francis. I grieved for so long for my mother and brother that I didn't think I would ever recover. When Jim came back from Windsor for Mother and Joe's funeral, he was stunned to see Mary Francis standing in the back of the church sobbing with grief, and I watched as Jim wrapped his arms around her to comfort her. Mary Francis had lost her daughter and now she lost what she thought was the only hope of finding love in this life. Jim grieved for her and the secret he knew. Jim asked Mary Francis to marry him and move to Detroit. He knew that her daughter Margaret that Joseph had fathered lived in Montreal and Jim thought this would be a good time to start fresh. Mary Francis gladly accepted and in October of 1923, she married Jim in Windsor, Canada leaving her grief and life as a spinster behind.

Now it's just me alone in this big farmhouse filled with memories. We lived a wonderful life with the parties and stories about growing up in Ireland, Father playing the fiddle and Grandmother singing. As any family has their trials and tribulations, for the most part, we had our share but we felt extremely close to one another. I miss my mother and father and siblings, aunts and uncles more than I can say. We are the last of the Doyle's from Wicklow, Ireland, as my father would proudly say with no heirs left behind. Maybe someone will magically discover and share our story…because it is a great story worth telling.

A Note on History
By Jim Rees

Author of: Surplus People, The Fitzwilliam Clearances 1847-1856 and A Farewell to Famine

The Irish potato famine of the second half of the 1840s has been described as the worse social disaster of 19th century Europe. Its scale was so vast that historians disagree on many of its aspects. How many died, how many emigrated, how much or how little was done by government to alleviate the suffering of millions; how great was its social and cultural impact. Was it famine or simply a series of crop failures? Was it the will of God or passive genocide? They cannot even agree on how long it lasted. Its duration is difficult to define because it didn't 'end' but rather petered out with some regions experiencing crop failures for seven consecutive years from 1845 to 1852.

So much has been written about that horrific time that it is sometimes tempting to think that there are no new angles from which to view it. That would be a great mistake. As historians dig deeper new facts leading to new interpretations come to light. It is unending. Also, when an event of such magnitude is looked at on a national level, the overall picture can only be brought into focus at the loss of localized detail. The potato crop failures of those years varied in intensity and geographical distribution and there has been an understandable tendency to concentrate on those areas which were hardest hit. Because of this tendency, many parts of the country have been overlooked or, at best, only briefly referred to.

One of those regions is County Wicklow which, in common with most of the eastern counties, figures scantily if at all in most of the major studies. This meager coverage is unintentionally misleading and perpetuates the misconception that Wicklow somehow managed to come through those years unscathed.

Studies over the past twenty years have shown that death from starvation and disease in Wicklow was more common than had been realized. The workhouses in Shillelagh, Rathdrum, Baltinglass and Rathdown were filled to overflowing. These institutions were as incapable as the workhouses in the west of Ireland of dealing with the demands made upon them. Government schemes, soup kitchens and local relief committees operated throughout the county. Eviction and emigration were also part of Wicklow's famine experience. It has been estimated that the population of the county decreased by 21.5% between 1841 and 1851. This decrease represented over 27,000 people. The proximity of the national capital offered an escape route for many and by 1851 'more than a fifth of all Wicklow-born people lived in Dublin'. There were also many thousands who went to Britain, the United States, and Canada. In 1850, the parish priest of the combined parish of Killaveny and Annacurra, in the south of the county, led over a thousand people to the American Mid-West at the behest of the Bishop of Little Rock in Arkansas.

Landlords, eager to rid their estates of 'surplus' tenantry, were engaged in 'assisted passages'. The most important of these was Lord Fitzwilliam, whose 80,000-acre estate was by far the largest in the county. Between 1847 and 1856, he removed almost six thousand men, women and children from his property and arranged passage for them to Canada. Most of them were destitute and arrived in Quebec and New Brunswick with little more than what they wore on their backs.

The problem with statistics is we sometimes lose track that these are not merely numbers - they are human beings, real men, women and children who had the same hopes, fears, loves hatreds, worries, ambitions, frustrations as we have. This was a human tragedy which in a very real sense touches millions of people of Irish descent all over the world.

CPSIA information can be obtained at www.ICGtesting.com
Printed in the USA
LVOW10s1502050216

473888LV00001B/42/P